PENGUIN  CL

T0201100

TALES OF BELKIN AND OTHE

ALEXANDER SERGEYEVICH PUSHKIN was born in Moscow in 1799. He
was liberally educated and left school in 1817. Given a sinecure in the Foreign
Office, he spent three dissipated years in St Petersburg, writing light, erotic
and highly polished verse. He flirted with several pre-Decembrist societies,
composing the mildly revolutionary verses which led to his disgrace and exile
in 1820. After a stay in the Caucasus and the Crimea, he was sent to Bessarabia,
where he wrote *The Prisoner of the Caucasus* and *The Fountain of Bakhchisarai*.
His work took a more serious turn during the last year of his southern exile,
when he began *The Gipsies* and *Eugene Onegin*. In 1824 he moved to his
parents' estate at Mikhaylovskoye in north-west Russia and wrote *The Gipsies*.
The following year he wrote his great historical drama *Boris Godunov* and
continued *Eugene Onegin*. With the failure of the Decembrists' rising in 1825
and the succession of a new Tsar, Pushkin recovered his freedom. During the
next three years he wandered restlessly between St Petersburg and Moscow.
He wrote an epic poem, *Poltava*, but little else. In 1829 he went with the Russian
army to Transcaucasia, and the following year he retired to a family estate at
Boldino, completing *Eugene Onegin*. In the autumn of 1830 he wrote *Tales of
Belkin* and his experimental 'Little Tragedies' in blank verse. In 1831 he married
the beautiful Natalia Goncharova. The rest of his life was plagued by debts
and the malice of his enemies. His literary output slackened, but he wrote
two prose works, *The Captain's Daughter* and *The Queen of Spades*, and folk
poems, including *The Golden Cockerel*. Towards the end of 1836 anonymous
letters goaded Pushkin into challenging a troublesome admirer of his wife to
a duel. Pushkin was mortally wounded and died in January 1837.

RONALD WILKS studied Russian language and literature at Trinity College,
Cambridge, after training as a Naval interpreter, and later Russian literature
at London University, where he received his Ph.D. in 1972. Among his trans-
lations for Penguin Classics are *My Childhood*, *My Apprenticeship* and *My
Universities* by Gorky, *Diary of a Madman* by Gogol, filmed for Irish Televi-
sion, *The Golovlyov Family* by Saltykov-Shchedrin, *How Much Land Does a
Man Need?* by Tolstoy, and six volumes of stories by Chekhov: *The Party and
Other Stories*, *The Kiss and Other Stories*, *The Fiancée and Other Stories*, *The
Duel and Other Stories*, *The Steppe and Other Stories* and *Ward No. 6 and Other
Stories*. He has also translated *The Little Demon* by Sologub for Penguin.

JOHN BAYLEY was Warton Professor of English Literature, Oxford University, from 1974–92. Among his many books are *The Romantic Survival: A Study in Poetic Evolution*, *The Characters of Love: A Study in the Literature of Personality*, *Tolstoy and the Novel*, *Pushkin: A Comparative Commentary*, *An Essay on Hardy*, *Shakespeare and Tragedy*, *Iris: A Memoir of Iris Murdoch* and a detailed study of A. E. Housman's poems. *Alice* (1994), *The Queer Captain* (1995) and *George's Lair* (1996) are his trilogy of novels. He has also introduced Pushkin's *Eugene Onegin* and edited James's *The Wings of the Dove* for Penguin Classics.

TALES OF BELKIN
AND OTHER PROSE WRITINGS

ALEXANDER PUSHKIN

Translated by RONALD WILKS
With an Introduction by JOHN BAYLEY

PENGUIN BOOKS

PENGUIN BOOKS

Published by the Penguin Group
Penguin Books Ltd, 80 Strand, London WC2R 0RL, England
Penguin Putnam Inc., 375 Hudson Street, New York, New York 10014, USA
Penguin Books Australia Ltd, 250 Camberwell Road, Camberwell, Victoria 3124, Australia
Penguin Books Canada Ltd, 10 Alcorn Avenue, Toronto, Ontario, Canada M4V 3B2
Penguin Books India (P) Ltd, 11 Community Centre, Panchsheel Park, New Delhi – 110 017, India
Penguin Books (NZ) Ltd, Cnr Rosedale and Airborne Roads, Albany, Auckland, New Zealand
Penguin Books (South Africa) (Pty) Ltd, 24 Sturdee Avenue, Rosebank 2196, South Africa

Penguin Books Ltd, Registered Offices: 80 Strand, London WC2R 0RL, England

www.penguin.com

First published in Russian in 1831
This translation first published in Penguin Classics 1998

022

Copyright © Ronald Wilks, 1998
Copyright © Introduction, John Bayley, 1998
All rights reserved

The moral right of the editors has been asserted

Set in 11/12.5pt Monotype Fournier
Typeset by Rowland Phototypesetting Ltd, Bury St Edmunds, Suffolk
Printed and bound in Great Britain by Clays Ltd, Elcograf S.p.A.

ISBN-13: 978-0-14-044675-3

www.greenpenguin.co.uk

MIX
Paper from
responsible sources
FSC   FSC® C018179
www.fsc.org

Penguin Books is committed to a sustainable
future for our business, our readers and our planet.
This book is made from Forest Stewardship
Council™ certified paper.

CONTENTS

There is a kind of genius in art who seems to embody a culture, a language, a created world. Examples are Shakespeare and Mozart. In some degree each national culture possesses one such genius: one who most obviously embodies and expresses it. For Russia it is Pushkin. His poems taught the Russian people to speak, to be themselves and rejoice in their language, to know who they were and how they felt. No cultivated Russian, familiar with his country's history and literature, would find such a claim extravagant.

And yet the absolute ascendancy of Pushkin's genius in Russian eyes and for Russian culture does continue to puzzle the rest of Europe. Pushkin is above all a poet, and so absolute a poet in his own language that he cannot be translated. Shakespeare is a poet too, of course; but he has so many other gifts that his native linguistic genius dilutes itself naturally into universal human channels. This is not the case with Pushkin. As a poet his dependence on his own language is complete. To see his real point you must be able to participate in the magic of the words of his poems. Those words lose their magic utterly in translation.

This strange fact has annoyed as well as puzzled writers and critics in western countries, who rightly supposed that they could always tell literary genius when they saw it. Flaubert in France was more than willing to accept his friend Mérimée's enthusiastic assessment of Pushkin as one of the greatest. But he soon changed his mind. '*Il est plat, votre poète*', he exclaimed disconsolately when Mérimée supplied him with translated samples of Pushkin's poetic masterpieces, put into accurate French. Mérimée could read Russian: Flaubert could not.

If Mérimée, on the other hand, had seen fit to supply his friend with translations of Pushkin's *Tales of Belkin*, Flaubert's reaction might well have been very different. In fact Mérimée did translate at least two of the tales, and one, 'The Shot', he virtually passed off as his own. One could say, in fact, that Pushkin's prose inspired the French writer in a way that Pushkin's poetry could not possibly have done. And yet Mérimée, as a man of letters who knew Russian, was well aware that Pushkin's greatness for his own countrymen was in his poetry, and so he attempted to persuade Flaubert. No good. It sounded flat; and the novelist was quite right to say so. But any Tale of Belkin would have sparkled in French, as it can in English. The humour, the understatement, the graphic simplicity all come over very well. Flaubert would have seen that and enjoyed it. He would at least have been valuing Pushkin as an admirable and versatile prose writer, even though he could not understand why he was a very much greater poet.

Dostoyevsky too made a valiant attempt, on a very much larger scale than Mérimée's, to persuade the world of the importance of his country's greatest genius. At the celebration of Pushkin's fiftieth anniversary in Moscow he made an impassioned speech, which he obviously hoped would be widely reported throughout Europe. In it he claimed that Pushkin was indeed a universal genius, who should be recognized as such wherever great books were read. Shakespeare, Cervantes – yes, very well, said Dostoyevsky, but neither had our Pushkin's power of projecting himself into every country, every culture, every class and kind of mind. This startling claim was based on the ideas and the situations that can be extrapolated from Pushkin's swift-moving poetic and dramatic narratives, and particularly from the so-called *Little Tragedies*, such as 'Mozart and Salieri'. In a sense the claim is just enough, for Pushkin's ideas and situations did indeed inspire subsequent Russian writers, and none more than Dostoyevsky himself.

But ideas and situations are commonplace in themselves. They must be transformed by the magic of art, and it is this art which – residing in the poetry as it does – is so difficult to bring across in a translation. Pushkin's lighter art, on the other hand, as it is expanded in prose stories – his humour, his pleasure in absurdity, his good-natured amusement at human beings – these things can come across very well. Yet it has never been easy to find translations of the prose pieces in which these qualities of a great writer are both paramount and accessible. Hence the pleasure with which the reader who has not come across Pushkin's prose before will welcome this excellent translation of most of his lesser known prose works.

Where prose was concerned Pushkin was above all a pioneer and experimentalist. The vogue for his poetry, especially his early poetry, had been sensational. In Russian literary circles he had become as famous as Byron had been in England and throughout western Europe. His poems were popular among ordinary folk too, in the same way that those of Burns became in his native Scotland. He had the common touch, and delighted in fairy tales and ballads, but he was also a dedicated and sophisticated artist who was never prepared to repeat a success, but was always exploring new effects and different forms. In his short life (he was killed in a duel at thirty-seven) he wrote a great deal, not in sheer bulk but in terms of versatility and variety. Furthermore, as he himself often stressed in a humorous way, he wrote for money. His early narrative poems had brought him in a good deal, but in the 1830s – he was born in the last year of the previous century – he understood very well that the fashion for romantic poetry was beginning to wane. A contemporary of his, an aspiring novelist in the manner of Sir Walter Scott, famously remarked that Russian readers had begun to get tired of poetry, as a child gets tired of its rattle: 'There is a general outcry – give us prose! Water, plain water!'

Pushkin was prepared to oblige. His first serious attempt at writing prose fiction was to begin a novel about his own ancestor: the boy, probably from Abyssinia, who had been presented by the Turkish sultan to Peter the Great, and who had risen to become a general in Peter's service. 'Precision and tidiness are the prime merits of prose', he had observed in one of his letters, and 'The Negro of Peter the Great' (1827) is perhaps almost too bald and simplistic in its narrative mode, although the account it gives of the period is a vivid and fascinating one. Probably the sheer impersonality of the narrative technique did not suit Pushkin, who in a narrative poem like *Eugene Onegin* had enjoyed playing deftly and humorously with every kind of literary convention and stylistic approach. In the unfinished Peter the Great story – it remains no more than a fragment – he ventured too boldly and too far towards the kind of omniscient and impersonal prose narration that would become common in the second half of the century – the heyday of the great novel. Possibly too he saw no way of making his leading character more significant and more interesting as the story of the young negro's career developed. And so, with characteristic decisiveness, he stopped writing it.

None the less he did not at once abandon its impersonal and omniscient method. When reading 'The guests were arriving at the dacha', and 'At the corner of a small square' – these are the opening sentences of a pair of fragments a good deal shorter than the 'Peter' one – one has the uncanny impression of entering the sort of highly sophisticated and complex social world which is to be found in the novels of Stendhal or Flaubert. The characters Pushkin rapidly sketches in seem immensely 'promising': in a page or two one is already quite absorbed by them. The two fragments, especially the first, fascinated Tolstoy, who was inspired by its opening sentence ('That is how prose should be written', he remarked) in beginning the first draft of *Anna Karenina*.

And yet one can see why Pushkin found himself unable to develop a situation that seemed so auspiciously begun. The simple deadpan method gave him no room in which to turn round, and to expand the fashionable and intricate social scene in which his characters appear to be moving, and of which they are evidently natural denizens.

Pushkin moved in that sophisticated urban world himself, especially after 1831, when he married the beautiful Nataliya Goncharova. His marriage was a happy one, but his wife's frivolity and flirtatiousness were to lead to the fatal duel seven years later, for Pushkin was by temperament intensely jealous, attributing this, like his own highly-sexed nature, to the remote African ancestor of whom he remained extremely proud. He loved society and gambling, and all the pleasures of the metropolis, but for two highly-productive autumns – the time he liked best to write – he withdrew to a small family manor house in the country at Boldino, shut himself up and wrote night and day for a month in a single continuous burst of inspiration. These 'Boldino autumns', as they are known to Pushkin scholars and admirers, produced astonishing achievements in verse, and at the same time in prose stories and the drama.

It was there he wrote his first prose masterpiece – the *Tales of Belkin*. This unique and delightful series of tales was first written straight out: it was afterwards that Pushkin invented the inimitable figure of Squire Belkin himself, as part of an elaborate mechanism of anonymity, and of a pretended *naïveté*. Pushkin was well aware too of a literary precedent, for both Walter Scott in *Tales of My Landlord* (1816–19) and the American Washington Irving in *Tales of a Traveller* (1824) had employed the same elaborately humorous narrative device. Pushkin's humour is more subtle, however, and Belkin himself an excellent 'character', seen both with amusement and with a kind of affectionate respect. He is the simple good-hearted Russian squire – *prostoy i dobry barin* – rather like the father of Tatiana Larin in the verse novel *Eugene Onegin*. It seems quite likely that he was the kind of inspiration that came not only from a Boldino autumn in the country but from some of the local landowners.

As the 'editor' of the late Mr Belkin's tales tells us in a footnote, their collector picked them up from various sources, in the course of his rural routines. A civil servant, a 'titular councillor', supplied 'The Postmaster'. 'The Shot' he had heard from a Lieutenant-Colonel, and 'The Undertaker' from a 'shop assistant', perhaps at second-hand. Miss K. I. T., herself perhaps the daughter of a local squire, had been the source of the two most obviously 'romantic' tales – 'The Blizzard' and 'The Squire's Daughter'.

It is obvious of course that Pushkin enjoyed himself in his own quiet artist's way by putting in touches appropriate to these various narrators. What is less obvious is the skill with which he has made his narrators not necessarily typical at all. His own theory of character (though one can hardly call the rapid, sparkling way in which he flung out ideas in his letters by the name of a 'theory') was that really great creators, notably Shakespeare, never created characters whose behaviour was consistent and all-of-a-piece. Shylock and

Macbeth, for instance, show personalities – Shylock a man of his word and a devoted father, Macbeth tormented by conscience and wholly unsuited by nature to murder and intrigue – which are quite at variance with their dramatic roles. Byron, on the other hand, says Pushkin, makes a conspirator 'even order a drink conspiratorially, and that's absurd'.

This sense of a true and unpredictable humanity was vital to Pushkin's creative genius. It appears most clearly in the *Little Tragedies*, where Salieri is as honourable and high-minded a murderer as Othello, and Don Juan irresistible not because he is an expert and cold-hearted seducer but because he really loves and appreciates women – all women. We can see the same impulse working in the complex comedy of the Belkin stories, most felicitously of all in 'The Postmaster'. For a start the narrator is himself by no means a 'typical' civil servant: he is a man of sense and sensibility, who understands and appreciates both the pathos of the situation from the old father's point of view, and how things must look to a pretty and intelligent daughter longing for a chance to make her way in the world. The consistency and predictability which Pushkin subtly undermines in his tale are here in fact those of the New Testament story of the Prodigal Son. So far from going to the bad, the Postmaster's daughter Dunya goes to the good, as it were. Everything turns out well for her; it is her old father who takes to drink and dies forlorn. And then she comes home, as he would not permit her while he was alive, to shed a tear on his grave. She is by no means an abandoned or a hard-hearted girl.

There is not a trace of sentimentality in the telling of the story, and yet this quiet and unemphatic presentation of an episode from Wordsworth's 'still sad music of humanity' is very moving. Romanticism tended of course to sentimentalize such things. Pushkin was very gently sending up the famous tear-jerker 'Poor Liza' (1792), by the older and distinguished Russian author Karamzin. The same sentimental formula would be exploited by Dickens. But temperamentally Pushkin was not in the least a romantic. He was, it would be true to say, much more a Shakespearean; and in his first wholly successful prose pieces he delighted in using the subtle arts of parody and comedy to produce an effect which was intelligently moving, and never superficial or sensationalized. As his critics have demonstrated, Pushkin's art is full of implication. In his own words there was 'no need to spell it out'.

The *Tales of Belkin* are thus in one sense a 'plain prose' equivalent of the dazzling poetic virtuosity he had displayed in *Eugene Onegin*. But there is no authorial presence in the tales, just as there is no sign of an omniscient narrator. The flashes of insight which transform the stories do not proceed from any individual in them, or, apparently, from the author himself. That anonymity seems to have been what Pushkin was trying to produce in prose. If so he succeeded in doing so with perfect unobtrusiveness. The ashamed and yet exasperated young hussar assures the postmaster that his daughter is very well off, and inadvertently he reveals exactly the truth which the parable of the Prodigal Son preferred to leave out. 'Neither of you will ever forget what has happened.' Nor is the old man dignified in his pathos. When the young hussar gives him money he indignantly throws it to the ground and walks away, but after a moment's reflection comes back to pick it up. Too late! – someone else has already removed it. So it all too often goes with preconceived moral gestures.

'The Blizzard' is a charming parodic variant on the contemporary vogue for tales of romantic elopements and demon bridegrooms returning from limbo. Miss K. I. T.'s other story, 'The Squire's Daughter', is also discreetly told from the feminine angle. The narrator takes pleasure in the fact that her hero should think of marrying a peasant girl for love; and he is seen from a woman's point of view, as Darcy and Bingham are seen in *Pride and Prejudice*. The shop assistant who is the anecdotalist of 'The Undertaker' takes for granted his protagonist's pride in trade and pleasure, in securing custom and cheating the customer. Once again, however, a sudden insight seems to come from nowhere in particular. The new cottage bought by the undertaker, which he has always longed for, does not after all make 'his heart . . . rejoice', as he is surprised to find. For trade and business are his whole life, though he had never realized it before.

Insofar as there is a meaning or even a moral in the *Tales*, and to find such things in Pushkin is in any event highly dubious, it is that the objective reality of things always remains outside the stories we tell about them, just as they remain outside the meanings we ourselves seek to impose. Silvio, in 'The Shot', has an absolute determination to impose his will upon the indifferent world of fact. His determination is magnificent but futile. He is a mystery man, a melodramatist cut off from the prosaic world, and it takes sober prose to reveal him, not as a hero but as the grotesquely isolated figure he has become. None the less he is surely still admired by the army officer who tells his story.

In Pushkin's prose the world seems alienated from the medium describing it by the very operation of that medium. As the Russian critic Lezhnev put it, 'poetry and truth cannot coexist' in this atmosphere, which is the point of prose. It is a property of the prose virtues which Pushkin is investigating, rather than something put in by his own personality. The *Tales of Belkin* are thus very different from the *contes* of Flaubert, Maupassant or Mérimée, where 'impersonality' is a product of the writer's own personal attitude. They are much more like James Joyce's *Dubliners*, and have the same play of parody mixed with realism. We could say that Pushkin, as an experimenter, honours the medium of prose by not slipping it on with the casual and familiar ease with which he had slipped on the garment of poetry. His successor Gogol, who much admired the Belkin tales, could be said to have made a kind of deliberate and often facetious mannerism of his own, out of this unobtrusive evasiveness which he found in Pushkin.

Pushkin, as we have seen, created the figure of Belkin himself as a kind of postscript to his stories, almost as an incongruous guarantee of their impersonality. When Belkin gets his head, he becomes, as if quite unintentionally, a character in his own right, both comic and endearing. As if to relax himself and his reader, Pushkin went on at once to write his inimitable 'History of the Village of Goryukhino'. We learn now that young Squire Belkin had always had literary ambitions; that he attempted at first to write a Russian epic, which caused him so much trouble that he turned it into a tragedy and finally into a ballad. Then he dropped the whole idea and started to compose aphorisms, which even he could see were a trifle banal. So he collected and embellished anecdotes – in fact the *Tales* which we have just been reading – and finally, still unsatisfied, he determines to write a proper history, like that of the Russian historian Polevoy or the celebrated Gibbon ('whose name I cannot remember').

So drolly effective is Pushkin's satire – if indeed something so good-natured can be called satire at all – that we could easily miss what must have amused his friends, and some of his fellow-authors, at the time. Belkin is struggling to do what the Russian writers of the great classic period, and not least Pushkin himself, had themselves all been trying to do. They had begun ambitious epics, turned to other kinds of poetry, and then finally to prose and to history. Belkin found the diary of his own great-grandfather, once lord of the manor, a preliminary inspiration.

May 4th. Snow. Trishka beaten for rudeness. 6th – the brown cow died. Senka flogged for drunkenness . . . 9th – rain and snow. Trishka flogged because of the weather.

And so forth. The diary, as Belkin observes, 'is distinguished for clarity and brevity of style' – just the qualities which Pushkin was seeking in his own prose.

Oppressed by the weight of things as they actually are, Belkin, unlike his great-grandfather, seeks relief in writing them down as they are not. And yet the gloomy history of Russian feudal serfdom, as also its more incidentally human side, appears both in his introduction and in the 'history' itself. Belkin suddenly becomes wholly natural when he describes his own homecoming, and how the birches on the estate have grown taller. 'I told the women unceremoniously, "How you've aged," and they replied with feeling, "And how plain you've become, master." ' But when writing 'history' Belkin attempts the proper magisterial tone, and in doing so makes, as if accidentally, an observation that is true in all nations and at all times, but especially true of what the poet Aleksandr Blok called the dark chronicle of Russia. It is because of that darkness that the Russian peasantry always looked back to what they thought of as a golden age. It was not until the age of Lenin and the Communist Party that they became conditioned to look forward instead – to what was promised and proclaimed to be the gleaming heights of socialism.

Pushkin's free and individual brand of interest in history, and how to write it, is also visible in the novel fragment 'Roslavlev'. It seems at least to have been projected as a novel, a kind of alternative version of his acquaintance Zagoskin's actual and orthodox historical fiction in the Sir Walter Scott manner, also called *Roslavlev*. The latter story concerns a young Russian lady, Polina, who has been in France before Napoleon's invasion of Russia, where she has fallen in love with a married man. Back in Russia during the invasion she meets him again, now widowed, and a prisoner of war. She herself is half-heartedly betrothed to a young Russian officer, Roslavlev, but she now deserts her home in the company of her former French lover, and they manage to reach the French army. Like the old-time heroine who has suffered a fate worse than death, and therefore cannot be allowed to survive the conclusion of a heroic narrative, Zagoskin's Polina is later killed with her lover during the Russian siege of Danzig.

Pushkin was clearly interested in the possibilities of Polina as a character, implying that she had been merely conventionalized in Zagoskin's narrative. Slight as his sketch is, he makes it clear that she is a young woman of fire and intelligence, able to think for herself and eager to read and to know about everything that is going on. He gives her, in fact, the qualities which he himself could admire in young women, and which he felt were more paramount in Russian society among women than men. His own Tatiana in *Eugene Onegin* would be a good example. Young Lieutenant Roslavlev, on the other hand, is the sort of good-natured rake who talks down to what he thinks is women's level, and who is quite unworthy of Polina's love. Senicour, the French prisoner, is a different proposition entirely. He is gentle, courteous and attractive. But Polina is a spirited and patriotic girl, who at the end of the fragment gives the news to the female narrator that her brother Roslavlev has been killed fighting heroically at Borodino.

So what might happen now? A potentially interesting situation, with Polina divided between admiration and growing love for the French prisoner, and her own strong patriotic feelings? Whatever resolution for the story Pushkin might have found, he clearly lost interest at this point in continuing the novel. It was Polina as a person, rather than her story as told by Zagoskin, which had interested him. He toyed with the idea of making her a friend and confidante of the great Madame de Staël, whose personality and intelligence she sees as a reproach to the whole of a philistine Russian upper class. It is of some interest, incidentally, that Madame de Staël's novel *Corinne* (1807), which Pushkin mentions more than once, is also mentioned by Tolstoy in *War and Peace*. Madame de Staël is the favourite novelist of the Russian General Kutuzov, and he is actually absorbed in her during the opening stages of the Battle of Borodino, presumably when he knows he can do no more than to let the events of the day take their course – a policy of wise passivity which Tolstoy approves in *War and Peace*; and which Pushkin, who took a great interest in military matters, and in the personalities of the war of 1812, would no doubt have approved of too.

Pushkin's interest in campaigning – in this case a campaign against the Turks – is evident in his unique chapters of autobiography, 'A Journey to Arzrum at the Time of the 1829 Campaign'. Not only does this give us one of the few pieces of Pushkin's personal writing, but it is written in a style of quite singular compression, purity and vividness. Many later Russian authors, including Lérmontov and Tolstoy himself, have taken it for a model. Though it is one of the most interesting of Pushkin's writings it is almost impossible to find in a translation, which makes its appearance in this selection particularly welcome.

As his early poems show, Pushkin loved the exotic for its own sake. The spirited tale 'Kirdzhali' shows that, but it is also a masterpiece of matter-of-fact simplicity which may remind us not only of one of Tolstoy's last and finest tales, *Hadji-Murad*, but of some of the best early stories of Hemingway (themselves much influenced by Tolstoy). Love for the exotic, as well as a humorous attitude towards it, is also a feature of that fascinating fragment 'Egyptian Nights'. Half serious and half playful, Pushkin plays in it with the idea of his own personality as a poet: or rather as two poets, the young Russian aristocrat Charsky, and the humble Italian improviser who possesses, in spite of his lowly status, that mysterious gift of the gods, a true poetic inspiration. Like Pushkin himself, he can produce finished verses on every subject. Nor is he concerned with what they mean, or with what he as a poet is 'trying to say'. The verses that come have their own value and give their own unique aesthetic satisfaction.

As well as the exotic Pushkin always rejoiced in what was quietly ironical. To test the improviser's powers Charsky suggests the theme that the poet, and no one else, should choose what subjects he should take to write on. Who is the laugh on here? Pushkin, like Charsky, believed passionately in the poet's independence, and yet another poet can produce verses on this very theme to order. It is the paradox of art, making the poet not only his own Priest and Tsar, but mountebank and chameleon. That solemn romantic dogma, the divine dignity of the poet, is being sent up by Pushkin, who knew quite well that the great artists and poets of the Renaissance would never have supposed they were forfeiting their independence by producing the kind of works which their patrons expected of them.

The story the improviser tells of Cleopatra and her lovers is taken from an anecdote of the classical author Aurelius Victor. The French poet Théophile Gautier wrote a complete poem about it, and the Russian symbolist poet Bryusov 'continued' Pushkin's poem in his own style, giving it a romantic aura of love and death and drawing a parallel between modern St Petersburg and ancient Alexandria. Like Gautier, Bryusov saves the third and youngest suitor, making an inevitable anticlimax, and a banal ending to the poem. Pushkin of course evades this by breaking off at the most suggestive moment.

And he had a genius for what was suggestive and fragmentary. Indeed it could be said that the idea of the 'romantic fragment' was not only the sole innovation that he took from romantic theory and practice – for he is temperamentally and at heart the most classically minded of authors – but the one he brought in his own style to its fullest perfection. He never needed to 'spell it out'. The same qualities of pungency and economy animate and give his individual stamp to the way he wrote prose. His versatility is amazing, ranging as it does from such already well-known stories as 'The Queen of Spades' and 'The Captain's Daughter', to the much less familiar but equally remarkable qualities of the Belkin tales, and the other pieces assembled in this book. Although he adored Shakespeare and Scott, Pushkin's English was rather rudimentary; but I fancy that he had enough to have appreciated the sober and effective style of Ronald Wilks's translation, and to have felt it does justice to his original.

John Bayley

FURTHER READING

John Bayley, *Pushkin: A Comparative Commentary* (Cambridge, 1971)
A. D. P. Briggs, *Alexander Pushkin: A Critical Study* (Bristol, 1991)
Paul Debreczeny, *The Other Pushkin: A Study of Alexander Pushkin's Prose Fiction* (Stanford, 1983)
A. Kodjak, *Pushkin's I. P. Belkin* (Columbus, Ohio, 1979)
J. Lavrin, *Pushkin and Russian Literature* (London, 1947)
D. S. Mirsky, *Pushkin* (London, 1926)
E. J. Simmons, *Pushkin* (New York, 1964)
W. N. Vickery, *Alexander Pushkin* (New York, 1970)

This selection of Pushkin's prose writings comprises: *The Tales of the Late Ivan Petrovich Belkin*, 'The History of the Village of Goryukhino', 'Roslavlev', 'Kirdzhali: A Tale', 'Egyptian Nights' and 'A Journey to Arzrum at the Time of the 1829 Campaign'.

The *Tales of Belkin* were written in the space of a few weeks at Boldino in Autumn 1830. The preface, 'From the Editor', was written the following year, when they were published, 'anonymously', under the initials 'A. P.' They are Pushkin's first completed works in prose, and the reception was very mixed. Asked by a friend from his schooldays, P. I. Miller, 'Who is this Belkin?', Pushkin is said to have replied, 'Whoever he is, this is the way to write stories: simply, briefly and clearly.' The *Tales* were first published under Pushkin's name in 1834.

'The History of the Village of Goryukhino' was also written at Boldino in Autumn 1830 after the completion of the *Tales of Belkin*. It was printed after Pushkin's death, in the *Contemporary*, in mutilated form: the full text, restored from his manuscripts, was published much later, in 1857. The work was probably left uncompleted because Pushkin felt that to continue with the peasant rebellion would have incurred the wrath of the censors.

Pushkin started work on 'Roslavlev' in 1831, and the novel remained unfinished. The beginning was published separately in 1836 under the title 'Fragment from the unpublished memoirs of a lady (1811)'. It is interesting to note how the descriptions of the mood of the aristocracy on the eve of the fall of Moscow, and of the banquet held for Madame de Staël, anticipate *War and Peace*. Pushkin was deeply interested in the events of 1812 and in 1829 produced a

fragment, 'At the beginning of 1812 our regiment was situated . . .'
'Roslavlev' is polemically directed against Zagoskin's historical work
of the same title (cf. Introduction, and first note to 'Roslavlev').

'Kirdzhali' was written in 1834 and published in the *Library for
Reading* that year. The story is linked to the Greek uprising of 1821,
in which Pushkin took a keen interest. He had contemplated a
narrative poem on the subject but abandoned it.

'Egyptian Nights' was probably written in 1835 at Mikhaylovskoye
and first printed in the *Contemporary* in 1837, after Pushkin's death.
Queen Cleopatra captured his imagination more than once. In 1824
he had written the draft of a poem about her. Pushkin returned to
this theme in 1828 when the text of the second improvisation was
written. In a prose fragment of 1835, 'We were spending the evening
at Princess D.'s dacha', which also combines prose with poetry,
Cleopatra is compared to other women with claims to fame. For the
first improvisation Pushkin reworked lines from his unfinished poem
'Ezersky' (1832–3).

In 'A Journey to Arzrum at the Time of the 1829 Campaign',
Pushkin describes his time in the Caucasus during the Russo-Turkish
War, and his subsequent experiences with the Russian army under
General Paskevich (who had been ordered to keep him under close
surveillance, chiefly because of his friendship with former Decembrists. Pushkin's coldness towards the General is apparent in this
work). Pushkin's record of his travels forms the basis of the present
account, and in 1830 a fragment was published in the *Literary Gazette*
with the title 'The Georgian Military Highway'. A complete account
was written in 1835 and published in the *Contemporary* in 1836.

Title-page of the first edition: *The Tales of the Late Ivan Petrovich Belkin*,
Published by A. P., St Petersburg, 1831

ПОВѢСТИ

ПОКОЙНАГО

ИВАНА ПЕТРОВИЧА БѢЛКИНА,

ИЗДАННЫЯ

А. П.

САНКТПЕТЕРБУРГЪ.
1831.

ПОВѢСТИ

THE TALES OF THE LATE
IVAN PETROVICH BELKIN

MRS PROSTAKOV: Oh yes, my dear sir. He's been keen on
   stories since he was a little boy.
SKOTININ: Mitrofan takes after me.

The Minor[1]

FROM THE EDITOR

Having undertaken the publication of the *Tales of Belkin*, which we
herewith offer to the public, we wished to preface them with at least
a brief biography of the late author, thereby satisfying the justifiable
curiosity of lovers of our native literature. To that end we approached
Marya Alekseyevna Trafilin, heiress of Ivan Petrovich Belkin and
his next of kin. But unfortunately she could not provide us with any
information at all, since she had never been acquainted with the
deceased. She advised us to consult on this matter a certain worthy
gentleman who had been a friend of Ivan Petrovich. We followed
her advice and received the following valued reply to our letter. We
print it here without any alterations or commentary, as a precious
memorial to a noble intellect and a touching friendship, and at the
same time as a most adequate biographical account.

My dear Sir,
I had the honour of receiving on the 23rd inst. your esteemed letter dated
the 15th, in which you express your desire to possess detailed information
regarding the dates of birth and death, the service career, the domestic
circumstances, as well as the occupations and character of the late Ivan

Petrovich Belkin, my former loyal friend and neighbour. It is with great pleasure that I comply with your request and I herewith forward to you, my dear Sir, all that I can recall, not only of his conversations but also of my own observations.

Ivan Petrovich Belkin was born of honourable and noble parents in the year 1798, in the village of Goryukhino. His late father, Second-Major Pyotr Ivanovich Belkin, was married to one Pelageya Gavrilovna, née Trafilin. He was not rich, but was abstemious in his habits and very able in managing his business affairs. Their son received his elementary education from the parish clerk. It was to this worthy gentleman, it would appear, that he owed his love of reading and interest in Russian literature. In 1815 he entered a regiment of chasseurs (I do not remember the number), in which he remained until the year 1823. The deaths of his parents, which were almost simultaneous, compelled him to resign his commission and to return to Goryukhino, his patrimonial estate.

Having embarked on the management of his estate, because of his inexperience and soft-heartedness, Ivan Petrovich soon allowed matters to fall into neglect, and he relaxed the strict regime that had been established by his late father. After dismissing the industrious and efficient bailiff with whom his serfs (as is their wont) were dissatisfied, he entrusted the management of the estate to his old housekeeper, who had won his confidence through her narrative skill. This stupid old woman could not distinguish a twenty-five from a fifty rouble note. The peasants, to all of whom she was godmother, had no fear of her whatsoever. The village-elder whom they had elected was so indulgent towards them, acting in concert with them to swindle their master, that Ivan Petrovich was compelled to abolish the corvée,[2] replacing it with an extremely moderate quit-rent.[3] Even so, the peasants, taking advantage of his weakness, elicited from him a special tax exemption in the first year and in the second paid more than two-thirds of the quit-rent in nuts, cranberries and the like. Notwithstanding, they were still in arrears.

Having been a friend of Ivan Petrovich's late father, I deemed it my duty to offer his son advice too, and on more than one occasion volunteered to restore the old order which he had allowed to fall into neglect. To that end I rode over to his place one day, requested the account books, summoned that rogue of an elder and began to examine them in the presence of Ivan

Petrovich. At first the young master followed me with the greatest attention and diligence; but as soon as it became clear from the accounts that, in the past two years, the number of peasants on the estate had increased, while the quantity of fowls and cattle had considerably decreased, Ivan Petrovich said that he was satisfied with these initial findings and no longer listened to me; at that very moment when, as a result of my investigations and stern interrogation, I had thrown that roguish elder into utmost confusion and reduced him to complete silence, to my extreme annoyance I heard Ivan Petrovich snoring vigorously in his chair. Thereafter I ceased interfering in his business affairs, entrusting these matters to the care of the Almighty.

However, this in no way harmed our friendly relations, inasmuch as I myself, while deeply regretting that weakness and ruinous negligence of his, so prevalent among our young noblemen these days, was genuinely fond of Ivan Petrovich. And it was indeed impossible not to like such a gentle and honest young man as he. For his part Ivan Petrovich showed respect for one of my years and had a heartfelt attachment for me. Right up to his death he would see me almost every day, greatly valuing my simple conversation, although, for the most part, we had hardly anything in common as regards habits, ways of thinking or temperament.

Ivan Petrovich lived the most modest of lives, avoiding excess of any kind. Not once did I see him the worse for drink (which in our parts can be accounted an unprecedented marvel); he had a strong inclination towards the female sex, but he was truly as shy as a young girl.*

Besides the tales which you are good enough to mention in your letter, Ivan Petrovich left a large number of manuscripts, some of which are in my possession and some of which were used by his housekeeper for various domestic needs. Thus all the windows in her wing of the house were pasted over last winter with the first part of a novel which he never completed. The above-mentioned tales were, it would appear, his first literary venture. As Ivan Petrovich used to maintain, for the most part they were true stories that he had heard from various people.† However, the names in almost all

---

* Here follows an anecdote which we have omitted, deeming it superfluous. However, we assure the reader that it contains nothing prejudicial to the memory of Ivan Petrovich Belkin. (A. S. Pushkin)

† In actual fact, over each tale in Mr Belkin's manuscript there is written in the author's hand: told to me by *such-and-such a person* (rank or title and initial letters

of them were invented by himself, but those of villages and hamlets were taken from our neighbourhood, which explains why my village too is mentioned somewhere. This was not from any malicious motives, but solely from want of imagination.

In the autumn of 1828 Ivan Petrovich caught a catarrhal chill which developed into a fever, and he died despite the untiring ministrations of our local doctor, a highly skilled gentleman, especially in the treatment of deep-rooted ailments such as corns and the like. He passed away in my arms in the thirtieth year of his life and is buried next to his parents in the churchyard at Goryukhino.

Ivan Petrovich was of medium height, with grey eyes, fair hair, straight nose; he had a light complexion and a thin face.

This is all, my dear Sir, that I can recall concerning the manner of life, occupations, temperament and appearance of my late neighbour and friend. But in case you should think fit to make use of this letter in any way, I most humbly beseech you not to mention my name: for although I have great respect and admiration for men of letters, I consider it inappropriate and indeed unseemly for one of my years to be included in their number. With my profound respects, etc.

November 16, 1830

Village of Nenaradovo.

Considering it our duty to respect the wishes of our author's esteemed friend, we convey our deepest gratitude to him for the information provided and hope that the public will appreciate his sincerity and good nature.

A. P.

---

of name and surname). We reproduce them here for the curious student. 'The Postmaster' was recounted to him by titular councillor A. G. N., 'The Shot' by Lieutenant-Colonel I. L. P., 'The Undertaker' by shop assistant B. V., 'The Blizzard' and 'The Squire's Daughter' by Miss K. I. T. (A. S. Pushkin)

THE SHOT

And so we fought a duel.   Baratynsky[1]

I vowed to kill him according to the code of duelling (it was
my turn to shoot).   'An Evening on Bivouac'[2]

I

We were stationed in the small town of ***. The life of an army
officer is well-known. In the mornings drill and riding-school; dinner
with the Colonel or at a Jewish inn; in the evenings punch and cards.
In *** there was not one open house, nor a single marriageable girl.
We would meet in each other's quarters, where all we saw was our
own uniforms.

Only one of our company was not in the army. He was about
thirty-five and therefore considered an old man. His experience gave
him many advantages over us; moreover, his habitual sullenness,
gruff disposition and spiteful tongue had a powerful effect on our
young minds. Some kind of mystery surrounded his life; he appeared
to be Russian, yet his name was foreign. Formerly he had served
with the hussars, and successfully at that. No one knew the reason
that had induced him to resign his commission and settle in a wretched
little town, where he lived poorly and extravagantly at the same
time. He invariably went about on foot, in a shabby black frock-coat,
but he kept open house for all the officers in our regiment.

True, his dinners consisted of only two or three courses, prepared
by an ex-soldier, but the champagne flowed like water. No one knew
what his circumstances were or what his income was, and no one

dared question him on the subject. He had a collection of books, chiefly on military subjects, and some novels. He willingly lent them to us and never asked for them back. On the other hand, he never returned to its owner any book that he had borrowed. His principal pastime was pistol-shooting. The walls of his room were riddled with bullet holes, so that they resembled a honeycomb. His rich collection of pistols was the sole luxury in that miserable clay-walled cottage where he lived. The skill he had acquired was simply incredible, and had he offered to shoot a pear from anyone's forage cap, not a man in our regiment would have hesitated to offer his head.

Our conversations often touched upon duelling. Silvio (as I shall call him) never became involved in them. If he were asked whether he had ever fought he would coldly reply that he had, but would never go into details, and it was obvious that he found such questions disagreeable. We assumed that he had on his conscience some hapless victim of his terrible skill. Besides, it never even occurred to us to suspect him of anything like cowardice. There are those whose mere appearance is enough to remove any such suspicion. But an unexpected event astounded us all.

One day about ten of our officers were dining at Silvio's. We drank as much as usual – that is, a great deal; after dinner we tried to persuade our host to hold the bank at cards. For some time he kept refusing, since he rarely played; at last, though, he ordered cards to be brought, poured out about fifty gold coins on to the table and sat down to deal. We stood around him and the game began. It was Silvio's habit to maintain complete silence when playing, never arguing or entering into any explanations. If a player happened to miscalculate Silvio either immediately paid him the difference or made a note of the surplus. We were well aware of this habit of his and never stopped him from having things his own way. But among us at that time was an officer recently transferred to our regiment. While playing this lieutenant absent-mindedly doubled his stake. Silvio took the chalk and corrected the score as he usually did. Thinking that Silvio had made a mistake the officer called for an explanation. Silvio continued dealing in silence. The lieutenant, losing patience, picked up the brush and rubbed out what he thought had been wrongly noted. Silvio took the chalk and adjusted the score. Heated by the wine, the game and his comrades' laughter, the officer considered himself grossly insulted and, in a fit of rage, seized a bronze candlestick from the table and hurled it at Silvio, who barely managed to get out of the way in time. We were all stunned. White with rage, Silvio stood up, his eyes flashing, and said, 'Sir, please be so good as to leave, and thank God that this has happened in my house.'

We had no doubts as to the consequences and already considered our new comrade a dead man. The officer left, declaring that he was ready to answer for the insult whenever it suited the gentleman holding the bank. We continued playing for a few minutes longer but, feeling that our host was no longer in the mood for cards, we withdrew one after the other and departed to our quarters, talking about the imminent vacancy in the regiment.

Next day, at riding-school, we were already asking each other if the poor lieutenant was still alive, when suddenly he appeared. We asked him the very same question. He replied that as yet he had had no word from Silvio. This astonished us. We went to Silvio's and found him in the courtyard, firing one bullet after another at an ace glued to the gate. He greeted us as usual, without saying a word about the incident of the previous evening. Three days passed and the lieutenant was still alive. Could it be possible, we asked in amazement, that Silvio was not going to fight? Silvio did not fight. He was satisfied with a very flimsy apology and made peace with the officer.

This did him enormous harm in the eyes of the young men. Lack of courage is the last thing to be excused by young people, who normally see valour as the summit of human virtue and as an excuse for every imaginable vice. Gradually, however, the whole affair was forgotten and Silvio regained his former influence.

I alone could no longer treat him on the same terms as before. Having a romantic imagination, I had become more attached than anyone else to this man, whose life was an enigma and who struck me as the hero of some mysterious tale. He was fond of me; at least, with me alone did he abandon his habitual sarcastic tone and converse about various subjects in a frank and unusually agreeable manner. But after that unfortunate evening, the thought that his honour had been stained and had remained uncleansed through his own fault would not leave me and prevented me from associating with him as before; I felt ashamed to look at him. Silvio was too intelligent and experienced not to notice this and not to guess the reason. It seemed to upset him; at least, on one or two occasions I could see that he wanted to explain everything to me. But I avoided such opportunities and Silvio did not keep company with me any longer. Subsequently I saw him only in the presence of other officers and our former frank conversations came to an end.

Those who live among the distractions of the capital can have no conception of the many sensations so familiar to inhabitants of villages or small towns – for example, waiting for the day when the mail arrives. On Tuesdays and Fridays our regimental office would be packed with officers, some expecting money, others letters or newspapers. Letters were usually opened on the spot, items of news exchanged and the office presented the liveliest of scenes. Silvio, whose letters were addressed to our regiment, was usually there. One day he received a letter whose seal he tore off with a look of the utmost impatience. His eyes gleamed as he ran through its contents. The other officers were too engrossed with their own letters to notice anything.

'Gentlemen,' Silvio told them, 'circumstances demand my immediate departure. I am leaving tonight. I hope that you will not refuse to dine with me for the last time. And I shall expect you too,' he added, turning to me. 'I shall expect you without fail.'

With these words he left in a hurry; after agreeing to meet at Silvio's the rest of us went our various ways.

I arrived there at the appointed time and found almost the entire regiment there. All his belongings were already packed. There remained only those bare, bullet-riddled walls. We sat down at the table. Our host was in exceptionally high spirits and before long his gaiety infected us all. Corks constantly popped, glasses foamed and hissed incessantly. With the utmost fervour we wished our departing host a safe journey and good fortune. It was late in the evening when we rose from the table. As we were sorting out our caps Silvio, who was bidding each of us farewell, took me by the arm and stopped me just as I was about to leave.

'I must have a word with you,' he said softly. I stayed behind.

The guests had all departed; the two of us were left alone, and we sat opposite each other and lit our pipes in silence. Silvio seemed very anxious; not a trace was left of that feverish gaiety. His grim pallor, his flashing eyes and the dense smoke issuing from his mouth made him look like the Devil incarnate. Several minutes passed and then Silvio broke the silence.

'We shall probably never meet again,' he told me, 'but before we part I would like to have a few words with you. You may have noticed that I care little for other people's opinion of me; but I like you and it would be painful for me to leave you with a false impression.'

He stopped and started refilling his pipe. I said nothing and looked down at the floor.

'You found it strange,' he continued, 'that I did not demand satisfaction from that drunken madcap R**. You will agree that, as I had the choice of weapons, his life was in my hands, while my own was in virtually no danger whatsoever. I could well ascribe my restraint to magnanimity alone, but I do not wish to lie. Had I been able to punish R** without risking my own life I would not have pardoned him for anything.'

I looked at Silvio in astonishment. Such a confession took me completely aback. Silvio continued,

'That's the precise truth: I have no right to put my life in danger. Six years ago I received a slap in the face and my enemy is still alive.'

My curiosity was greatly aroused.

'Did you not fight him?' I replied. 'Circumstances kept you apart, I suppose.'

'I did fight him,' Silvio replied, 'and here is a souvenir of our duel.'

Silvio stood up and took from a cardboard box a braided red cap with a gold tassel (the sort the French call *bonnet de police*). He put it on; a bullet had pierced it about two inches above the forehead.

'You know,' Silvio continued, 'that I used to serve in the *** hussar regiment. You know all about my character. I'm accustomed to taking first place in everything, but since I was young it has been a veritable passion with me. In our times wild behaviour was all the rage, and I was the wildest officer in the whole army. We would boast of our drinking-bouts – once I outdrank the famous Burtsov, of whom Denis Davydov sang in his poetry.[3] In our regiment duels were a regular occurrence: in all of them I was either witness or participant. My comrades idolized me, but the regimental commanders, who were constantly being replaced, looked upon me as a necessary evil.

'I was calmly (or not so calmly) basking in my reputation, when a young man from a rich and noble family joined the regiment (I do not want to mention his name). Never in my life had I met such a brilliant child of fortune. Picture for yourself – youth, intelligence, good looks, the most unbridled gaiety, the most reckless courage, a distinguished name, more money than he could count and of which he was never short – and you can gauge the impression he was bound to make on us. My supremacy was shaken. Fascinated by my reputation, he started seeking my friendship; but I treated him coldly and so, without the least regret, he avoided me. I came to hate him. His successes in the regiment and in female company reduced me to despair. I began to pick quarrels with him. To my epigrams he replied with epigrams that always struck me as more spontaneous and sharper than my own and which, needless to add, were infinitely more amusing: he jested while I fumed. Finally, at a ball given by a Polish landowner, when I saw that he was the centre of attention of all the ladies, particularly of the hostess herself, with whom I was having an affair, I whispered some crude insult in his ear. He flushed and slapped my face. We reached for our sabres; the ladies fainted; we were dragged apart, but that same night we rode out to fight.

'Dawn was breaking. I stood at the appointed place with my three seconds. With indescribable impatience I awaited my opponent. The spring sun had risen and the heat was making itself felt. I saw him in the distance. He was on foot, his jacket draped over his sabre, and he was accompanied by one second. We went to meet him. He approached, carrying his cap which was filled with cherries. The seconds measured twelve paces for us. I was to fire first, but so violent was my feeling of anger that I could not hope to depend on a steady hand, and in order to give myself time to cool down I allowed him first shot. But my opponent would not agree to this. So we decided to cast lots. The winning number fell to him, that eternal favourite of fortune. He took aim and sent a bullet through my cap. Now it was my turn. At last his life was in my hands. I looked at him, eagerly trying to detect the faintest sign of nervousness . . . But he stood there facing my pistol, picking the ripe cherries from his cap and spitting out the stones, which flew to where I was standing. His nonchalance maddened me. What is the use of depriving him of life, I thought, when he holds it so cheap? A spiteful thought flashed through my mind. I lowered my pistol. "You don't appear to be in the mood for death just now," I told him. "You want to have your breakfast; I have no wish to disturb you."

' "You're not disturbing me in the least," he retorted. "Please go ahead and shoot – or do as you please. The next shot is yours. I shall always be at your service."

'I turned to my seconds, announcing that I had no intention of firing that day, and with that the duel was over.

'I resigned my commission and retired to this small town. Since that time not a day has passed without my contemplating revenge. Now my time has come . . .'

Silvio took from his pocket the letter he had received that morning and gave it to me to read. Someone (apparently his business agent) had written to him from Moscow that a *certain individual* was shortly going to marry a young and beautiful girl.

'You can guess who this *certain individual* is,' Silvio said. 'I am going to Moscow. We shall see if he accepts death now, on his wedding eve, just as nonchalantly as he once waited for it while eating cherries!'

With these words Silvio stood up, threw his cap on the floor and started pacing the room like a tiger in its cage. I listened without moving an inch; strange, conflicting emotions agitated me.

A servant entered and announced that the horses were ready. Silvio grasped my hand firmly and we embraced. He climbed into his carriage where two suitcases were lying, one with his pistols, the other with his personal effects. We bade each other farewell once again and the horses galloped off.

II

Several years passed and domestic circumstances forced me to settle in a poor little village in N** district. Although busy with farming, I never ceased to sigh for my former boisterous and carefree life. Most difficult of all was having to get used to spending autumn and winter evenings in complete solitude. I somehow managed to drag out the time until dinner, chatting with the village elder, driving around to inspect work in progress or visiting new projects; but the moment dusk began to fall I just did not know what to do with myself. The few books that I had found in cupboards or in the storeroom I already knew by heart. All the tales that my housekeeper, Kirilovna, could remember had been recounted time and time again; the peasant women's singing utterly depressed me. I almost took to drinking unsweetened liqueurs, but they made my head ache. And indeed I must confess that I was scared of becoming one who drinks to drown his sorrows, that is, the saddest type of drunkard, of whom our district provided plenty of examples. I had no close neighbours, except for two or three hardened drinkers, whose conversation consisted chiefly of hiccups and sighs. Solitude was preferable to their company.

About two miles away was a rich estate belonging to a Countess B**, but only the manager lived there. The countess had visited her estate only once, in the first year of her marriage, and she stayed less than a month. However, in the second spring of my seclusion the rumour circulated that the countess and her husband were coming to spend the summer there. And in fact they arrived at the beginning of June.

The arrival of a rich neighbour is an important event in the lives of country-dwellers. Landowners and their servants talk about it for two months beforehand and for three years afterwards. For my part I do confess that the news of the arrival of a young and beautiful neighbour affected me deeply. I was burning with impatience to see her, and so, on the very first Sunday after their arrival, I set off after dinner for the village of *** to introduce myself to their Excellencies as their nearest neighbour and most humble servant.

A footman showed me into the count's study and then went off to announce me. The spacious study was furnished with every possible luxury; bookcases lined the walls and on the top of each one stood a bronze bust; above the marble fireplace was a wide mirror; the floor was covered with a green cloth, with carpets scattered over it. Unaccustomed to luxury in my own humble abode and not having seen other people's wealth for a long time, I began to feel nervous and awaited the count with some trepidation, just as a provincial petitioner awaits the entrance of a minister. The doors were opened and a handsome man of about thirty-two entered. The count approached me with an open, friendly air. I tried to regain my composure and was about to introduce myself when he anticipated me. We sat down. His easy, friendly conversation soon dispelled my sullen bashfulness. I was just beginning to feel myself again, when suddenly the countess entered and I became more embarrassed than ever. She was indeed beautiful. I wanted to appear at ease, but the more I tried to assume a relaxed air the more awkward I felt. To give me time to recover and become used to my new acquaintances they started talking to each other, treating me as if I were a good neighbour and without any formality. Meanwhile I started pacing up and down the study, examining the books and paintings. I am no expert on paintings, but one caught my attention. It depicted a Swiss scene; however, it was not the painting that struck me, but the fact that there were two bullet holes in the canvas, one right next to the other.

'That was a good shot,' I said, turning to the count.

'Yes,' he replied, 'a most remarkable shot. Are you a good marksman?' he continued.

'Fairly good,' I replied, delighted that the conversation had at last touched upon a subject that was dear to my heart. 'I can hit a card at thirty paces without fail – that is, of course, using a pistol I'm familiar with.'

'Really?' said the countess with a look of the greatest interest. 'And could you, my dear, hit a card at thirty paces?'

'Some day I'll try. In my time I wasn't a bad shot, but it's four years since I handled a pistol.'

'Oh,' I remarked. 'In that case I'll wager that your Excellency couldn't hit a card at twenty paces: pistol-shooting calls for daily practice. That I know from my own experience. I was considered one of the finest shots in the regiment. Once it so happened that I didn't touch a pistol for a whole month – mine were being repaired. And what do you think, your Excellency? The first time I started shooting again I missed a bottle four times in a row – at twenty-five paces! We had a cavalry captain, a witty and amusing fellow; he happened to be nearby and he told me, "It is clear, my friend, that your hand refuses to attack a bottle!" No, your Excellency, you must not neglect to practise or you'll soon lose the knack. The best marksman I ever met used to shoot every day, at least three times before dinner. It was as much a part of his daily routine as a glass of vodka.'

The count and countess were pleased that I had found my tongue.

'And what kind of a shot was he?' the count asked.

'Let me tell you, your Excellency. If he saw a fly on the wall – you laugh, Countess? I swear it's true. If he spotted a fly he'd shout, "Hey, Kuzka, my pistol!" Kuzka would bring him a loaded pistol. Bang! – and he'd flatten the fly against the wall.'

'Amazing!' said the count. 'And what was his name?'

'Silvio, your Excellency.'

'Silvio,' cried the count, leaping up. 'You knew Silvio?'

'How could I help knowing him? We were friends: he was accepted in the regiment as one of us. But it's five years since I had any news of him. So your Excellency knew him too?'

'Yes, I knew him very well. Did he ever tell you about . . . no, I don't think he could have. Did he ever tell you about one very strange incident?'

'The slap in the face he received, your Excellency, from some madcap at a ball?'

'Did he ever tell you the name of that madcap?'

'No, your Excellency, he never mentioned it,' I continued, realizing the truth. 'Forgive me . . . I didn't know . . . could it have been *you*?'

'Yes, it was I,' replied the count with a look of the utmost distress. 'And that picture with the bullet hole is a memento of our last meeting . . .'

'Ah, my dear,' said the countess, 'for heaven's sake don't tell him about it. It would be too awful for me to listen to.'

'No,' retorted the count, 'I shall tell everything. He knows how I insulted his friend, so let him know how Silvio took his revenge on me.'

The count drew up an armchair for me, and with the liveliest curiosity I listened to the following story.

'Five years ago I got married. The first month, the honeymoon,[4] we spent here, on this estate. To this house I owe the happiest moments of my life – as well as one of its most painful memories.

'One evening we went riding together. For some reason my wife's horse suddenly turned obstinate. She became frightened, handed me the reins and returned home on foot. I rode on ahead. In the courtyard I saw a wagon and was told that sitting in my study was a man who did not want to give his name but who simply said that he had business with me. I came into this room, and in the darkness I could see a man covered in dust and with a thick growth of beard; he was standing here, by the fireplace. I went up to him, trying to recall those features.

' "You do not recognize me, Count?" he asked in a trembling voice.

' "Silvio!" I cried, and I confess I felt my hair was standing on end.

' "Exactly," he went on. "I'm due one shot and I've come to discharge my pistol. Are you ready?"

'A pistol was protruding from one of his side pockets. I measured out twelve paces and stood in the corner, over there, imploring him to hurry up and shoot before my wife returned. He took his time and asked for a light. Candles were brought in. I closed the door, gave instructions that no one was to enter and again begged him to fire. He drew his pistol and took aim . . . I counted the seconds . . . I thought of her . . . A terrible minute went by! Then Silvio lowered his arm.

' "I'm sorry," he said, "that my pistol is not loaded with cherry stones . . . bullets are so heavy. It strikes me, however, that this is not a duel, but murder: I am not accustomed to aiming at unarmed men. Let us begin all over again. We shall cast lots as to who fires first."

'My head was spinning . . . I think that I objected . . . Finally we loaded another pistol; we folded two pieces of paper; he put them in that very same cap through which I had once fired; again I drew the lucky number.

' "You have the luck of the devil, Count," he said with a grin that I shall never forget. I don't understand what came over me or how he could have forced me into it . . . but I fired and hit that picture over there." (The count pointed at the perforated picture; his face was burning like fire; the countess was paler than her own handkerchief. I could not help crying out.)

' "I fired," continued the count, and "thank God I missed; then Silvio . . . (at that moment he was terrible to look at) Silvio began to take aim at me. Suddenly the door opened, Masha rushed in and with a scream threw her arms around my neck. Her presence restored all my courage.

' "My dear," I told her, "can't you see we're joking? How frightened you look! Go and drink some water and then come back. I shall introduce you to an old friend and comrade."

'But Masha still did not believe me.

' "Tell me, is my husband telling the truth?" she asked, turning to the menacing Silvio. "Is it true that you are both joking?"

' "He is always joking, Countess," Silvio replied. "Once he slapped me on the face for a joke, fired a bullet through this cap for a joke and just now he missed – for a joke. Now *I* feel the urge to have a little joke . . ."

'With these words he started to take aim . . . in front of her! Masha threw herself at his feet.

' "Get up, Masha, aren't you ashamed!" I shouted furiously. "And will you, Sir, will you stop mocking a poor woman? Are you going to fire or not?"

' "No, I am not," Silvio replied. "I am satisfied: I have witnessed your dismay, your loss of nerve. I have forced you to fire at me and that is enough. You will remember me. I leave you to your conscience."

'At this point he turned to leave, but stopped in the doorway, looked back at the picture through which my bullet had passed and fired at it, almost without aiming, after which he vanished. My wife lay in a faint; the servants did not dare stop him and looked at him in horror; he went out on to the front steps, summoned his coachman and drove off before I had time to collect myself.'

The count fell silent. Thus I came to hear the end of that story whose beginning had once made such a deep impression on me. I never met its hero again. Rumour has it that Silvio was killed at the Battle of Skulyani, during the uprising under Alexander Ypsilanti, while commanding a detachment of Hetairists.[5]

THE BLIZZARD

Trampling the snow in drifts so deep,
The horses race in headlong flight,
And as across the slopes they sweep
A lonely church comes into sight

A great blizzard suddenly flings
Tufted flakes along the way;
A black raven with whistling wings
Hovers over the sleigh.
Its woeful cry forebodes but doom;
With manes upraised the steeds make haste
Peering into the distant gloom,
As they cross the snowy waste . . .
                                    Zhukovsky[1]

At the end of 1811, during an epoch so memorable for us, there lived on his estate at Nenaradovo the worthy Gavrila Gavrilovich R**. He was famous throughout the district for his hospitality and cordiality. His neighbours were constantly visiting him, either to eat or drink, or to play Boston[2] at five copecks a hand with his wife; but there were some who came to look at their daughter Marya Gavrilovna, a pale, slim girl of seventeen. She was considered a wealthy match and many intended her for themselves or their sons.

Marya Gavrilovna was brought up on French novels and consequently was in love. Her chosen one was a poor ensign who was then on leave in his village. There is no need to say that the young man was burning with equal passion and that the parents of his beloved, having observed their mutual inclination, forbade their daughter even to consider him and gave him a worse reception than if he were a retired court assessor.

Our lovers wrote to each other and every day met secretly in the pine grove or near the old chapel. There they vowed eternal love to each other, bemoaned their cruel lot and made various plans. Corresponding and conversing in this way they (very naturally) came to the following conclusion: since we cannot live without each other and the will of our hard-hearted parents is barring our happiness, then why can we not ignore it.

Of course, there is no need to mention that it was to the young man that this happy thought first occurred and that it was intensely gratifying to Marya Gavrilovna's romantic imagination.

Winter came and put an end to their meetings; but their correspondence became all the more lively. In every letter Vladimir Nikolayevich implored her to entrust herself to him, to marry him secretly, to stay in hiding with him for a while, after which they would throw themselves at the feet of her parents who, quite naturally, would at last be moved by the heroic constancy and unhappiness of the lovers and would be bound to tell them: 'Children! Let us embrace you.'

Marya Gavrilovna hesitated for some time; she rejected most of the plans for the elopement. Finally she agreed to the following: on the appointed day she would excuse herself from supper and retire to her room on the pretext of a headache. Her maid was party to the plot; both of them were to go by the back stairs out into the garden, at the bottom of which they would find a sleigh waiting for them, get into it and drive the three miles from Nenaradovo to the village of Zhadrino, straight to the church there, where Vladimir would be waiting for them.

On the eve of the decisive day Marya Gavrilovna did not sleep the whole night. She spent the time packing, tied up some of her linen and dresses, wrote a long letter to a sentimental lady-friend and another to her parents. She bade them farewell in the most touching terms, excused her actions, which were governed by the invincible power of passion, and concluded with the remark that she would consider it the happiest moment of her life when she would be allowed to throw herself at the feet of her dear parents. After sealing both letters with a Tula[3] seal, on which were engraved two flaming hearts with a suitable inscription, she threw herself on her bed just before dawn and fell into a light slumber. But terrible dreams constantly aroused her. First she dreamt that, at the very moment when she seated herself in the sleigh to drive off to be married, her father stopped her, dragged her over the snow with agonizing speed and cast her into a dark, bottomless dungeon ... and she flew headlong with an indescribable sinking of the heart. Then she saw Vladimir lying on the grass, pale and bloody. As he died he implored her in a piercing voice to make haste and marry him ... and a succession of hideous, absurd visions drifted past. Finally she rose from her bed, paler than usual – and with a genuine headache. Her mother and father noticed her uneasiness; their tender solicitude and incessant enquiries: 'What's wrong, Masha? Are you ill, Masha?' rent her heart. She endeavoured to reassure them and look cheerful, but she could not. Evening came. The thought that this was the last day she would be spending with her family lay heavily on her heart. She felt barely alive; secretly she bade farewell to everyone, to all the objects that surrounded her.

Supper was served; her heart beat violently. In a trembling voice she announced that she did not want any supper and took leave of her father and mother. They kissed her and gave her their usual blessing: she very nearly started crying. As soon as she reached her room she threw herself into a chair and burst into tears. Her maid urged her to be calm and to take heart. Everything was ready. Within half an hour Marya Gavrilovna was to leave her parents' house, her room, her quiet girlish life for ever ... Outside a blizzard was raging; the wind howled and the shutters shook and rattled; everything seemed a threat, a bad omen. Soon all was quiet in the house; everyone was asleep. Masha wrapped herself in a shawl, put on a warm cloak, took her box in her hands and went out by the back stairs. Her maid followed her with two bundles. They went down into the garden. The blizzard had not abated; the wind blew in their faces, as if trying to stop the young criminal. They struggled to the bottom of the garden. On the road the sleigh was waiting for them.

The chilled horses just would not keep still; Vladimir's coachman was walking up and down by the shafts trying to restrain the restive steeds. He helped the young lady and her maid to seat themselves and stow away the bundles and box, grasped the reins, and the horses flew off. Having entrusted the young lady to the care of fate and to the skill of Teryoshka, the coachman, let us return to our young lover.

All day long Vladimir had been driving around. In the morning he called on the priest at Zhadrino; after much difficulty he managed to come to an agreement with him; then he rode off to look for witnesses among the neighbouring landowners. The first person he called upon was Dravin, a retired forty-year-old cornet, who agreed with alacrity. The whole adventure, he affirmed, reminded him of the old days and his pranks in the hussars. He persuaded Vladimir to stay for dinner and assured him that he would have no trouble finding another two witnesses. And in fact there arrived immediately after dinner the surveyor Schmidt, with moustache and spurs, and the son of the district police chief, a lad of sixteen who had recently joined the uhlans. Not only did they accept Vladimir's proposal, but they even vowed that they were ready to lay down their lives for him. Vladimir embraced them rapturously and rode home to make his preparations.

It had been dark for some time. Vladimir dispatched his trusty Teryoshka to Nenaradovo with his troika and with detailed, lengthy instructions, ordered the little one-horse sleigh for himself and drove off without any coachman to Zhadrino, where Marya Gavrilovna was due to arrive in about two hours. He knew the road well, and it was only a twenty-minute drive.

But hardly had Vladimir driven out on to the open road when the wind rose and such a blizzard began to rage that he could see nothing. In one minute the road was covered with snow. The landscape all around disappeared in a murky yellowish fog through which white snowflakes flew; sky merged with earth. Vladimir found himself driving over fields and he tried in vain to get back on to the road again. His horse made its way by guesswork, every moment mounting a snowdrift or sinking into a hole, so that the sleigh kept turning over. Vladimir's only concern was not to lose his way. But more than half an hour seemed to have passed already and still he had not reached Zhadrino Wood. Another ten minutes or so passed; still he could not see the wood. Vladimir drove over a field criss-crossed by deep gullies. The blizzard did not abate, the sky showed no sign of clearing. The horse began to tire, and the sweat poured from Vladimir, despite the fact that he was constantly waist-deep in snow.

Finally Vladimir saw that he was travelling in the wrong direction. He stopped to consider, to try and remember, to work it out and felt convinced that he should have turned right. So now he did turn right. His horse could barely move one leg in front of the other. He had been on the road for more than an hour. Zhadrino could not be far away. But on and on he went, and still the field did not come to an end. Nothing but snowdrifts and gullies; the sleigh was constantly turning over – and constantly he set it upright again. Time was passing; Vladimir became deeply worried.

At last he could see something black to one side. Vladimir turned towards it. As he approached he saw that it was a wood. Thank God, he thought, it's not far now. He skirted the wood, hoping to come out on the familiar road any moment, or to pass right round the wood. Zhadrino was just beyond it. Soon he found a road and drove into the dark wood, whose trees had been stripped of their leaves by winter. The wind could not rage here; the road was smooth; the horse took heart and Vladimir felt calmer.

But on and on he drove – and still there was no sign of Zhadrino; there was no end to the wood. Vladimir was horrified to see that he had driven into an unfamiliar wood. He was gripped with despair. He struck the horse; the poor animal broke into a trot but soon began to tire and after a quarter of an hour slowed to a walk, despite all the efforts of the hapless Vladimir.

Gradually the trees began to thin out, and finally Vladimir emerged from the wood; but there was no sign of Zhadrino. It must have been about midnight. Tears streamed from his eyes; he drove on, trusting in guesswork. In the meantime the blizzard had abated, the clouds dispersed and before him stretched a plain covered with a white, undulating carpet. The night was quite clear. Not far off he saw a hamlet, consisting of four or five cottages. Vladimir drove towards it. At the first cottage he leapt from the sledge, ran to the window and started knocking. After a few minutes the wooden shutter was raised, and an old man poked his grey beard out. 'What d'ye want?' 'Is Zhadrino far from here?' 'Zhadrino? Far from here?' 'Yes, yes! Is it far?' 'Not far, about six miles I reckons.' At this reply Vladimir clutched his hair and stood motionless, like a man condemned to death.

'And where are you from?' continued the old man. Vladimir did not have the spirit to reply to the question. 'Old man,' he said, 'can you find me some horses to take me to Zhadrino?' 'What horses do you think we have here?' the old man replied. 'Well, can't I at least take a guide? I shall pay him whatever he asks.' 'Wait,' said the old man, lowering the shutter, 'I'll send my son out, he'll guide you.' Vladimir stood and waited. Barely had a minute elapsed before he started knocking again. The shutter was raised and the beard reappeared. 'What d'ye want?' 'Where's your son?' 'He's coming right away; he's just putting on his boots. Are you cold? Come inside and warm yourself.' 'No thank you. Send your son out, and quickly.'

The door creaked. A young lad came out with a cudgel and went on ahead, now pointing out, now looking for the road among the deep snowdrifts. 'What time is it?' Vladimir asked. 'It'll soon be daylight,' the boy replied. Vladimir did not say another word.

The cocks were crowing and it was already light when they reached Zhadrino. The church was locked. Vladimir paid his guide and drove into the priest's courtyard. His troika was not there. And what news awaited Vladimir!

But let us return to our worthy landowners of Nenaradovo and see what is happening over there.

Nothing.

The old couple awoke and went into the drawing-room. Gavrila Gavrilovich was in his nightcap and flannel jacket, Praskovya Petrovna in her quilted dressing-gown. The samovar was brought in and Gavrila sent a servant girl to ask how Marya Gavrilovna was feeling and what kind of night she had spent. The girl returned and announced that the young lady had not slept well, but that she was feeling better now and would soon join them in the drawing-room. And indeed the door opened and Marya Gavrilovna entered and greeted her father and mother.

'How is your head, Masha?' asked Gavrila Gavrilovich. 'Better, Papa,' Masha replied. 'It must have been the fumes from the stove, Masha,' said Praskovya Petrovna. 'Probably, Mama,' Masha replied.

The day passed happily, but during the night Masha was taken ill. They sent to town for a doctor. He arrived towards evening and found the sick girl delirious. A severe fever developed, and for two weeks the poor girl lay at death's door.

No one in the house knew of the proposed elopement. The letters she had written the previous evening had been burnt; fearing her master's wrath, the maid had not breathed a word to a soul. The priest, the retired cornet, the moustached surveyor and the young uhlan kept a discreet silence – and not without reason. Teryoshka the coachman did not utter one word too many, even when drunk. Thus the secret was kept by more than half a dozen conspirators. But Marya Gavrilovna herself, in her constant delirium, revealed her secret. However, what she said was so incoherent that her mother, who never quitted her bedside, could only make out that her daughter was hopelessly in love with Vladimir Nikolayevich and that in all probability her being in love was the cause of her illness. She consulted her husband and several neighbours, and in the end all unanimously concluded that such was Marya Gavrilovna's destiny, that marriages are made in heaven, that poverty is no crime, that one should live not with riches but with a person and so on. Moral commonplaces are amazingly useful when we can find little in ourselves with which to justify our actions.

Meanwhile the young lady began to recover. Vladimir had not been seen for a long time in Gavrila Gavrilovich's house. He was afraid of the usual reception. So they decided to send for him and tell him a piece of unexpected good news: their consent to the marriage. Imagine the astonishment of the Nenaradovo landowners when, in reply to their invitation, they received a half-insane letter from him! He informed them that he would never set foot in their house again and asked them to forget a poor wretch for whom the only hope was death. A few days later they learnt that Vladimir had gone to join the army. This was in the year 1812.

For a long time they dared not speak about it to Masha, who was now convalescing. Not once did she mention the name of Vladimir. Several months later, finding his name in a list of those who had distinguished themselves and had been gravely wounded at Borodino,[4] she fainted, and it was feared the fever might return. However, thank goodness, her fainting fit had no serious consequences.

A fresh misfortune befell her: Gavrila Gavrilovich died, leaving her heiress to the entire estate. But coming into her inheritance offered no consolation. She shared genuinely in the grief of poor Praskovya Petrovna and vowed never to be parted from her. Both of them left Nenaradovo, scene of such sad memories, and went to live on another estate at ***.

And there too suitors swarmed around that charming and rich prospective bride, but she did not hold out the slightest hope to any of them. Occasionally her mother tried to persuade her to make a choice. Masha would shake her head and become thoughtful. Vladimir no longer existed: he had died in Moscow, on the eve of the entry of the French. His memory seemed sacred to Masha; at least, she kept everything that might remind her of him: books he had once read, drawings, music and poetry he had copied out for her. When the neighbours learnt about this, they marvelled at her constancy and awaited with curiosity the hero who would finally triumph over the sad fidelity of this virginal Artemisia.[5]

Meanwhile the war ended gloriously. Our regiments were returning from abroad. The people ran to greet them. Bands played songs of the conquered enemy: *Vive Henri-Quatre*,[6] Tyrolean waltzes and airs from *Joconde*.[7] Officers who had left for the wars as mere boys returned having grown to manhood in the martial air, with medals hanging from their tunics. Soldiers gaily chatted to each other, constantly introducing German and French words into their speech. An unforgettable time! A time of glory and enthusiasm! How violently did Russian hearts beat at the word *fatherland*! How sweet were the tears of reunion! How we all combined, with such unanimity,

a feeling of national pride with love for the Tsar! And for him what
a moment it was!

The women – Russian women – were beyond comparison at that
time. Their habitual coldness disappeared. Their enthusiasm was
truly intoxicating when, greeting the victors, they cried 'Hurrah!'

And tossed their bonnets into the air.[8]

What officer of that time does not admit that it was to Russian
women that he was obliged for his best and most precious reward . . . ?

At this brilliant time Marya Gavrilovna was living with her mother
in *** province and did not see how the return of the troops was
celebrated in both capitals. But in the provinces and villages the
general enthusiasm was perhaps even stronger. The appearance of
an officer in these parts was a genuine triumph for him and the
frock-coated lover had no chance when he was in the vicinity.

We have already said that, despite her aloofness, Marya Gavrilovna
was, as before, surrounded by suitors. But all of them had to withdraw
when the wounded Colonel Burmin of the Hussars, with the Order
of St George in his buttonhole and with an 'interesting pallor' as the
young ladies of the locality put it, appeared at the manor-house. He
was about twenty-six. He had been given leave to visit his estate,
which was in close proximity to Marya Gavrilovna's. She singled
him out for special attention. In his company her habitual pensiveness
was replaced by cheerfulness. It could not be said that she actually
flirted with him; but the poet, observing her behaviour, would have
said:

Se amor non è che dunque? . . .[9]

Burmin was really a most charming young man. He possessed the
type of mind that is so pleasing to women: urbane and observant,
without any pretensions, and given to gentle mockery. His behaviour
towards Marya Gavrilovna was unaffected and natural. But whatever
she said or did, his heart and eyes invariably followed her. He seemed
to be of a mild, inoffensive disposition; it was rumoured that he had
once been a terrible rake, but that did him no harm in the eyes of
Marya Gavrilovna who (like all young ladies) took pleasure in

excusing his misdemeanours, which testified to the boldness and fieriness of his character.

But more than anything else . . . more than his gentleness, more than his pleasant conversation, more than his 'interesting pallor', more than his bandaged arm – it was the young hussar's silences that excited her curiosity and imagination. She could not but admit to herself that he liked her very much. And most probably he too, with his intelligence and experience, had already noticed that she had singled him out for special attention. So why was it that, as yet, she had not seen him at her feet and heard him declare his love? What was holding him back? Timidity, inseparable from true love, or the flirtatiousness of a cunning philanderer? It was a mystery to her. After long reflection she decided that timidity was the sole cause of his reserve and proposed to encourage him by greater attentiveness and, should circumstances warrant it, even by a display of tenderness. She prepared the most surprising denouement and impatiently awaited the moment of romantic declaration. Secrets of any kind always weigh heavily on the female heart. Her military tactics had the desired effect: at least, Burmin lapsed into such a reverie and his black eyes rested on Marya Gavrilovna with such fire that the decisive moment seemed imminent. Her neighbours spoke of the marriage as a foregone conclusion, and the good Praskovya Petrovna rejoiced that her daughter had finally found a worthy suitor.

One day the old lady was sitting alone in the drawing-room, laying out cards for *grande patience*, when Burmin entered and immediately asked for Marya Gavrilovna.

'She's in the garden,' replied the old lady. 'Go to her, I shall wait for you here.'

Burmin went out and the old lady crossed herself and thought: 'Perhaps it will all be settled today!'

Burmin found Marya Gavrilovna under a willow near the pond, in a white dress, with a book in her hand – a true heroine from a novel. After the first questions she deliberately allowed the conversation to flag, thus increasing the mutual embarrassment, from which the only possible escape was by a sudden and decisive declaration of love. And that is what happened: Burmin, sensing the difficulty of his position, announced that he had long been seeking an opportunity to open his heart to her and requested a moment's attention. Marya Gavrilovna closed her book and looked down as a sign of consent.

'I love you,' Burmin said. 'I love you passionately . . .' (Marya Gavrilovna blushed and lowered her head even more.) 'I have behaved imprudently by indulging myself in the charming habit of seeing and hearing you daily . . .' (She recalled the first letter of St Preux.[10]) 'Now it is too late to resist my fate; the memory of you, your charming, incomparable image, will henceforth be the torment and the joy of my life. But there still remains a painful duty for me to perform – to reveal a terrible secret, thereby placing an insurmountable barrier . . .' 'It has always existed,' Marya Gavrilovna interrupted with animation. 'I could never have been your wife . . .' 'I know,' he replied quietly. 'I know that once you were in love, but death and three years of mourning . . . Dear, kind Marya Gavrilovna! Do not attempt to deprive me of my last consolation: the thought that you would have agreed to make me happy if only . . . do not speak, for heaven's sake, do not speak! You are tormenting me. Yes, I know, I feel that you would have been mine, but . . . I am the most wretched of creatures . . . I am married!'

Marya Gavrilovna looked at him in astonishment.

'I am married,' Burmin continued. 'I have been married four years and I do not know who my wife is, where she is or whether I shall ever see her again!'

'What are you saying?' exclaimed Marya Gavrilovna. 'How very strange this is! Please continue; I shall tell you my story later, but please continue, I beg you.'

'At the beginning of 1812,' Burmin began, 'I was hurrying to Vilna, where our regiment was stationed. Arriving late one evening at a post-station I ordered horses to be harnessed without delay, when suddenly there was a terrible blizzard, and the postmaster and drivers advised me to wait. I followed their advice, but an inexplicable anxiety took hold of me: it seemed as if someone was pushing me forward. Meanwhile the blizzard did not abate. I lost patience, again ordered horses to be harnessed and rode off straight into the blizzard. The coachman took it into his head to follow the course of the river, which should have shortened the journey by about a mile and a half. The banks were covered with snow; the coachman passed the spot where we would have come out on the main road, and as a result we found ourselves in unknown territory. The blizzard did not let up. I saw a light and ordered the driver to head towards it. We reached a village; in a wooden church a light was burning. The church was open and by the fence stood several sleighs; people were walking up and down the porch. "Over here! Over here!" cried several voices. I ordered the coachman to drive up. "For heaven's sake, why have you taken so long?" someone asked me. "The bride has fainted, the priest does not know what to do; we were just about to go back. Come as quickly as you can." Without saying a word I sprang from my sleigh and entered the church, which was dimly lit by two or three candles. A young girl was sitting on a bench in a dark corner of the church; another girl was rubbing her temples. "Thank God," the latter said. "At last you've come. You very nearly killed my mistress." The old priest came over to me and asked, "Do you wish me to begin?" "Yes, begin, do begin, Father," I answered absently. They lifted the young lady to her feet. She seemed not bad-looking. Prompted by an incomprehensible, unpardonable light-headedness, I took my place at her side before the pulpit; the priest was in a hurry; three men and a maid supported the bride and concerned themselves only with her. We were married. "Kiss each other," we were told. My wife turned her pale face towards me. I was about to kiss her . . . She cried out, "Oh, it is not he! It is not he!" – and she fell senseless. With fear in their eyes the witnesses stared at her. I turned around, walked out of the church unimpeded, threw myself into the sleigh and shouted, "Drive off!" '

'Good God!' cried Marya Gavrilovna. 'And do you have any idea what became of your poor wife?'

'I do not know,' Burmin replied. 'Nor do I know the name of the village where I was married. I cannot remember the name of the post-station from which I set out. At the time I attached so little importance to my criminal prank that I fell asleep when I drove away from the church and I did not wake up until I was at the third station, the following morning. The servant who was with me at the time died during the campaign, so that I have no hope at all of ever finding that woman upon whom I played such a cruel joke and who has now taken such cruel vengeance.'

'Good God! Good God!' cried Marya Gavrilovna, grasping his hand. 'So it was *you*! Do you not recognize me?'

Burmin turned pale and threw himself at her feet . . .

THE UNDERTAKER

Do we not behold coffins every day,
The grey hairs of an ageing universe?
Derzhavin[1]

The last of the undertaker Adrian Prokhorov's belongings were piled
on to the hearse and for the fourth time the two scrawny-looking
horses dragged themselves from Basmannaya Street to Nikitskaya
Street,[2] where the undertaker had moved with his whole household.
After locking his shop he nailed to the gate a notice announcing that
the house was for sale or rent, and set off on foot for his new abode.
As he approached the little yellow house that for so long had captured
his imagination and which he had bought at last for a tidy sum, the
old undertaker was amazed to find that his heart did not rejoice.
When he crossed the unfamiliar threshold and found his new home
in chaos, he sighed for his old tumbledown shack where, for eighteen
years, the strictest order had prevailed. He started scolding his two
daughters and maidservant for being so slow and set about helping
them himself. Soon order was established; the icon case, the crockery
cupboard, the table, the sofa and the bed occupied their appointed
places in the back room; in the kitchen and parlour the master's
wares were placed: coffins of every colour and size, as well as
cupboards filled with mourning hats, cloaks and torches. Over the
gate hung a sign depicting a plump cupid with a downturned torch
in his hand and bearing the inscription: 'Plain and painted coffins
sold and upholstered here. Coffins also let out for hire and old ones
repaired.' The girls retired to their room. After making a tour of

inspection of his new dwelling Adrian sat by the window and ordered the samovar to be prepared.

The enlightened reader knows that Shakespeare and Walter Scott both portrayed their grave-diggers as cheerful, jocular characters so that the contrast might strike our imagination all the more forcibly. Out of respect for the truth we are unable to follow their example and have to admit that the temperament of our undertaker harmonized perfectly with his lugubrious vocation. Adrian Prokhorov was habitually gloomy and pensive. He would break his silence only to scold his daughters when he found them idly staring out of the window at passers-by, or to demand an exorbitant price for his wares from those who had the misfortune (or occasionally the good fortune) to need them. And so Adrian, seated by the window and drinking his seventh cup of tea, was, as usual, absorbed by sad reflections. He was brooding over the torrential rain which, a week before, had poured down at the funeral procession of a retired brigadier. Because of the rain, many cloaks had shrunk, many hats had lost their shape. He foresaw unavoidable expenses, since his old stock of funeral apparel was in a sorry state. He had hoped to recoup his losses with the funeral of old Tryukhina, the merchant's wife, who had been at death's door for over a year. But Tryukhina lay dying at Razgulyai,[3] and Prokhorov was afraid that her heirs, despite their promise, would not bother to send for him from so far away and would make their arrangements with the nearest undertaker.

These reflections were unexpectedly interrupted by three Masonic knocks at the door. 'Who's there?' asked the undertaker. The door opened and a man who could immediately be recognized as a German craftsman entered the room and approached the undertaker with a cheerful look. 'Excuse me, my good neighbour,' he said in that accented Russian which to this day we cannot hear without laughing, 'excuse me for disturbing you . . . I wanted to make your acquaintance as soon as possible. I'm a shoemaker, my name is Gottlieb Schultz and I live across the street, in the little house opposite your windows. Tomorrow I shall be celebrating my silver wedding, and I've come to invite you and your daughters to have dinner with us.' The invitation was graciously accepted. The undertaker asked the shoe-

maker to sit down and have a cup of tea, and thanks to Gottlieb
Schultz's open-hearted disposition they were soon having the most
amicable of conversations. 'How is business, my dear sir?' Adrian
asked. 'Oh,' replied Schultz, 'so-so. I really can't complain. Of course
my goods are not like yours: the living can do without shoes, but
the dead can't do without a coffin.' 'That's so true,' observed Adrian.
'However, if a living person has no money for shoes then, begging
your pardon, he goes around barefoot. But a dead beggar gets his
coffin for nothing.' The conversation continued in this vein for some
time. Finally the shoemaker stood up, renewed his invitation and
took his leave of the undertaker.

Next day, at precisely twelve o'clock, the undertaker and his
daughters passed through the gate of their newly purchased house
and went to visit their neighbour. I shall not stop to describe Adrian's
Russian caftan, nor Akulina and Darya's European attire, in this
respect departing from the normal practice of contemporary novelists.
At the same time, however, I do not consider it superfluous to remark
that both girls had put on the yellow hats and red shoes which they
wore only on very important occasions.

The shoemaker's cramped room was packed with guests, mainly
German craftsmen with their wives and apprentices. There was only
one Russian official there, namely a constable, Yurko the Finn who,
despite his lowly calling, enjoyed the host's particular favour. For
twenty-five years he had discharged his duties honestly and loyally,
like Pogorelsky's postman.[4] The fire of 1812, which had destroyed
the ancient capital, had also destroyed his yellow sentry-box. But
immediately after the expulsion of the enemy, a new one appeared
in its place, painted grey and with white Doric columns, and Yurko
once again paced up and down before it 'axe in hand and in armour
of coarse cloth'.[5] He was known to the majority of Germans living
near the Nikitsky Gate, and some of them had even happened to
spend Sunday night at his place. Adrian immediately made himself
acquainted with him as someone who, sooner or later, might have
need of his services, and when the guests took their places at the
table they sat beside one another.

At dinner Herr and Frau Schultz and their seventeen-year-old daughter Lottchen waited on their guests and helped the cook to serve the food. The beer flowed. Yurko ate enough for four and in no way did Adrian lag behind; his daughters conducted themselves with due decorum. The conversation, which was in German, became noisier every minute. Suddenly the host called for his guests' attention and, as he uncorked a sealed bottle, said loudly in Russian, 'To the health of my good Luisa!' The sparkling wine foamed. The host tenderly kissed the fresh face of his forty-year-old spouse and the guests noisily toasted good Luisa's health. 'To the health of my dear guests!' proclaimed the host as he uncorked a second bottle; and the guests thanked him as they drained their glasses again. Then one toast followed another: they drank the health of each guest; they drank to the health of Moscow and a round dozen little German towns; they drank to the health of all guilds in general and each one in particular; they drank to the health of the masters and apprentices. Adrian drank zealously and became so merry that he proposed some humorous toast himself. Suddenly one of the guests, a fat baker, raised his glass and exclaimed, 'To the health of those for whom we work, *unserer Kundleute!*'[6] This proposal, like all the others, was joyfully and unanimously welcomed. The guests began to bow to one another – the tailor to the shoemaker, the shoemaker to the tailor, the baker to both of them, the whole assembly to the baker and so on. Amidst the mutual salutations Yurko cried out, turning to his neighbour, 'Come on, my dear friend! Drink to the health of your corpses!' Everyone burst out laughing, but the undertaker considered himself insulted and frowned. No one noticed, the guests carried on drinking and the bells were already ringing for vespers when they left the table.

It was late when the guests departed and most of them were tipsy. The fat baker and the bookbinder, whose face

Seemed to be bound in red morocco,[7]

led Yurko by the arm to his sentry-box, on this occasion observing the Russian proverb, 'One good turn deserves another.' The undertaker arrived home drunk and angry. 'Why is it?' he deliberated aloud, 'that my profession is less honourable than any other? Is an undertaker brother to the hangman? What were those heathens laughing at? Is an undertaker a clown at a Christmas party? I'd really like to invite them to a house-warming and give them a splendid feast. But no! I'll invite those for whom I work – the Christian dead.'

'What are you saying, master?' asked his maidservant, who was just then helping him off with his boots. 'Cross yourself! Fancy inviting the dead to a house-warming! How awful!' 'By God I shall invite them!' Adrian continued. 'And tomorrow too! Do me the favour, my benefactors, come and feast with me tomorrow evening. I shall regale you with whatever I have.' With these words the undertaker went to bed and he was soon snoring.

It was still dark outside when Adrian was roused from his slumbers. Tryukhina, the merchant's wife, had died that very night, and a special messenger, sent on horseback by her steward, had galloped over to Adrian with the news. The undertaker gave him ten copecks for some vodka, hurriedly dressed and took a cab to Razgulyai. The police were already standing at the door of the dead woman's house, while tradesmen walked up and down like ravens scenting a dead body. The deceased lay on a table, yellow as wax but as yet not disfigured by decay. Relatives, neighbours and servants had crowded round her. All the windows were open; candles were burning; priests were reading prayers for the dead. Adrian went up to Tryukhina's nephew, a young merchant in a fashionable frock-coat, and informed him that the coffin, candles, pall and other funeral accessories would be immediately delivered, and in perfect condition. The heir thanked him absently, saying that he would not haggle about the price and had complete confidence that the undertaker would be guided by his conscience. The undertaker, as was his custom, swore that he would not charge a copeck too much, exchanged meaningful glances with the steward and went home to make the arrangements.

The entire day was spent travelling back and forth from Razgulyai to the Nikitsky Gate. By evening he had seen to everything and, after dismissing the cab, returned home. It was a moonlit night. The undertaker safely reached the Nikitsky Gate. By the Church of the Ascension he was hailed by our friend Yurko who, when he recognized the undertaker, wished him good-night. It was late. The undertaker was approaching his house when suddenly he thought he could see someone go up to his gate, open the wicket and disappear within. 'What could this mean?' wondered Adrian. 'Who could be needing my services again? Can it be a thief who's come to rob me? Or perhaps my stupid daughters have lovers coming to visit them? It can bode nothing good!' And the undertaker was already thinking of summoning the assistance of his friend Yurko. At that moment someone else approached the wicket-gate and was about to enter. However, seeing the master of the house running towards him he stopped and raised his three-cornered hat. His face seemed familiar to Adrian, but he was in such a hurry he had no time to take a close look at it. 'You've come to visit me, then,' Adrian said breathlessly. 'Do go in, I beg you.' 'Don't stand on ceremony, old chap,' the other replied in a hollow voice. 'You go in first and show your guests the way!' Adrian had no time to stand on ceremony. The wicket-gate was open; he climbed the steps, with the other following him. Adrian thought he could hear people walking around in the rooms. 'What the hell's going on?' he thought and hurried in . . . but then his legs gave way. The room was full of corpses. The moon shone through the windows and illuminated their yellow and blue faces, sunken mouths, dim, half-closed eyes and prominent noses. To his horror Adrian recognized them as people he himself had buried and in the guest who had entered with him the brigadier who had been buried in the pouring rain. All of them, ladies and gentlemen, surrounded the undertaker with bows and greetings, except for one poor devil recently buried free of charge and who, ashamed of his rags and feeling shy, dared not approach him but stayed meekly in one corner. All the others were decently dressed: the females in bonnets and ribbons, the officials in uniform, but with beards unshaven, and the merchants in their Sunday best. 'You see, Prokhorov,' said the brigadier on behalf of the whole honourable company, 'we have all risen in response to your invitation; only those who were unable to attend have remained at home, those who have completely fallen to bits and of whom there is nothing left but fleshless bone. But one of them could not hold himself back, so keen was he to come and see you . . .' At this moment a small skeleton forced its way through the crowd and went up to Adrian. The skull smiled warmly at the undertaker. Shreds of bright green and red cloth and rotting linen hung on him here and there, as if on a pole, while the bones of his feet rattled in his large jackboots like pestles in mortars. 'You don't recognize me, Prokhorov,' said the skeleton. 'Don't you remember Pyotr Petrovich Kurilkin, retired Guards sergeant, that very same person to whom, in 1799, you sold your first coffin – and in cheap pine instead of what should have been oak?' With these words the skeleton held out its arms in bony embrace, but Adrian, bracing himself, shrieked and pushed it away. Pyotr Petrovich staggered, fell and completely disintegrated. A murmur of indignation arose amongst the corpses; all of them stood up and defended the honour of their comrade, attacking Adrian with such abuse and threats that the poor host, deafened by their shouts and almost crushed to death, lost his nerve, fell on to the bones of the retired Guards sergeant and fainted clean away.

The sun had long been shining on the bed upon which the undertaker lay. At last he opened his eyes and saw his maidservant before him, heating the samovar. With horror Adrian recalled all the events of the previous day. Tryukhina, the brigadier and Sergeant Kurilkin dimly appeared in his mind. Silently he waited for the maid to start the conversation and tell him of the consequences of the previous night's adventures.

'How you've overslept, Adrian Prokhorovich,' said Aksinya as she handed him his dressing-gown. 'Your neighbour the tailor called and the district constable dropped in to say that today's the inspector's name-day, but you were sleeping so soundly, and we didn't want to wake you.'

'Did anyone come for me from the late Tryukhina?'

'The *late*? Is she dead?'

'Stupid girl! Didn't you yourself help me yesterday with the arrangements for her funeral?'

'Have you gone out of your mind or are you still tipsy from yesterday? *What* funeral was there yesterday? You spent the whole day celebrating at the German's place, came back drunk, fell on to your bed and slept until now, when the bells have already rung for Mass.'

'Is that so?' said the overjoyed undertaker.

'Oh yes, master,' replied the maid.

'Well, if that's the case hurry up with my tea and call my daughters.'

THE POSTMASTER

> The collegiate registrar, with iron hand,
> Dictator of every post-stage in the land.
> Prince Vyazemsky[1]

Who has not cursed postmasters, who has never quarrelled with them? Who, in a moment of rage, has not demanded from them that fatal book in order to record in it futile complaints of heavy-handedness, rudeness and inefficiency? Who does not look upon them as the scum of the earth, the equal of scriveners of old,[2] or at least of the brigands of Murom?[3] Let us be fair, however; let us try to put ourselves in their position and perhaps then we shall come to judge them much more leniently. What is a postmaster? A veritable martyr of the fourteenth grade, protected by his rank[4] only from blows and then not always. I appeal to the conscience of my readers.

What are the duties of this dictator, as Prince Vyazemsky has humorously called him? Is not his work tantamount to hard labour? All the vexation that has accumulated during a tiresome journey is vented by travellers on postmasters. If the weather is intolerable, if the road is execrable, the driver obstinate, the horses stubborn – the postmaster is to blame. When he enters the postmaster's poor abode the traveller looks upon him as an enemy; the postmaster is lucky if he manages to rid himself quickly of his uninvited guest; but if there are no horses . . . Heavens! What torrents of abuse, what threats are showered down upon his head! In rain or in slush he is obliged to run from one house to another. During a storm or biting January frosts he must take refuge out in the entrance hall, in order to enjoy a moment's respite from the shouting and jostling of an infuriated

41

traveller. A general arrives. The trembling postmaster gives him the last two troikas, including that reserved for the special courier. The general departs without a word of thanks. Five minutes later a sleigh bell rings ... and the courier throws down on the table his order for fresh horses.

If we take all this into consideration our hearts will be filled with genuine compassion instead of indignation. And I shall say a few more words on the subject. Over a period of twenty years I have travelled the length and breadth of Russia, in every direction; almost all the post-roads are familiar to me. I am acquainted with several generations of drivers. There are few postmasters I do not know by sight and few with whom I have not had business. I hope to publish the interesting stock of observations made during my travels before long. For the moment I shall merely remark that postmasters have been presented to the public in an exceedingly false light. These much-maligned postmasters are, on the whole, peaceful individuals, obliging by nature, inclined to be sociable, modest in their pretensions to honours and not particularly mercenary. From their conversation (unjustly scorned by travellers) much can be learnt that is both interesting and edifying. For my part I confess that I prefer their talk to that of some high-ranking official travelling on government business.

It will easily be guessed that I have friends among the honourable company of postmasters. Indeed, the memory of one is precious to me. Circumstances once brought us together, and it is of him that I now intend telling my amiable readers.

In the year 1816, in the month of May, I happened to be travelling through *** province, along a post-road now abandoned. At that time I held a low rank, and had a travelling allowance for two horses only.[5] Consequently postmasters treated me with little ceremony, and often I had to take by force what, in my opinion, was mine by right. As I was young and hot-tempered, I would become indignant at the baseness and cowardice of postmasters when the latter harnessed horses that had already been prepared for me to the carriage of some high-ranking official. It took me just as long before I could get used to being passed over by some discriminating lackey at a governor's dinner-table.[6] Nowadays both one and the other seem to be in the order of things. Indeed, what would become of us if, instead of the generally accepted rule, *let rank honour rank*, another were to be introduced, for example, *let brains honour brains*. What arguments that would provoke! And whom would the servants serve first then? But to return to my story.

It was a hot day. About two miles from the post-station a light drizzle began, and within a few minutes this turned into a torrential downpour and I was soaked to the skin. On arriving at the post-station my first concern was to change my clothes as quickly as possible; my second, to ask for some tea.

'Hey, Dunya!' cried the postmaster. 'Prepare the samovar and fetch some cream.'

At these words a girl of about fourteen appeared from behind the partition and ran into the hall. I was struck by her beauty.

'Is that your daughter?' I asked the postmaster.

'That's my daughter, sir,' he replied with a look of satisfied pride. 'She's so sensible and quick, just like her late mother.'

Here he started entering my order for fresh horses, and I occupied myself by examining the paintings that adorned his humble but tidy abode. They depicted the Parable of the Prodigal Son: in the first, a venerable old man in night-cap and dressing-gown was saying farewell to a restless young man who was hastily accepting his blessing and a bag of money. In the next the dissipated conduct of the young man was vividly portrayed: he was seated at a table, surrounded by false friends and shameless women. Further on the ruined youth, in rags and with a three-cornered hat on his head, was tending swine and sharing a meal with them; his face expressed deep sorrow and remorse. The last picture portrayed his return to his father: the worthy old man, in the same night-cap and dressing-gown, ran out to meet him; the prodigal son was on his knees; in the background the cook was killing the fattened calf, and the elder brother was asking the servants the reason for such rejoicing. Under each picture I read some appropriate verses in German. All this I have preserved to this day in my memory, including the pots of balsam, the bed with the brightly coloured curtains and the other objects that were all around me. I can see, as if it were now, the master of the house himself, a man of about fifty, healthy and fresh-looking, in his long green frock-coat with three medals hanging from it on faded ribbons.

I had hardly settled my account with my elderly driver when Dunya returned with the samovar. The little coquette saw at second glance the impression she had made on me. She lowered her big blue eyes. I started talking to her; she replied without the least shyness, like a girl who has seen the world. I offered her father a glass of punch, handed Dunya a cup of tea, and the three of us started chatting together as if we had known each other all our lives.

The horses had long been ready, but I was reluctant to part from the postmaster and his daughter. Finally I took my leave of them. The father wished me a pleasant journey and the daughter accompanied me to my coach. In the porch I stopped and asked permission to kiss her: Dunya agreed . . .

> Many are the kisses I can count,
> Since first I dabbled in such things

but not one of them has left so sweet, so lasting a memory.

Several years passed and circumstances led me along that same road, to the same neighbourhood. I remembered the old postmaster's daughter and was overjoyed at the thought of seeing her again. 'But,' I thought, 'perhaps the old postmaster has been replaced; and Dunya is probably married by now.' The thought that one or other of them might have died flashed through my mind as well, and I approached the *** post-station with sad forebodings.

The horses drew up before the little post-house. Entering the room I immediately recognized the pictures depicting the Parable of the Prodigal Son; the table and bed stood in the same places as before; but no longer were there flowers in the windows, and everything indicated decay and neglect. The postmaster was asleep under his sheepskin coat; my arrival woke him and he stood up . . . it was certainly Semyon Vyrin, but how he had aged! While he was copying my order for fresh horses, I looked at his grey hair, at the deep wrinkles on his unshaven face, at his bent back, and I was truly amazed that three or four years could have transformed such a healthy and vigorous person into a feeble old man.

'Don't you recognize me?' I asked him. 'We are old acquaintances.'

'That's possible,' he replied gloomily. 'This is a main road. Many travellers pass through here.'

'Is your Dunya well?' I continued.

The old man frowned. 'God knows,' he replied.

'Is she married now?' I asked.

The old man pretended not to hear my question and went on reading out my order for horses in a low voice. I stopped questioning him and ordered some tea. Curiosity began to disturb me, and I hoped that some punch would loosen my old acquaintance's tongue.

I was not mistaken: the old man did not refuse the glass which I offered him. I could see that the rum dispelled his moroseness. With the second glass he became talkative; he either remembered or pretended to remember me, and I heard from him a story that both intrigued and deeply moved me at the time.

'So you knew my Dunya?' he began. 'Who didn't know her? Oh Dunya, Dunya! What a girl she was! Whoever came here would sing her praises, no one had a word to say against her. Ladies used to give her presents, sometimes a handkerchief, or a pair of ear-rings. Gentlemen passing through would stop on purpose, as if they wanted dinner or supper, but in reality all they wanted was to take a longer look at her. However angry a gentleman happened to be, he would calm down when she was there and would speak civilly to me. Would you believe it, sir: government couriers and special messengers would chat with her for half an hour at a time. The whole place depended on her: she tidied up, prepared everything, took care of everything. And I, old fool, never tired of looking at her and simply doted on her. Didn't I love my Dunya? Didn't I cherish my child? Didn't she have a happy life here? But no, there's no escaping misfortune; what will be, will be.'

At this point he started telling me about his sorrows in detail. Three years earlier, one winter's evening, when the postmaster was ruling lines in a new register and his daughter was making a dress behind the screen, a troika drove up, and a traveller with a shawl around his neck, a Circassian cap on his head, and wearing a military greatcoat came into the room and demanded horses. They were all out. When he heard this the traveller was about to raise his voice and his whip; but Dunya, accustomed to such scenes, ran out from behind the screen and graciously asked the traveller if he would care for something to eat. Dunya's appearance had its usual effect. The traveller's anger subsided; he agreed to wait for the horses and ordered supper. When he had removed his wet, shaggy cap, unwound his shawl and taken off his greatcoat the traveller turned out to be a handsome hussar with a small black moustache. He made himself comfortable and started gaily chatting away with the postmaster and his daughter. Supper was served. Meanwhile the horses arrived, and the postmaster ordered them to be harnessed immediately, without even being fed, to the traveller's sledge. But when he came back to the post-house he found the young hussar lying almost unconscious on the bench. He felt bad, his head ached and he was in no state to travel. What was to be done? The postmaster gave up his own bed to him, and it was decided that if the sick man did not improve by the morning they would send to S** for the doctor.

Next day the hussar was worse. His batman rode into town for a doctor. Dunya wrapped a handkerchief soaked in vinegar around his head and sat at his bedside with her sewing. In the presence of the postmaster the sick man groaned and hardly said a word, although he did drink two cups of coffee and, still groaning, ordered some dinner. Dunya did not leave his side. Constantly he asked for a drink, and Dunya would bring him a jug of lemonade she had just made herself. The sick man moistened his lips, and every time he handed back the jug he would weakly squeeze Dunya's hand in gratitude. Towards dinner time the doctor arrived. He felt the sick man's pulse, spoke to him in German and declared in Russian that all he needed was rest and that within two days or so he would be fit to continue his journey. The hussar paid him twenty-five roubles for his visit, and invited him to have dinner with him. The doctor accepted. Both ate with great appetite, drank a bottle of wine and parted very satisfied with each other.

Another day passed and the hussar had completely recovered. He was extraordinarily cheerful, joked incessantly, now with Dunya and then with the postmaster; he whistled tunes, chatted with travellers, copied their warrants into the register and so endeared himself to the worthy postmaster that on the third morning he felt sad at the prospect of having to part with his amiable guest.

It was a Sunday; Dunya was preparing to go to Mass. The hussar's sleigh was brought round. He bade the postmaster farewell, generously rewarded him for the board and lodging, and said goodbye to Dunya, offering to drive her to the church, which was at the far end of the village. Dunya stood there in a quandary.

'What are you afraid of?' her father asked. 'His Honour is no wolf; he won't eat you. Now, drive to church with him.'

Dunya seated herself in the sleigh beside the hussar, the batman leapt on to the coachman's box, the driver whistled and the horses galloped off.

The poor postmaster could not understand how he could have allowed his Dunya to drive off with the hussar, how he could have been so blind and what he could have been thinking of at the time. Half an hour had barely passed when his heart began to ache, and he became so agitated that he could no longer restrain himself and went off to the church. As he approached he saw that the congregation was already leaving; but Dunya was neither in the churchyard nor in the porch. He hurried into the church: the priest had left the altar, the sexton was putting out the candles, two old women were still praying in one corner; but there was no sign of Dunya. Her poor father could barely bring himself to ask the sexton whether she had attended Mass. The sexton replied that she had not been to church. The postmaster returned home more dead than alive. One hope remained for him: Dunya, in the recklessness of youth, had perhaps decided to drive to the next post-station, where her godmother lived. In torments of anxiety he awaited the return of the troika with which he had let her go. But it did not return. Finally, towards evening, the driver returned, alone and drunk, bearing the devastating news: 'Dunya drove on from the next station with that hussar.'

The old man's misfortune was too much for him; he immediately took to that very same bed where the day before that young deceiver had lain. And now, after considering all the facts of the matter, the postmaster guessed that the illness had been faked. The poor man contracted a severe fever; he was taken to S** and for a while another postmaster was appointed in his place. He was treated by the same doctor who had called on the hussar. He assured the postmaster that the young man had been perfectly well and that he had suspected his evil intention all along, but had remained silent for fear of his whip. Whether the German was speaking the truth or only wanted to boast of his far-sightedness, his words brought no consolation to his poor patient. Barely had the postmaster recovered from his illness than he obtained two months' leave of absence from the postmaster at S** and, without breathing a word to anyone about his plans, set off on foot to look for his daughter. From the warrant for fresh horses he learnt that Captain Minsky had travelled from Smolensk to St Petersburg. The driver who had taken him told him that Dunya had wept the whole way, although she appeared to have gone of her own free will. 'Perhaps,' thought the postmaster, 'I shall bring my stray lamb home.' With this thought he stayed at the barracks of the Izmailovsky regiment, in the house of an old comrade, a retired non-commissioned officer, and embarked on his search. He soon discovered that Captain Minsky was in St Petersburg and living at Demut's hotel.[7] The postmaster decided to call on him.

Early in the morning he went into Minsky's ante-room and asked for His Honour to be informed that an old soldier wanted to see him. The batman, who happened to be polishing a boot on a boot-tree, announced that his master was still asleep and that he never received anyone before eleven o'clock. The postmaster departed and returned at the appointed time. Minsky himself came out to him in his dressing-gown and red skull-cap.

'Well, what do you want, my friend?' he asked.

The old man's heart boiled with indignation, tears welled up in his eyes, and he could only reply in a trembling voice, 'Your Honour, please be so good as to do me the favour! . . .'

Minsky glanced swiftly at him, flushed, led him by the arm into his study and locked the door.

'Your Honour!' continued the old man. 'It's no use crying over

THE POSTMASTER

spilt milk; but at least give me back my poor Dunya. You've had your pleasure with her, don't ruin her needlessly.'

'What's done cannot be undone,' the young man said, in extreme confusion. 'I am guilty before you and am pleased to ask your forgiveness. But do not think that I could forsake Dunya. She will be happy, I give you my word on it. Why do you want her? She loves me, she has grown out of her former life. Neither of you will ever forget what has happened.' Then, pushing something up the old man's sleeve, he opened the door, and the postmaster, without recalling how, found himself out in the street.

For a long time he stood motionless until finally he saw a roll of paper under the cuff of his sleeve. He pulled it out and unrolled several crumpled five- and ten-rouble notes. Once again the tears welled up in his eyes – tears of indignation! He rolled the notes into a ball, flung them on to the ground, stamped on them with his heel and walked off . . . After a few paces he stopped, pondered . . . and went back . . . but by now the notes were gone. A well-dressed young man, noticing him, dashed to a cab, hurriedly seated himself and shouted, 'Drive on!' The postmaster did not pursue him. He decided to go back to his station, but before doing so he wanted to see his poor Dunya just once more. To that end he returned to Minsky's rooms a couple of days later, but the batman gruffly informed him that his master was receiving nobody, shoved him out of the entrance hall and slammed the door in his face. The postmaster stood there a long long time – and then he went away.

That same day, in the evening, he was walking along Liteiny Street, having attended a service at the Church of Our Lady of Sorrows. Suddenly an elegant droshky flew past and the postmaster recognized Minsky. The droshky stopped at the entrance to a three-storeyed house and the hussar ran up the steps. A happy thought flashed through the postmaster's mind. He turned back and went up to the coachman.

'Whose horse is that, my friend?' he asked. 'Doesn't it belong to Minsky?'

'Yes it does,' replied the coachman. 'And what business is it of yours?'

49

'I'll tell you what: your master ordered me to deliver a note to his Dunya, but I've forgotten where this Dunya lives.'

'She lives here, on the second floor. You're a bit late with that note, old friend. He's already with her upstairs.'

'It doesn't matter,' replied the postmaster with an inexplicable flutter of the heart. 'Thanks for letting me know, but I must do as I was told.'

And with these words he climbed the staircase.

The door was locked. He rang, and after an agonizing wait of a few seconds the key rattled and the door opened.

'Does Avdotya[8] Samsonovna live here?' he asked.

'Yes,' answered a young housemaid. 'What do you want with her?'

Without replying the postmaster went into the hall.

'You mustn't go in, you mustn't!' the maid cried after him. 'Avdotya Samsonovna has visitors.'

But the postmaster ignored her and went straight on. The first two rooms were in darkness, but in the third there was a light. He went up to the open door and stopped. In the beautifully furnished room sat Minsky, deep in thought. Dunya, dressed splendidly in the latest fashion, was sitting on the arm of his chair, like a horsewoman on an English saddle. She was gazing tenderly at Minsky, winding his black curls around her glittering fingers. Poor postmaster! Never had his daughter struck him as so beautiful; he could not help feasting his eyes on her.

'Who's there?' she asked, without raising her head . . . and with a shriek she fell on to the carpet. The frightened Minsky rushed to lift her up but, suddenly catching sight of the old postmaster in the doorway, left Dunya and went up to him, quivering with anger.

'What do you want?' he asked, clenching his teeth. 'Why do you keep sneaking after me everywhere like a thief? Do you want to cut my throat? Clear off!'

And with a powerful hand he grabbed the old man by the collar and pushed him down the stairs.

The old man returned to his lodgings. His friend advised him to make an official complaint; but the postmaster, after pondering for a moment, gave it up as a lost cause and decided to take no further action. Two days later he left St Petersburg for his post-station to resume his duties.

'It's three years now since I've been living without Dunya,' he concluded, 'and not a word has been heard of her. Heaven knows whether she's alive or dead. So many things can happen. She's not the first, and nor will she be the last, to be seduced by a passing rake, kept for a while and then abandoned. There are many young fools like her in St Petersburg, dressed in satin and velvet today and tomorrow sweeping the streets with tavern riff-raff. At times, when I think that Dunya too might meet that fate, I can't help sinfully wishing her in her grave.'

Such was the story of my friend the old postmaster, a story interrupted more than once by tears which he picturesquely wiped away with his jacket sleeve, like the zealous Terentych in Dmitriyev's beautiful ballad.[9] The tears were partly brought on by the punch, of which he had drunk five glasses during the course of his narrative; however, they moved me deeply. After I had bidden him farewell it was long before I could get that old postmaster out of my mind, and for a long time I thought of poor Dunya . . .

Not very long ago, as I was passing through the small town of *** I remembered my friend. I discovered that the post-station of which he had been in charge was now abandoned. To my question, 'Is the old postmaster still alive?', no one could give me a satisfactory answer. So I decided to visit that familiar place and, having hired some privately owned horses, I set out for the village of N**.

It was autumn. Greyish clouds covered the sky; a cold wind blew across the harvested fields, bearing red and yellow leaves from the trees along its path. I reached the village at sunset and stopped at the postmaster's little house. A plump woman came out on to the porch (where once poor Dunya had kissed me) and in reply to my questions told me that it was about a year since the old postmaster had died, that a brewer now lived in the house and that she was the brewer's wife. I started regretting the wasted journey and the seven roubles I had spent in vain.

'Of what did he die?' I asked the brewer's wife.

'Of drink, sir,' she replied.

'And where is he buried?'

'On the village outskirts, next to his late wife.'

'Could someone take me to his grave?'

'Well, of course. Hey, Vanka! You've played with that cat long enough. Take the gentleman to the cemetery and show him the postmaster's grave.'

At these words a ragged, red-haired, one-eyed boy ran up to me and immediately led me to the outskirts of the village.

'Did you know the dead man?' I asked him on the way.

'Oh yes! He taught me to carve whistles, he did. Whenever he came out of the tavern (God rest his soul!) we would shout after him, "Grandpa! Grandpa! Give us some nuts!" And he would give us all nuts. He was always playing with us.'

'Do travellers remember him?'

'There's few travellers nowadays. Now and then the assessor might drop in, but he's not interested in the dead. Last summer a lady came here. She asked about the old postmaster and then visited his grave.'

'What kind of lady?' I asked inquisitively.

'A really beautiful lady,' the boy replied. 'She was riding in a carriage with six horses and with her were three young boys, a nanny and a little black pug-dog. And when she heard that the old postmaster was dead, she started crying and told the boys, "Now, you sit still while I go to the cemetery." I offered to take her there, but the lady said, "I know the way myself." And she gave me a silver five-copeck piece – such a kind lady!'

We arrived at the cemetery, a bare place, completely unfenced, dotted with wooden crosses that were not shaded by a single tree. Never had I seen such a miserable cemetery.

'Here's the old postmaster's grave,' the boy told me, leaping on to a heap of sand into which was stuck a black cross with a copper image.

'And did the lady come here?' I asked.

'Yes she did,' replied Vanka. 'I watched her from the distance. She lay down here – and she stayed like that for a long time. And then she went back to the village, sent for the priest, gave him some money and drove off. And she gave me a silver five-copeck piece – such a nice lady!'

I too gave the lad a five-copeck piece, and no longer did I regret the journey or the seven roubles I had spent on it.

You look pretty, Dushenka, in any dress you wear.

Bogdanovich[1]

In one of our remote provinces was situated the estate of Ivan Petrovich Berestov. In his youth he had served in the Guards, but he resigned his commission at the beginning of 1797, returned to his estate and since then had never left it. He married a poor gentlewoman who died in childbirth while he was away on a hunting trip. He soon found consolation in busying himself with the administration of his estate. He built a house to his own plan, established a textile mill, trebled his income and soon began to consider himself the cleverest man in the entire district – and in this he was not contradicted by the neighbours who came to visit him with their families and dogs. On weekdays he went around in a velveteen jacket, and on holidays he would wear a frock-coat of homespun cloth. He kept an account of his expenses himself and never read anything besides the *Senate Gazette*.[2] On the whole he was liked, although he was considered proud. Only Grigory Ivanovich Muromsky, his closest neighbour, was not on good terms with him. The latter was a true Russian gentleman. Having squandered the major part of his fortune in Moscow, and having become a widower at the same time, Muromsky retired to his last remaining estate where he continued to fritter away his fortune, but in a novel way. He laid out an English garden, on which he lavished almost his entire remaining capital. His stable-boys were dressed like English jockeys. His daughter had an English governess. He cultivated his fields according to the English method:

But Russian grain fares badly when alien methods are observed[3]

54

and, despite a significant reduction in expenditure, Grigory Ivanovich's income did not increase; even in the country he found ways
of incurring new debts. For all that he was considered no fool, since
he was the first landowner in his province to think of mortgaging
his estate with the Board of Guardians,[4] a proceeding considered at
the time extremely complex and daring. Berestov was the severest
of all his critics. Hatred of innovation was his distinguishing feature.
He was unable to speak calmly about his neighbour's Anglomania
and constantly sought occasion to criticize him. If he happened to
be showing a visitor around his property he would answer praise of
the way he ran his estate by saying with a crafty smile, 'Ah, yes, sir!
I don't manage my affairs like my neighbour Grigory Ivanovich.
Why should we ruin ourselves English style? As long as we have
enough to eat, Russian style!' These and similar jests, thanks to the
zeal of his neighbours, were brought to the ears of Grigory Ivanovich
greatly embellished. The Anglomaniac endured criticism just as
impatiently as our journalists do. He was furious and called his
carping critic a boor and a country bumpkin.

Such were the relations between these two landowners when
Berestov's son returned to his father's estate. He had been educated
at the University of *** and was intending to go into the army, but
his father would not consent to this. The young man felt completely
unsuited for the civil service. Neither would give way, and for the
time being Aleksey led the life of a gentleman, letting his moustache
grow, in case he should need one.[5]

Aleksey was really a fine young man. Indeed, it would have been
a pity if, instead of being able to show off on a charger, he had been
forced to spend his youth poring over official documents. When the
neighbours saw him always riding at the head of the hunt, galloping
regardless of where he was going, they all agreed that he would
never make a decent chief clerk. Young ladies would take a good
look at him, and some were lost in admiration; but Aleksey did not
bother about them very much, and they ascribed his aloofness to
some love-affair. Indeed, a piece of paper with the address from one
of his letters was passed from hand to hand:

To Akulina Petrovna Kurochkin in Moscow, opposite the Alekseyev Monastery, at Savelyev the coppersmith's house, humbly requesting her to hand this letter to A. N. R.

Those of my readers who have never lived in the country cannot imagine how delightful these provincial young ladies are! Brought up in the fresh air, in the shade of the apple trees in their gardens, they derive their knowledge of the world and life from books. Solitude, freedom and reading develop in them, at an early age, sentiments and passions unknown to our beauties living among the distractions of the city. For a young country lady the jingle of harness bells is an event in itself, a trip to the nearest town is a landmark in her life and a visit from a friend leaves long and sometimes lasting memories. Of course, anybody may choose to laugh at some of their eccentricities if they so wish, but the jokes of a superficial observer cannot nullify their essential qualities, of which the most important is that unique originality of character (*individualité*), without which, in Jean-Paul's opinion,[6] there can be no human greatness. In the capital cities[7] women possibly receive a better education; but the life of society quickly effaces character and makes their souls as uniform as their head-dresses. Let this not be said in judgement or in censure. However, *nota nostra manet*,[8] as one of the ancient commentators wrote.

The impression Aleksey was bound to make in the circle of our young ladies is easy to imagine. He was the first to appear to them gloomy and disenchanted, the first to speak of lost joys and faded youth; moreover, he wore a black ring engraved with a death's head. All of this was something quite novel in that province. The young ladies went mad over him.

But no one was as interested in him as Liza (or Betsy as Grigory Ivanovich called her), the daughter of our Anglomaniac. Since the parents were not on visiting terms, she had not yet seen Aleksey, but with the young ladies of the neighbourhood he was the sole topic of conversation. Liza was seventeen years old. Black eyes enlivened her dark-complexioned, extremely pleasant face. She was an only and therefore a spoilt child. Her liveliness and constant pranks delighted her father and were the despair of her governess, Miss Jackson, a prim old maid of forty, who powdered her face, dyed her eyebrows and read the whole of *Pamela*[9] twice a year, for which she was paid two thousand roubles a year, and who was dying of boredom in this 'barbarous Russia'.

Liza was waited upon by Nastya who, although a little older, was just as high-spirited as her mistress. Liza was very fond of her, shared all her secrets with her and joined her in planning her pranks. Briefly, Nastya was a far more significant person in the village of Priluchino than any confidante in a French tragedy.

'May I go out on a visit today?' Nastya asked one day as she was dressing her mistress.

'Certainly. But where to?'

'To Tugilovo, to the Berestovs. It's the name-day of the cook's wife, and yesterday she came over and invited us to dinner.'

'Well!' said Liza. 'The masters are at loggerheads, yet the servants are entertaining each other.'

'And what do we have to do with the masters?' retorted Nastya. 'Besides, I belong to you, not your papa. You haven't quarrelled so far with the young Berestov. Let the old ones fight each other if that's what they enjoy.'

'Try to catch a glimpse of Aleksey Berestov, Nastya, and then you can tell me exactly what he looks like and what kind of man he is.'

Nastya promised to do so and Liza waited impatiently all day long for her return. Nastya appeared in the evening.

'Well, Lizaveta Grigoryevna,' she said, entering the room. 'I've seen young Berestov. I managed to have a really good look at him. He was with us the whole day.'

'How was that? Tell me everything, exactly as it happened.'

'Well, we set off, myself, Anisya, Nenila, Dunka . . .'

'Yes, yes, I know. And then?'

'Please wait a moment. I shall tell you everything, just as it happened. We all arrived just in time for dinner. The room was full of people. The folk from Kolbino were there, from Zakharyevo, the steward's wife and her daughters, folk from Khlupino . . .'

'Go on! And what about Berestov?'

'Please wait a moment. We sat down at the table. The steward's wife had the place of honour, I sat next to her . . . her daughters sulked, but I couldn't have cared less about them.'

'Oh, Nastya, how tedious you are with your interminable details!'

'And how impatient you are! So we left the table . . . we had been sitting down for about three hours, and it was a wonderful dinner; there was red, blue and striped blanc-mange . . . So we left the table and went into the garden to play catch, and then the young master appeared.'

'Well? Is it true that he is so handsome?'

'Extremely handsome, a real beauty you might say. Tall, a fine figure, and with rosy cheeks.'

'Really? And I thought that his face would be pale. Well, how did he strike you? Sad and thoughtful?'

'Oh no! I've never seen such a wild one in my life. He decided to join in the game with us.'

'Play catch with you? Impossible!'

'Oh, very possible! And what he thought of next! Whenever he caught someone he'd kiss her!'

'Come now, Nastya, you're fibbing.'

'No I'm not. I had a hard job getting away from him. He spent the whole day with us.'

'But why is it they say he's in love and that he doesn't look at anyone?'

'I don't know about that, but I do know that he looked at me a lot, far too much, and at Tanya the steward's daughter too, and at Pasha from Kolbino. But the truth is, he didn't ignore anyone. Such a scamp he was!'

'That's extraordinary! And what do they say about him in the manor-house?'

'They say he's a fine master. He has one fault, though. He's far too fond of running after the girls. But if you ask me there's no harm in that. He'll settle down in time.'

'How I would love to see him!' sighed Liza.

'What's so difficult about that? Tugilovo's not far from here, only about two miles. Why not walk there, or go over on horseback. You'll be bound to meet him. Early every morning he goes hunting with his gun.'

'No, that wouldn't be right. He might think that I'm running after him. Besides, our parents have fallen out, so I can't possibly get to know him . . . Oh, Nastya! Do you know what? I shall dress up as a peasant girl!'

'That's a good idea. Put on a coarse smock, a sarafan,[10] and boldly walk to Tugilovo. I give you my word that Berestov will not pass you by.'

'And I can imitate the way the peasants speak here. Oh, Nastya, my dear Nastya! What an excellent idea!'

And Liza went to bed with the firm intention of carrying out her bright scheme.

On the very next day she started to put it into action. She sent to the market for some coarse cloth, blue nankeen and brass buttons and with Nastya's help cut out for herself a smock and a sarafan. Then she set all the maids to work on the sewing and by evening all was ready. Liza tried on her new clothes and had to admit to herself before the mirror that never had she looked so charming. She rehearsed her part, curtseying low while walking and then nodding several times, like those china cats with moving heads; she spoke in peasant fashion and laughed behind her sleeve, for which she earned Nastya's whole-hearted approval. Only one thing proved troublesome: when she tried to walk over the courtyard barefoot the turf pricked her tender feet, and she found the sand and gravel unbearable. Here too Nastya immediately came to her assistance. She measured Liza's feet, ran off to the fields to find Trofim, the shepherd, and ordered a pair of bast shoes from him to fit Liza. Next day Liza was already awake at crack of dawn. Everyone else in the house was still asleep. Nastya was at the gate, waiting for the shepherd. A horn sounded and the village flock slowly moved past the manor-house in a long line. As he passed by Trofim gave Nastya a pair of small, brightly coloured bast shoes, for which he was rewarded with fifty copecks. Liza quietly put on her peasant costume, whispered instructions regarding Miss Jackson to Nastya, left by the back door and ran through the kitchen garden into the fields.

The east was filled with the glow of dawn, and golden ranks of clouds seemed to be awaiting the sun, like courtiers awaiting their sovereign. The clear sky, the morning freshness, the dew, the gentle breeze and the singing of the birds filled Liza's heart with childlike gaiety. The fear that she might meet someone she knew made her fly along, it seemed, rather than walk. As she approached the grove on the boundary of her father's estate, Liza walked more slowly. Here she was to wait for Aleksey. Her heart beat violently and she knew not why. But the principal charm of the pranks of our youth lies in the sense of danger that accompanies them. Liza entered the dark grove. She was welcomed by the deep, broken murmuring of the trees, and her gaiety vanished; gradually she abandoned herself to blissful reverie. She was thinking . . . but who can accurately determine what a seventeen-year-old girl can be thinking about when she is all alone, in a grove, between five and six o'clock on a spring morning? And so, lost in thought, she walked along the path, which was shaded on either side by tall trees, when suddenly a handsome setter ran up to her barking. Liza cried out in fear. But at that moment a voice rang out: 'Tout beau, Sbogar, ici . . .',[11] and a young hunter appeared from behind a clump of bushes. 'Don't be afraid, my dear,' he told Liza, 'my dog does not bite.' Liza had already recovered from her fright and immediately took full advantage of the situation. 'But, sir,' she said, assuming a half frightened, half timid expression, 'I'm afraid. He might rush at me again.'

Meanwhile Aleksey (the reader will have recognized him) stared at the young peasant girl.

'I shall go with you if you are afraid,' he said. 'Will you allow me to walk by your side?'

'Who's stopping you?' Liza replied. 'A man is free to do as he likes – and it's a public road.'

'Where are you from?'

'Priluchino. I'm Vassily the blacksmith's daughter. I'm going to pick mushrooms.' (Liza was carrying a small bark basket on a piece of string.) 'And you sir? Are you from Tugilovo?'

'Yes,' replied Aleksey. 'I'm the young master's valet.'

Aleksey wanted to put their relationship on an equal footing. But Liza looked at him and laughed.

'You're telling me fibs,' she said. 'I'm not such a fool as you take me for; I can see that you're the young master himself.'

'What makes you think that?'

'Everything about you tells me.'

'But what?'

'Well, as if it's impossible to tell a master from a servant. The way you dress is different, the way you talk is different and you don't call your dog the way we do.'

With every moment that passed Aleksey began to like Liza more and more. Being unaccustomed to standing on ceremony with pretty village girls, he tried to embrace her. But Liza drew back and suddenly assumed such a stern, cold expression that, although he was much amused, Aleksey did not attempt any further advances. 'If you want us to stay good friends,' she said solemnly, 'then please be good enough not to forget yourself.' 'Who taught you to be so clever?' asked Aleksey, laughing out loud. 'Can it have been my friend Nastenka, your mistress's maid? So that's how enlightenment spreads these days!'

Liza felt that she had begun to speak out of character and immediately acted the peasant girl again.

'Do you really think,' she said, 'that I never visit the manor-house? I've seen and heard all sorts of things there, I have,' she continued. 'But I shall never get any mushrooms picked if I stay here chattering to you. Now you go your way, young sir, and I'll go mine. If you don't mind . . .'

Liza wanted to go but Aleksey seized her by the hand.

'What's your name, my dear?'

'Akulina,' replied Liza, trying to free her fingers from Aleksey's grasp. 'Let me go, sir, it's time I went home.'

'Well, Akulina my friend, I shall most certainly visit your father, Vassily the blacksmith.'

'What did you say?' exclaimed Liza excitedly. 'For Heaven's sake, please don't do that. If they were to find out at home that I'd been talking to a young gentleman, alone in a copse, I'd really be in trouble. My father Vassily the blacksmith would beat me to death, he would.'

'But I really do want to see you again, whatever happens.'

'Well, I'll be coming here again for mushrooms.'

'When?'

'Well, tomorrow perhaps.'

'Dear Akulina. I would like to kiss you, but I dare not. Tomorrow then, at the same time?'

'Yes, yes.'

'And you will not deceive me?'

'I'll not deceive you.'

'Swear it.'

'I swear by Holy Friday that I'll come.'

The young couple parted. Liza walked out of the copse, crossed the fields, stole into the garden and rushed headlong into the farm building where Nastya was waiting for her. There she changed out of her costume, absently answering her impatient confidante's questions, after which she appeared in the drawing-room. The table was laid, breakfast was ready and Miss Jackson, already powdered and tightly laced so that she resembled a wine glass, was buttering thin slices of bread. Her father praised her for her early morning walk.

'There's nothing healthier,' he said, 'than getting up at dawn.'

And he quoted several examples of human longevity, gleaned from English journals, remarking that everyone who had lived to be more than a hundred had abstained from vodka and risen at dawn, winter and summer. But Liza did not listen to him. In her mind she was running through all the circumstances of the meeting that morning, the whole of Akulina's conversation with the young hunter, and her conscience began to torment her. In vain did she try to convince herself that their conversation had not exceeded the bounds of propriety, that her prank would have no serious consequences – but her conscience spoke louder than her reason. The promise she had given for the following day troubled her more than anything else. She very nearly decided not to keep her solemn vow. But Aleksey, after waiting for her in vain, might then come to the village and seek out Vassily the blacksmith's daughter, the real Akulina, a fat, pock-marked wench, and so he would find out about the thoughtless trick she had played on him. The very idea horrified Liza, and she decided to go to the grove next morning disguised as Akulina.

For his part Aleksey was in raptures. All day long he thought only of his new acquaintance; the image of that dark-complexioned beauty haunted his imagination, even in his dreams.

Dawn had barely broken when he was already dressed. Without even stopping to load his gun, he went off to the fields with his loyal Sbogar and hurried to the place of the promised rendezvous. About half an hour passed in unbearable waiting. At last he glimpsed a blue sarafan amongst the bushes, and he rushed to meet his charming Akulina. She smiled at his ecstatic gratitude; but Aleksey immediately noticed signs of dejection and anxiety on her face. He wanted to know the reason. Liza admitted that her behaviour struck her as frivolous, that she regretted it, that on this occasion she had not wanted to go back on her word, but this meeting would be the last, and she asked him to end a friendship which could lead to no good for either of them. All this, of course, was said in peasant speech; but such feelings and thoughts, so unusual in a simple peasant girl, startled Aleksey. He employed all his eloquence to deflect Akulina from her purpose. He assured her that his intentions were honourable, promised that he would never give her any cause for regret, to obey her in everything and entreated her not to deprive him of the joy of seeing her alone, if only every other day, or twice a week. He spoke the language of real passion and at that moment he was truly in love. Liza listened to him in silence.

'Give me your word,' she said at length, 'that you will never go and look for me in the village, or enquire about me. Give me your word that you will not seek any meetings with me besides those that I myself will arrange.'

Aleksey swore by Holy Friday, but she stopped him with a smile.

'I don't need solemn vows,' Liza said. 'Your word is enough.'

After this they chatted amicably as they strolled together through the wood, until Liza told him, 'It's time for me to go home.'

They parted and when Aleksey was left on his own he just could not understand how a simple peasant girl could have succeeded in acquiring such real power over him in the course of two meetings. For him his relationship with Akulina had all the charm of novelty, and although the strange peasant girl's demands seemed very severe, the thought of breaking his word never once entered his head. The fact was that Aleksey, despite his macabre ring, his mysterious correspondence and his air of gloomy disenchantment, was a fine, spirited young man with a good heart, capable of appreciating innocent pleasures.

Were I to follow my own inclinations I should embark on a detailed description of the young people's meetings, their growing mutual attraction and trust in each other, how they occupied themselves, their conversations. But I know that the majority of my readers would not share my pleasure. On the whole, such details are bound to appear excessive; therefore I shall omit them, with just a brief mention of the fact that before two months had gone by Aleksey was head over heels in love, and that Liza, although she did not show it so much, was equally smitten. Both were happy with the present and gave little thought to the future.

The thought of indissoluble ties frequently flashed through their minds, but they never mentioned it to each other. The reason was clear: however deep Aleksey's attachment to his dear Akulina, he was always conscious of the distance that separated him from the poor peasant girl, while Liza was aware of the hatred that existed between their fathers, and she dared not hope that they might be reconciled with one another. Moreover, her vanity was secretly aroused by the vague, romantic hope of finally seeing the heir to Tugilovo at the feet of the daughter of the Priluchino blacksmith. Suddenly an important event took place that threatened to change their mutual relations.

One cold, bright morning (one of those mornings with which our Russian autumn is so abundantly blessed), Ivan Petrovich Berestov went for a ride on horseback, taking with him, in case he should need them, six greyhounds, a whipper-in and several stable-boys with rattles. At exactly the same time, Grigory Ivanovich Muromsky, tempted by the fine weather, ordered his bob-tailed mare to be saddled and trotted off to view his English-style domains. As he approached the wood he saw his neighbour proudly seated on his horse, wearing a Cossack jacket lined with fox-fur and waiting for a hare which his stable-boys were driving out of a clump of bushes with their shouts and rattles. Had Grigory Ivanovich been able to foresee this encounter he would certainly have turned in another direction; but he had come across Berestov so unexpectedly that he suddenly found himself no more than a pistol-shot away. There was nothing he could do. Being a civilized European, Muromsky rode up to his adversary and politely greeted him. Berestov replied with all the enthusiasm of a chained bear saluting the public on its keeper's orders. At that moment the hare darted out of the wood and made for the open fields. Berestov and his whipper-in shouted at the tops of their voices, unleashed the greyhounds and galloped off in hot pursuit. Muromsky's horse, which had never hunted, took fright and bolted. Muromsky, who claimed to be an excellent rider, gave it free rein and inwardly rejoiced at the incident that had freed him from such disagreeable company. But his horse, having reached a ditch it had not noticed before, suddenly shied and Muromsky was thrown from his saddle. Falling heavily on the frozen ground, he lay there cursing his bob-tailed mare which, as if coming to its senses, had stopped immediately it realized it was riderless. Ivan Petrovich galloped up to him to enquire if he had injured himself. In the meantime the whipper-in had secured the guilty horse and led it by the bridle. He helped Muromsky into the saddle and Berestov invited him to his house. Muromsky could not refuse the invitation, and thus Berestov returned home covered in glory, having caught a hare and brought back his adversary wounded and almost a prisoner-of-war.

The neighbours conversed in most friendly fashion over breakfast. Muromsky asked Berestov to lend him a droshky since, he was bound to confess, he was in no state to return home on horseback because of his bruises. Berestov conducted him down the front steps, and Muromsky would not take his leave until he had obtained his word of honour that he would drive over next day (with Aleksey Ivanovich Berestov) to dine with him at Priluchino. Thus a long-standing and deep-rooted enmity was apparently terminated as the result of the skittishness of a bob-tailed mare.

Liza ran out to greet Grigory Ivanovich. 'What's happened, papa?' she asked in amazement. 'Why are you limping? Where is your horse? Whose droshky is this?'

'You'll never guess, my dear,' Grigory Ivanovich replied and he then related everything that had happened. Liza could not believe her ears. Without giving her time to collect herself, Grigory Ivanovich announced that both Berestovs would be coming to dine with him the following day.

'What are you saying!' she exclaimed, turning pale. 'The Berestovs, father and son, dining with us tomorrow! No, papa, you do as you please, but on no account shall I show myself.'

'What's the matter? Have you taken leave of your senses?' retorted her father. 'Since when have you been so shy? Or do you nurture a hereditary hatred towards the Berestovs, like some romantic heroine? Now, enough of this silliness!'

'No, papa, not for anything in the world, not for any treasures shall I appear before the Berestovs.'

Grigory Ivanovich shrugged and did not argue any more with her. Knowing full well that he would gain nothing by contradicting her, he went to have a rest after that memorable ride.

Liza went to her room and summoned Nastya. The two of them spent a long time discussing tomorrow's visit. What would Aleksey think when, in a well-bred young lady, he discovered his Akulina? What opinion would he have of her conduct, her morals, her common sense? On the other hand, Liza dearly wanted to see what impression such an unexpected encounter would have on him . . . Suddenly an idea flashed through her mind. Immediately she communicated it to Nastya. Both were delighted with it, as if it were a godsend, and they decided to put it into action come what may.

Next day at breakfast Grigory Ivanovich asked his daughter

whether it was still her intention to hide from the Berestovs.

'Papa,' replied Liza, 'I shall receive them if you wish, but on one condition: however I may appear before them, whatever I may do, you will not scold me or show the least sign of surprise or displeasure.'

'Up to your tricks again!' laughed Grigory Ivanovich. 'Oh, very well, very well; I agree. Do what you like, my dark-eyed mischievous child.' With these words he kissed her forehead and Liza ran off to get herself ready.

At exactly two o'clock a home-made carriage, drawn by six horses, entered the courtyard and drove around the rich green circle of the lawn. The elder Berestov climbed the steps with the help of Muromsky's two liveried footmen. After him came his son, who had arrived on horseback, and together they entered the dining-room, where the table had already been laid. Muromsky greeted his neighbours with the utmost cordiality, suggested they inspect the garden and menagerie before dinner and led them along the carefully tended paths covered with sand. The elder Berestov inwardly regretted the time and effort expended on such useless fancies, but remained silent out of politeness. His son shared neither that thrifty landowner's disapproval, nor the Anglomaniac's enthusiasm, but impatiently awaited the appearance of the host's daughter, of whom he had heard so much; and although his heart, as we know, was already engaged, a beautiful young woman would always lay claim to his imagination.

Returning to the drawing-room, all three sat down. The old men recalled earlier times and related anecdotes of army days, while Aleksey reflected on the role he should play in Liza's presence. He decided that an air of cold aloofness would be most appropriate in the circumstances and prepared himself accordingly. The door opened and he turned his head with such indifference, with such nonchalance that the heart of the most hardened coquette might have quaked. Unfortunately, instead of Liza it was the elderly Miss Jackson who entered, powdered, tightly corseted, eyes downcast, and with a small curtsey, and thus Aleksey's splendid military manoeuvre was wasted. Barely had he succeeded in mustering his strength again when the door opened once more and this time Liza entered. Everyone stood up; her father was about to introduce her to his guests, when suddenly he stopped in his tracks and hurriedly bit his lip ... Liza, his dark-complexioned Liza, was powdered up to the ears and more heavily made up than Miss Jackson herself; false curls, far fairer than her own hair, were fluffed out like the peruke of Louis XIV; her sleeves, *à l'imbécile*,[12] stuck out like the hooped petticoats of Madame de Pompadour;[13] her waist was tightly laced so that she resembled the letter 'X', and all her mother's jewels that had not yet been pawned sparkled on her neck and ears. It was impossible for Aleksey to recognize his Akulina in that grotesquely dazzling young lady. His father kissed her hand and Aleksey followed suit; when his lips touched her little white fingers he had the impression that they were trembling. Meanwhile he managed to catch a glimpse of her little foot, intentionally thrust forward and embellished by the most coquettish of shoes one could imagine. This reconciled him somewhat to the rest of her attire. As for the paint and powder it must be admitted that, in his simplicity of heart, he had not noticed them at first, and he did not suspect them even later. Grigory Ivanovich remembered his promise and tried not to show surprise; but his daughter's prank struck him as so amusing he could barely hold back his laughter. But that prim English governess was in no mood for laughter. She guessed that the powder and paint had been purloined from her dressing-table, and a deep flush of anger showed through the artificial pallor of her face. She cast fiery glances at the young mischief-maker who, postponing any explanation until another day, pretended not to notice them.

They sat down at the table. Aleksey continued to play his absent-minded, pensive role. Liza spoke mincingly, in a sing-song voice, and only in French. Her father kept looking at her, unable to understand what her intention was, but finding it all most amusing. The English governess sat silently fuming. Only Ivan Petrovich seemed at home: he ate for two, drank his fill, laughed at his own jokes and conversed with increasing jollity.

At last everyone rose from the table; the guests departed and Grigory Ivanovich gave free rein to laughter and questions.

'Whatever were you thinking of, making fools of them like that?' he asked Liza. 'And do you know what? The powder suits you admirably. I shall not pry into the secrets of a lady's toilette, but if I were you I would start using powder regularly. Not too much, of course, just a little.'

Liza was delighted at the success of her scheme. She embraced her father, promised to consider his advice and then ran off to pacify the furious Miss Jackson, who was most reluctant to open her door and listen to her excuses. Liza was ashamed to appear before strangers with such a dark complexion; she did not dare ask . . . She was convinced that dear, kind Miss Jackson would forgive her . . . and so on. Once reassured that Liza had not intended making a laughing-stock of her, Miss Jackson calmed down, kissed Liza and as a token of reconciliation presented her with a small jar of English powder which Liza accepted with an expression of sincere gratitude.

The reader will guess that next morning Liza lost no time in keeping her rendezvous at the grove.

'You were at our master and mistress's house last night, sir, weren't you?' she asked Aleksey right away. 'What did you think of our young mistress?'

Aleksey replied that he had not noticed her.

'It's a pity,' Liza replied.

'Why is that?' asked Aleksey.

'Because I was wanting to ask you if what they say is . . .'

'What do they say?'

'That it's true that I look like her.'

'What nonsense! Compared with you she's a positive freak.'

'Oh, sir, it's not right that you should say such things. Our young mistress is so fair, so elegant. How could I compare myself with her!'

Aleksey swore that she was more beautiful than all the fair young ladies in creation and in order to set her mind completely at rest began describing her mistress in such comical terms that Liza laughed fit to burst.

'However,' she sighed, 'our young lady may be ridiculous, but in comparison with her I'm a poor ignorant fool.'

'Really?' said Aleksey, 'that's nothing to get upset about! If you like I'll start teaching you to read and write at once.'

'Do you mean it?' Liza asked. 'Well, why don't I give it a try?'

'If you like we can start now.'

They sat down. Aleksey took a pencil and notebook from his pocket, and Akulina learnt the alphabet with astonishing speed. Aleksey could not but marvel at her powers of comprehension. The following morning she wanted to try writing; at first her pencil would not obey her, but within a few minutes she was able to trace letters quite competently.

'How amazing!' Aleksey said. 'We're making better progress than if we used the Lancaster system.'[14] Indeed, by the third lesson Akulina could already work her way through *Natalya the Boyar's Daughter*,[15] making observations while she read that truly astounded Aleksey, after which she filled a whole page with aphorisms chosen from the story.

One week passed and they started writing to each other. Their post office was the hollow of an old oak tree, and Nastya secretly performed the duties of a postman. It was here that Aleksey brought letters written in a bold hand; it was here that he found the scribblings on plain blue paper of his beloved. Akulina, evidently, had swiftly accustomed herself to expressing herself more elegantly, and her powers of comprehension underwent a marked development and improvement.

Meanwhile the recent acquaintance between Ivan Petrovich Berestov and Grigory Ivanovich Muromsky grew stronger and stronger, and soon became real friendship, as a result of the following circumstances. Muromsky had often reflected that upon Ivan Petrovich Berestov's death all his property would pass into the hands of Aleksey, in which case he would become one of the wealthiest landowners in the province and that there would be no reason why Aleksey should not marry Liza. But although the elder Berestov, for his part, acknowledged a certain extravagance of behaviour (or, as he put it, 'English folly') in his neighbour, he readily admitted that he possessed many excellent qualities – for example, an uncommon resourcefulness. Grigory Ivanovich was a close relative of Count

Pronsky, a most distinguished and powerful gentleman. The count could be very useful to Aleksey, and Muromsky (so thought Ivan Petrovich Berestov) would probably rejoice at the opportunity of making such a good match for his daughter. After mulling over this matter in private the old men finally came to discuss it with one another, embraced, promised to see everything was properly arranged, and each got busy in his own way. But one difficulty confronted Muromsky: how to persuade his Betsy to become better acquainted with Aleksey, whom she had not seen since that memorable dinner. It did not appear that they liked each other very much; at least Aleksey never came back to Priluchino and Liza would retire to her room every time Ivan Petrovich honoured them with a visit.

'But,' thought Grigory Ivanovich, 'if Aleksey were to visit us every day Betsy would be bound to fall in love with him. That is in the order of things. Time will settle everything.'

Ivan Petrovich was not so anxious about the success of his plans. That same evening he summoned his son to his study, lit his pipe and, after a brief silence, said,

'It's a long time Aleksey, since you mentioned a military career. Or does a hussar's uniform no longer tempt you?'

'No, father,' Aleksey replied respectfully. 'I understand that you wouldn't want me to join the hussars and it is my duty to obey you.'

'Good,' replied Ivan Petrovich. 'I see that you're an obedient son and that's a great comfort to me. I don't want to force you to do anything against your will. I shall not compel you – at least not for now – to enter the civil service. However, I do intend you to get married.'

'To whom, father?' asked Aleksey in astonishment.

'To Lizaveta Grigoryevna Muromsky,' Ivan Petrovich replied. 'A splendid match, don't you agree?'

'I'm not thinking of marrying just yet, father.'

'You're not thinking, so I've done the thinking for you – and I've thought a great deal about it.'

'As you please, but I do not like Liza Muromsky at all.'

'But you will later. Love is just a matter of habit.'

'I don't feel I'm capable of making her happy.'

'Don't worry about making her happy, that's not your problem. Well? Is this how you respect your father's wishes? A fine thing!'

'As you like, but I do not wish to marry and I shall not marry.'

'You *shall* marry or I'll curse you. As for the estate, I shall sell it and squander all the money and not leave you with a copeck. As God is my witness! I'm giving you three days to think about it and in the meantime keep out of my sight.'

Aleksey knew that once his father got an idea into his head then, as Taras Skotinin[16] put it, not even a nail could force it out. But Aleksey took after his father and was just as stubborn when it came to an argument. He retired to his room and began to reflect upon the limits of paternal authority, Liza Muromsky, his father's solemn vow to cut him off completely and finally Akulina. For the first time he saw quite clearly that he was passionately in love with her. The romantic idea of marrying a peasant girl and living on the fruits of his labours crossed his mind, and the more he thought about such a decisive step, the more sensible it seemed. There had been no meeting in the grove for some time on account of the rainy weather. He wrote to Akulina in the clearest handwriting and most frenzied style, telling her of the ruin that was threatening them and offering her his hand, there and then. He took the letter immediately to the 'post office' in the tree hollow and went to bed exceedingly pleased with himself.

Early next morning Aleksey, firm of resolve, rode over to Muromsky for a frank discussion. He was hoping to arouse his magnanimity and win him over to his side.

'Is Grigory Ivanovich at home?' he asked, bringing his horse to a stop at the front steps of the Priluchino manor-house.

'No, sir,' replied the servant. 'Grigory Ivanovich rode out early this morning.'

'How annoying!' thought Aleksey. 'Is Liza Grigoryevna at home then?'

'Yes, sir.'

Aleksey sprang from his horse, handed the reins to the footman and entered the house unannounced.

'All will be decided now,' he thought as he made his way to the drawing-room. 'I shall explain everything personally.'

He entered . . . and stood there as if stunned! Not Liza . . . but Akulina, dear, dark-complexioned Akulina, not in a sarafan but in a white morning frock, was sitting by the window reading his letter; she was so engrossed that she had not heard him enter. Aleksey could not restrain a cry of joy. Liza started, raised her head, cried out and attempted to escape from the room. But Aleksey rushed to hold her back.

'Akulina, Akulina!'

Liza tried to break free from his grasp.

'Mais laissez-moi donc, Monsieur; mais êtes-vous fou?'[17] she said, turning away from him.

'Dear Akulina! My dear Akulina!' he repeated, kissing her hands. Miss Jackson, a witness to this scene, did not know what to make of it. At that moment the door opened and Grigory Ivanovich entered.

'Aha!' said Muromsky, 'so it's all settled between you two . . .'

Readers will spare me the unnecessary duty of describing the denouement.

END OF THE TALES OF BELKIN

THE HISTORY OF THE VILLAGE
OF GORYUKHINO

Should God grant me readers, perhaps they will be curious to know how it was that I decided to write the history of the village of Goryukhino. To that end I must enter into a few preliminary details.

I was born of upright and honourable parents in the village of Goryukhino on 1 April 1801 and received my elementary education from our parish clerk. It is to this worthy gentleman that I am indebted for what was to develop later into my love of reading and of literary pursuits in general. My progress was slow, but sound, since I knew at the age of ten everything that has since remained in my memory which is weak by nature and which, on account of my equally weak health, I was not allowed to overburden.

The calling of a man of letters has invariably struck me as the most enviable of all. My parents, respectable but simple people and educated according to old-fashioned methods, never read anything, and with the exception of an alphabet that they bought for me, some almanacs and the latest *Manual of Letter Writing*,[1] there were no other books to be found in the entire house. Reading the *Manual* was for a long time my favourite exercise. Although I knew it by heart, every day I discovered gems that I had not noticed before. After General Plemyannikov,[2] to whom my father was once adjutant, Kurganov struck me as the greatest of men. I questioned everyone about him, but unfortunately no one was able to satisfy my curiosity, no one knew him personally and the sole reply I received to all my questions was that Kurganov had written the latest *Manual of Letter Writing*, which I knew well enough already. He was lost in the mists of obscurity, like some ancient demigod; sometimes I even doubted whether he actually existed. His name struck me as pure invention

75

and the legend surrounding him as an empty myth awaiting the investigations of some new Niebuhr.[3] For all that, Kurganov still haunted my imagination. As I tried to give some form to that figure, I finally decided that he must resemble the district assessor Koryushkin, a little old man with red nose and sparkling eyes.

In 1812 I was taken to Moscow and placed in Karl Ivanovich Meyer's boarding-school, where I spent no more than three months as we were sent home just before the enemy invasion, and so I returned to the country. After the Twelve Nations[4] had been driven out, my parents wanted to take me back to Moscow again to see whether Karl Ivanovich Meyer had returned to his former abode and, if he had not, to send me to some other school; but I begged my mother to let me stay in the country, claiming that my poor health did not permit me to get up at seven o'clock in the morning, which is the normal practice in all boarding-schools. And so, when I had reached the age of sixteen, my standard of education was still at the same elementary stage as before, and I was still playing ball games with my friends in the village – this was the sole science in which I had acquired an adequate grounding during my residence at boarding-school.

At this time I enlisted as a cadet in the *** infantry regiment, in which I remained until last year, 18**. My time with the regiment left me with few agreeable impressions, apart from being commissioned and winning 245 roubles when all I had in my pocket was sixty copecks. The deaths of my beloved parents obliged me to resign my commission and retire to the estate I had inherited.

This period of my life is so important to me that I intend going into great detail, craving in advance the forgiveness of my gracious reader if I should abuse his indulgent attention.

It was an overcast day in autumn. After arriving at the post-station where I had to turn off for Goryukhino, I hired some fresh horses and drove off down the country road. Although I am placid by nature, my impatience to see again those places where I had spent my happiest years gripped me so strongly that I constantly urged on my coachman, first promising him a tip, then threatening him with blows: since it was easier for me to prod him in the back than to take out and untie my purse, I do confess that I struck him two or three times, something I had never done in my life, since the class of drivers – why, I do not know – is particularly dear to me. The driver urged his troika on, but I had the impression that – faithful to the habit of drivers – while exhorting the horses and waving his whip, he was at the same time tightening the reins. At length I caught sight of Goryukhino Copse; within ten minutes we were driving into the manor-house courtyard. My heart beat violently as I looked around with indescribable emotion: it was eight years since I had set eyes on Goryukhino. The birch saplings that had been planted near the fence at the time I lived there had grown into tall, spreading trees. The courtyard, once embellished by three regularly shaped flower-beds, between which ran a broad, sand-strewn path, was now an unmown meadow on which grazed a brown cow. My brichka[5] stopped at the front steps. My servant went to open the door, but it was boarded up, although the shutters were open and the house appeared to be inhabited. A woman came out of one of the peasant cottages and asked whom I wanted to see. When she learnt that her master had arrived, she ran back into her cottage, and soon I was surrounded by the household servants. I was touched to the very depths of my heart when I saw faces familiar and unfamiliar – and I kissed all of them in friendly fashion: my boyhood friends were now men, and young girls who had once sat on the floor waiting to run errands were now married women. The men wept. I told the women unceremoniously, 'How you've aged,' and they replied with feeling, 'And how plain you've become, master.' I was taken to the back entrance, where my old wet-nurse wept and sobbed as she came out to greet me, just as if I were the long-suffering Odysseus. They rushed off to heat a bath for me. The cook, who now had nothing to do and had let his beard grow, offered to prepare dinner – rather, a late supper – for me, since it was already dark. The rooms formerly occupied by my wet-nurse and my late mother's maids were immediately prepared for me, and so I found myself in my parents' humble abode and fell asleep in that same room in which I was born twenty-three years before.

About three weeks passed in all kinds of fuss and bother – I was busy with assessors, marshals of the nobility and every imaginable kind of provincial official. Finally I came into my inheritance and took possession of my patrimony; I had peace of mind, but soon the boredom of inactivity began to torment me. I was not yet acquainted with my worthy and respected neighbour ***. Running an estate was something quite foreign to me. The conversation of my wet-nurse, whom I had promoted to housekeeper and manageress, consisted of fifteen domestic anecdotes, all very interesting for me, but as she was in the habit of always telling them in the same way, she became for me another *Manual of Letter Writing*, in which I knew where each line would be on any of its pages. That good old *Manual* I found in the store-room, amidst junk of all kinds, and in a sorry state. I brought it out into the light and started to read, but Kurganov had lost his former charm – I read him once more, after which I never opened the book again.

In this extremity it occurred to me that I should endeavour to write something of my own. My gracious reader knows already that I was educated on a pittance and that I never had the chance of acquiring on my own what had once been neglected, playing as I did up to the age of sixteen with servants' sons and then moving from province to province, from billet to billet, spending my time with Jews and sutlers, playing on torn billiard tables and tramping through the mud.

Moreover, to be a writer struck me as so complicated, so unattainable for us the uninitiated, that the thought of taking pen in hand at first frightened me. Dare I hope to become a writer one day, when my burning desire to meet just one of them had never been fulfilled? But this reminds me of an incident which I intend relating as evidence of my undying passion for our native letters.

In 1820, while I was still a cadet, I happened to be in St Petersburg on government business. I stayed there a week and, despite the fact that I did not know a soul there, spent an extremely jolly time. Every day I would go off to the theatre and sit in the fourth row of the gallery. I got to know all the actors by name and fell passionately in love with ***, who one Sunday played with great skill the part of Amalia in the drama *Hatred and Repentance*.[6] In the mornings, when I returned from Headquarters, I used to drop in at a little coffee-house and read the literary journals over a cup of chocolate. One day I was sitting there engrossed in a critical article in *Good Intentions* when a gentleman in a pea-green overcoat came up to me and gently took from under my journal a copy of the *Hamburg Gazette*. I was so absorbed in my article that I did not so much as look up. The stranger ordered a beefsteak and sat opposite me; I carried on reading without paying him any attention; meanwhile he ate his lunch, angrily scolded the waiter for slovenliness, drank half a bottle of wine and left. Two young men were also having lunch at the time. 'Do you know who that was?' one asked the other. 'That was B.,[7] the writer.' 'The writer!' I could not help exclaiming, and, leaving my journal unfinished and my chocolate half-drunk, rushed to pay my bill and without waiting for the change dashed into the street . . . looking all around I spotted the pea-green overcoat in the distance and set off after it along Nevsky Avenue, half-running. After a few paces I suddenly felt I was being stopped – I looked round and there was a Guards officer pointing out to me that I should not have knocked him off the pavement, when the correct thing was to stop and stand to attention. After this reprimand I was more careful; unfortunately for me I kept meeting an officer every minute, and every minute I was made to stop, so that the writer drew further and further ahead. Never in my life had my army overcoat seemed so heavy, never had I been so jealous of those with epaulettes. At length, at the Anichkin Bridge, I caught up with the pea-green overcoat.

'May I enquire,' I asked, saluting, 'if you are that Mr B. whose fine articles I have had the pleasure of reading in the *Amateur of Enlightenment*?'

'No sir,' he replied. 'I am not a writer, but an attorney. But I know *** very well; only a quarter of an hour ago I met him at the Politseisky Bridge.'

And so my respect for Russian literature cost me thirty copecks in lost change, an official reprimand – almost an arrest – and all for nothing.

Despite all the objections of my reason, the daring idea of becoming a writer crossed my mind constantly. Finally, no longer able to resist my natural inclination, I made myself a thick exercise book with the firm intention of filling it with anything I could think of. I investigated and evaluated all genres of poetry (since I had not yet considered humble prose), and I decided to write an epic poem, drawn from the history of our fatherland. It did not take me very long to find a hero. I chose Rurik[8] – and set to work.

I had acquired a certain skill in verse by copying out notebooks that circulated among us officers – for example, *The Dangerous Neighbour*,[9] *Critique of a Moscow Boulevard*, *Presnensky Ponds*[10] and so on. For all that, my poem made slow progress and I abandoned it at the third verse. I concluded that the epic genre was not for me and so I began a tragedy about Rurik. But tragedy just did not work. I attempted to make a ballad out of it – but for some reason I did not succeed with this genre either. Finally inspiration dawned upon me, and I started and successfully completed an inscription to the portrait of Rurik.

Despite the fact that my inscription was by no means unworthy of attention, particularly as it was the first composition of a young poet, I none the less felt that I was not born to be a poet and contented myself with this first attempt. But my creative endeavour had made me so attached to literary activity that no longer was I able to part from my exercise book and ink-pot. I felt the urge to descend to prose. At first, not wishing to busy myself with preliminary study, with setting out a plan, linking all the sections together and so on, I decided to record individual thoughts, in any order, at random, just as they entered my head. Unfortunately the thoughts would not come to mind, and in the course of two whole days the only observation that occurred to me was as follows:

He who does not obey the laws of reason and is accustomed to following the promptings of his passions, often goes astray and subjects himself to tardy repentance.

A just thought, of course, but far from original. So, abandoning such reflections, I attempted stories, but as I am unpractised in setting out fictional events in logical sequence, I selected some remarkable anecdotes that I had heard at different times from various people, and tried to embellish the truth with lively narration, and on occasion with the flowers of my own imagination. In composing these stories I gradually fashioned my style and learnt to express myself correctly, pleasantly and fluently. But soon my stock of anecdotes was exhausted and once again I started searching for a fitting subject for my literary activity.

The idea of abandoning these trivial and dubious anecdotes for the narration of true and great events excited my imagination. To be the judge, observer and prophet of epochs and nations struck me as the summit of achievement for a writer. But, with my pitiful education, what historical events could I write about, where erudite, conscientious scholars had not anticipated me? What aspect of history had not already been exhausted by them? Should I write a history of the world – but is there not already Abbé Millot's[11] immortal work? Should I address myself to Russian history? But what could I say after Tatishchev,[12] Boltin and Golikov? And was I the kind of man to burrow into chronicles and attempt to fathom the secret meaning of a dead language when I had never been able even to learn the Slavonic numerals? I contemplated a history on a smaller scale, for example, a history of the provincial capital; but even here there were so many insuperable obstacles as far as I was concerned! A journey to the capital, visits to the Governor and the Bishop, a request for admission to the archives, monastery store-rooms and so on. A history of our local town would have been easier for me, but it would have been of no interest for either a scholar or a layman and would offer scant material for fine rhetoric. *** had acquired the status of town in 17** and the only event of note recorded in the town chronicles was the terrible fire that broke out ten years before, destroying the market and administrative offices.

An unexpected event put an end to my perplexity. While hanging up linen in the attic, an old woman servant found an old basket full of wood shavings, litter and books. The whole house knew of my love of reading. At that very moment when I was sitting over my exercise book, nibbling my pen and thinking of attempting rural sermons, my housekeeper triumphantly entered the room, dragging the basket and joyfully exclaiming, 'Books!' 'Books!' I repeated rapturously and threw myself on the basket. And in effect I saw a whole pile of books with green and blue paper covers – this was a collection of old almanacs. This discovery cooled my delight; nevertheless I was pleased at the unexpected find: after all, they were books, and I generously rewarded my laundress's zeal with a silver half-rouble. Left on my own, I started inspecting the almanacs and before long was deeply engrossed in them. They formed an unbroken series, covering the years from 1744 to 1799, that is, exactly fifty-five years. The blue sheets of paper that are usually bound into almanacs were covered with old-fashioned handwriting. As I examined these pages I was amazed to see that they included not only observations about the weather and household accounts, but also historical fragments concerning the village of Goryukhino. Without delay I started sorting through these most valuable records and soon discovered that they comprised a complete history of the estate I had inherited, over the course of almost an entire century, in the strictest chronological order. In addition, they constituted an inexhaustible fund of economic, statistical, meteorological and other scholarly observations. Ever since, the study of these records has occupied me to the exclusion of all else, as I saw the possibility of extracting from them an orderly, interesting and instructive narrative. As I made myself sufficiently familiar with these precious records, I started searching for new sources for the history of the village of Goryukhino. Soon I was amazed at the abundance of such sources. After devoting six whole months to preliminary study, I finally embarked on my long-awaited task and with God's help completed the said work on November 3, 1827.

Now – just as a certain historian[13] similar to myself and whose name I cannot remember – having completed my arduous task, I lay down my pen and sadly wandered into my garden to reflect on what I had accomplished. It seems to me that, having finished my *History of Goryukhino*, I am no longer needed in this world, that my duty is done and that it is time for me to go to my rest!

Hereunder is appended a list of sources used by me in the composition of my *History of Goryukhino*.

1. A collection of old almanacs, in fifty-four parts. The first twenty parts were covered with old-fashioned writing, in abbreviated script. This chronicle was composed by my great-grandfather Andrey Stepanovich Belkin. It is distinguished for clarity and brevity of style – for example: May 4th. Snow. Trishka beaten for rudeness. 6th – the brown cow died. Senka flogged for drunkenness. Clear weather. 9th – rain and snow. Trishka flogged because of the weather. 11th – fine weather. Fresh snowfall. Hunted three hares, and so on, without any comments at all . . . The remaining thirty-five parts were written in different hands, most of them in so-called 'shopkeeper's hand', with and without abbreviations, on the whole quite lengthy, disconnected and with no regard for orthography. Here and there a female hand is noticeable. In this section are included notes written by my grandfather Ivan Andreyevich Belkin and my grandmother Yevpraksiya Alekseyevna, as well as the steward Garbovitsky.

2. Chronicle of the Goryukhino sexton. This curious manuscript was found by me at the house of my priest, who married the daughter of the chronicler. The first sheets had been torn out and used by the priest's children for making kites. One such kite fell into the middle of the courtyard. I picked it up and was about to return it to the children when I noticed that there was writing on it. From the very first lines I could see that the kite had been made out of a chronicle, and fortunately I managed to save the rest. This chronicle, which I had acquired for a quarter of oats, is notable for profundity of thought and remarkable magniloquence.

3. Oral legends. I did not disregard any piece of information. But I am particularly obliged to Agrafena Trifonovna, mother of Avdey the clerk and (so it is said) the former mistress of the steward Garbovitsky.

4. Census lists, with comments by former village-elders concerning the morals and condition of the peasants.

———————

The region that is named Goryukhino after its capital occupies more than six hundred acres of this earthly globe. The number of inhabitants extends to sixty-three souls. To the north the region borders on the villages of Derikhovo and Perkukhovo, whose inhabitants are poor, gaunt and undersized, and whose landowners are devoted to the martial exercise of hunting hares. To the south the River Sivka separates the village from the possessions of the free farmers of Karachevo, restless neighbours notorious for the unbridled cruelty of their natures. Bounding it to the west are the flowering fields of Zakharino, thriving under the sway of wise and enlightened landowners. To the east it borders upon wild, uninhabited land, an impassable bog, where only the cranberry grows, where only the monotonous croaking of frogs is heard and where, according to superstitious tradition, some demon has his abode.

Note   This bog is called *Demon's Bog*. It is said that a certain half-witted shepherdess was tending a herd of pigs not far from this isolated spot. She became pregnant and was quite unable to give a satisfactory explanation of this state of affairs. Popular opinion blamed the demon of the bog; but this fable is unworthy of an historian's attention and after Niebuhr it would be inexcusable to give it credence.

From time immemorial Goryukhino has been famed for its fertility and salubrious climate. Rye, oats, barley and buckwheat thrive in its rich fields. A birch grove and fir forest provide its inhabitants with timber for building and fallen branches for heating their homes. There is no shortage of nuts, cranberries, whortleberries and bilberries. Mushrooms grow in extraordinary profusion and when fried in sour cream they provide pleasant, although unhealthy nourishment. The pond is teeming with carp, while pike and burbot are to be found in the River Sivka.

For the main part the inhabitants of Goryukhino are of medium height, and of sturdy, manly build; their eyes are grey and their hair fair or red. The women are noted for their slightly upturned noses, prominent cheekbones and ample proportions.

NB   *muscular peasant woman*: this expression is often found in the village-elder's comments on the census lists. The men are of good character, industrious (especially in their own fields), brave and warlike; many of them have fought bears single-handed and are renowned in the district as fist fighters; in general all show an inclination for the sensual pleasures of drunkenness. In addition to domestic work, the women share a large portion of their husbands' work; and they are not inferior to them as regards courage – very few of them fear the village-elder. They constitute a powerful community guard, keeping constant vigil in the manor-house court-yard, and they are called *spear-women* (from the Slavonic word *spear*). The chief duty of these spear-women is to beat a cast-iron plate with a stone, thereby striking fear into those of evil intent. They are as chaste as they are pretty; to the advances of the insolent they respond severely and unequivocally.

The inhabitants of Goryukhino have long carried on a rich trade in bast baskets and shoes. In this they are helped by the River Sivka, which they cross in the spring in dug-outs, like the ancient Scandinavians, at other times of the year wading across it, having rolled up their trousers to the knees beforehand.

The language spoken in Goryukhino is definitely a branch of Slavonic, but differs from it as much as Russian does. It is filled with abbreviations and truncations – some letters have been left out altogether or replaced by others. However, a Great Russian[14] has no difficulty in understanding anyone from Goryukhino, and vice versa.

The men used at the age of thirteen to marry girls of twenty. The wives would beat their husbands for four or five years. Subsequently the husbands would beat their wives; and thus both sexes enjoyed their period of authority and a correct balance was maintained.

Funeral ceremonies were performed in the following way. On the day of death the deceased was taken directly to the cemetery so that his corpse should not unnecessarily take up space in his cottage. As a result, it often happened that the corpse, to the indescribable joy of the relatives, would sneeze or yawn just as it was being conveyed out of the village in its coffin. Wives would bewail their husbands, howling and muttering, 'Light of my life, my brave darling! Whom have you left me to? How shall I keep your memory sacred?' After the return from the cemetery a wake in honour of the deceased would commence, and relatives and friends would be intoxicated for two or three days, even for an entire week, depending on their zeal and degree of attachment to his memory. These ancient rites have been preserved to this day.

The dress of the people of Goryukhino consisted of shirts worn over breeches – this is a distinguishing feature of their Slav origins. In winter they wore sheepskin jackets, but more for show than from need, since they usually slung them over one shoulder and then discarded them when doing the slightest work which called for bodily movement.

From earliest times, the arts and poetry have been in a fairly flourishing state in Goryukhino. Besides the priest and junior deacons, there have always been literate men in the village. The chronicle records a clerk by the name of Terenty, who lived around 1767 and who could write not only with his right hand but also with his left. This remarkable man became famous throughout the whole neighbourhood for being able to compose all kinds of documents, letters, petitions, civil passports and so on. Having suffered more than once on account of his skill and readiness to oblige, and for having taken part in various remarkable events, he died in ripe old age just when he was learning to write with his right foot, since the script of both his hands had become too well known. As the reader will see below, he plays an important role in the history of Goryukhino.

Music has always been the favourite art of the educated people of Goryukhino, the sound of the balalaika and bagpipes bringing delight to sensitive hearts, and they can be heard to this day in their dwellings, especially in the ancient communal hall, embellished with branches of spruce and the emblem of the two-headed eagle.[15]

At one time poetry flourished in ancient Goryukhino. To this day the poems of Arkhip the Bald are preserved in the memory of posterity.

In tenderness they are in no way inferior to the eclogues of the celebrated Virgil and in beauty of imagery they far surpass the idylls of Mr Sumarokov.[16] And although in elaborateness of style they do not emulate the latest productions of our muses, they are equal to them in inventiveness and wit. Let me quote as an example the following satirical poem:

> To the great boyar's mansion
> Wends his way the Elder, Anton,
> In his bosom he carries
> For the boyar his monthly tallies;
> The boyar looks on with vacant face,
> He can make nothing of this case;
> Oh, Anton you've cleaned the boyar out,
> Of that there is no doubt;
> Through you the village has naught to eat,
> While the Elder's wife is replete.

Having thus acquainted my reader with the ethnographic and statistical position of Goryukhino and with the customs and habits of its inhabitants, I shall now proceed to the narrative itself.

Legendary Times

Trifon the Village-Elder

The system of government in Goryukhino has changed several times. It was in turn under the authority of leaders elected by the village community, then of stewards who were appointed by the landowners and finally directly under the authority of the landowners themselves. The advantages and disadvantages of these various forms of administration will be examined by me in the course of my narrative.

The foundation of Goryukhino and its original settlement are shrouded in mystery. According to vague legends, at one time Goryukhino was a wealthy and large village, all its inhabitants were prosperous, tithes were collected once a year and taken to some unknown person in several cart-loads. At that time everything was bought cheaply and sold expensively. There were no stewards then, village-elders took advantage of no one, the inhabitants did little work and lived in clover – even the shepherds wore boots as they tended their flocks. But we must not let ourselves be carried away by this charming picture. The idea of a golden age is common to all nations and demonstrates only that people are never content with the present and, from experience having little hope for the future, they embellish the irrevocable past with all the colours of their imagination. The truth, however, is as follows:

From earliest times the village of Goryukhino belonged to the distinguished Belkin family. But my ancestors, who owned many other estates, ignored this remote part of the country. Goryukhino paid little tribute and was administered by elders elected by the people at an assembly called the Council of Peasants.

But in the course of time the ancestral estates of the Belkins broke up and fell into decline. The impoverished grandchildren of the rich grandfather were unable to cast off their luxurious habits and demanded the full income that had been previously received, from an estate that had decreased to one-tenth of its former size. Menacing orders followed, one after the other. The village-elder read them out at the assembly; other leaders in the village delivered speeches, the people grew agitated, while the masters, instead of twofold tithes, received cunning excuses and humble complaints written on soiled paper and sealed with a half-copeck.

A dark cloud hung over Goryukhino, but no one gave any thought to it. In the final year of the rule of Trifon, the last elder to be chosen by the people, on the day of the patronal festival, when the entire populace was either noisily crowding around the House of Entertainment (known as *pot-house* in the vernacular), or wandering up and down the streets, embracing and loudly singing the songs of Arkhip the Bald, there drove into the village a wicker brichka drawn by a pair of half-dead nags; a Jew in rags was sitting on the box, while from the brichka a head with a peaked cap on it poked out and seemed to be looking with curiosity at the people who were making merry. The inhabitants greeted the brichka with laughter and crude taunts.

Note   With the lapels of their jackets turned up, the crazy people mocked the Jewish coachman and exclaimed jeeringly, 'Jew, Jew, go and eat a pig's ear!' – *Chronicle of the Goryukhino Sexton.*

But how amazed they were when the brichka stopped in the middle of the village and the visitor jumped out and called out in an imperious voice for Trifon the village-elder. This dignitary happened to be in the House of Entertainment, whence two elders respectfully escorted him, supporting him under the arms. The stranger, after giving him a menacing look, handed him a letter and ordered him to read it immediately. The elders of Goryukhino were not in the habit of reading anything for themselves. The village-elder could neither read nor write. So they sent for Avdey the clerk. They found him not far away, sleeping under a fence in an alley, and he was brought before the stranger. But either from the sudden shock or from some grim foreboding, he found the words of the letter, which was in fact clearly written, blurred and consequently he could not make them out. Cursing dreadfully, the stranger sent Trifon the village-elder and Avdey the clerk off to bed, postponed the reading of the letter until the next day and went into the steward's cottage, the Jew following with his small trunk.

The people of Goryukhino watched this unusual event in mute astonishment, but soon the carriage, Jew and stranger were forgotten. The day finished noisily and merrily – and Goryukhino fell asleep, not suspecting what lay in store for it.

Next day, at sunrise, the inhabitants were awakened by a knocking at their windows and a summons to the Council of Peasants. One after the other the villagers appeared in the yard of the steward's cottage, which served as a council meeting-place. Their eyes were bloodshot and bleary, their faces swollen; yawning and scratching themselves, they looked at the man in the peaked cap – now wearing an old blue tunic – who was solemnly standing on the front steps to the clerk's hut, and they tried to recall those features that they thought they had seen before. Trifon the village-elder and Avdey the clerk were standing by him, hatless, each with an expression of servility and profound distress. 'Is everyone here?' asked the stranger. 'Is everyone here?' repeated the village-elder. 'Every single one of us,' replied the villagers. Then the village-elder announced that a document had been received from the squire and he ordered the clerk to read it out so that the whole assembly should hear.

Note   The chronicler writes: 'This dread document I copied at the house of Trifon the village-elder, and it is kept there in an icon-case, together with other memorials of his dominion over Goryu-khino.' I myself could not find the original of this curious letter.

Trifon Ivanov!

The bearer of this letter, my agent **, is travelling to my patrimonial village of Goryukhino in order to take charge of the administration of same. Immediately after his arrival he is to assemble all the peasants and announce my, their master's, wishes, namely: the peasants are to obey the orders of my agent ** as if they were my own, and to carry out whatever he may demand of them unquestioningly. In the event of their failing to do so, ** is empowered to treat them with the utmost severity. It is their shameless disobedience, together with your roguish indulgence, Trifon Ivanov, that has compelled me to take these steps.

Signed NN.

And then, spreading out his legs like the letter 'X' and standing with arms akimbo, ** delivered the following brief, compelling speech.

'You had better watch out: don't try and be clever with me. I know that you are a spoilt lot, and I can knock any nonsense out of your heads quicker than you can get over yesterday's hangover.' But no one was suffering from any hangover. The people of Goryu-khino, as if thunderstruck, hung their heads and returned to their homes, horrified.

The Rule of the Steward **

** assumed the reins of government and proceeded to put his political system into practice; it is deserving of special scrutiny.

It was chiefly based on the following axiom:

The richer a peasant, the more spoilt he is; the poorer, the humbler he is. Consequently ** strove towards maintaining humility on the estate, as the principal peasant virtue. He demanded a list of all the peasants and divided them into rich and poor.

1. Arrears of rent were allocated among the prosperous peasants and exacted from them with the utmost severity.

2. Those who were poorly-off or idle pleasure-seekers were immediately sent out to plough, and if, in his opinion, their work was unsatisfactory, he would send them out to labour for other peasants, who paid him a voluntary tribute for this service, while those delivered into serfdom had the full right to buy back their freedom by paying twice the annual tithes, over and above any arrears that might be due. The costs of all public services fell upon the well-to-do peasants. Recruitment for the army was the principal triumph of that mercenary administrator, since, according to that system, all the rich peasants were able to buy themselves out of it, one by one, until there remained only scoundrels or those who had been ruined.

Note That accursed steward put Anton Timofeyev in irons, but old Timofey bought out his son for one hundred roubles; the steward then put Petrushka Yeremeyev in irons, and he was bought out for sixty-eight roubles by his father; and that accursed man wanted to put Lekha Tarasov in irons, but he fled into the forest, which made the steward sorely distressed and he poured forth his anger in words; and then Vanka the drunkard was taken away to town and handed over as a recruit. (From a report by the peasants of Goryukhino.)

The peasant assemblies were abolished. The steward collected the tithes piecemeal all year round. Into the bargain he instituted sudden tax collections. It appears that the peasants did not pay much more than they had done previously; but they were quite unable to earn or save enough money for their needs. Within three years Goryukhino became utterly destitute.

Goryukhino sank into gloom and dejection, the market became deserted, the songs of Arkhip the Bald were heard no more. Village children ran around begging. Half of the peasants were sent out to plough, while the other half were used for hired labour; and the day of the church festival became, as the chronicler expresses it, not a day of joy and exultation, but an anniversary of sadness and woeful remembrance.

ROSLAVLEV

While reading *Roslavlev*[1] I saw to my amazement that its plot was based on a true happening, all too familiar to me. I had once been a friend of the unfortunate woman chosen by Mr Zagoskin as the heroine of his tale. He turned the public's attention anew to a forgotten event, aroused feelings of indignation that had been lulled by time and disturbed the peace of the grave. I shall be the protectress of that 'shade' – and the reader will forgive the feebleness of my pen, having respect for the sincerity of my motives. I shall be compelled to speak a great deal about myself, because my destiny was long bound up with the fate of my poor friend.

I was brought out into society in the winter of 1811. I shall not describe my first impressions. It is easy to imagine what a sixteen-year-old girl must feel after exchanging schoolroom and tutors for a life constantly filled with balls. I surrendered myself to the whirl of gaiety with all the vivacity of my years and did not pause to reflect . . . A pity: those times were worthy of observation.

Among the young girls who came out with me, Princess ** stood out from the others (Mr Zagoskin called her Polina so I shall leave her with this name). We soon became friends for the following reason.

My brother, a young man of twenty-two, belonged to the company of contemporary dandies; he was working in the Foreign Office and lived in Moscow, leading a life of dancing and riotous behaviour. He fell in love with Polina and begged me to bring our two households together. My brother was the idol of the whole family, and he did what he liked with me.

After making friends with Polina just to please him, I soon formed a genuine attachment for her. There was much that was strange about her, and even more that was attractive. Before I came to understand her, I loved her. Unconsciously I began to see with her eyes and to think with her thoughts.

Polina's father was a worthy gentleman, that is, he drove in a coach and six and wore a key and a star;[2] nevertheless, he was easy-going and unpretentious. Her mother, on the other hand, was a sedate woman, distinguished for her self-importance and common sense.

Polina appeared everywhere; she was surrounded by admirers who courted her, but she was bored and her boredom gave her a proud, aloof appearance. This suited her Grecian profile and black eyebrows remarkably well. I felt triumphant when my satirical remarks brought a smile to that bored face with those perfectly proportioned features.

Polina read an extraordinary amount and quite indiscriminately. She had the key to her father's library. This library consisted mainly of the works of eighteenth-century authors. She was familiar with French literature, from Montesquieu[3] to the novels of Crébillon.[4] She knew Rousseau[5] by heart. There was not a single Russian book in her library – apart from the works of Sumarokov,[6] which Polina never opened. She used to tell me that she had difficulty in reading Russian print, and she probably never read anything in Russian, not even the verses dedicated to her by Muscovite versifiers.

Here I allow myself a brief digression. It is already thirty years now, thank goodness, since we wretched women were reproved for never reading anything in Russian and for being unable, it would appear, to express ourselves in our native language.

Note   It is quite wrong of the author of *Yury Miloslavsky*[7] to keep on repeating his vulgar accusations. We all read this book, and, it seems, it is to one of us females that he is indebted for the translation of his novel into French.

The fact is, we would be glad to read Russian; but our literature appears to be no older than Lomonosov[8] and as yet is extraordinarily limited. It of course offers us a few excellent poets, but one really cannot expect from every reader an exclusive liking for poetry. As regards prose, all we have is Karamzin's *History*;[9] the first two or three novels appeared two or three years ago, whereas in France, England and Germany, books appear one after the other, each more remarkable than the last. We do not even see any translations; and if we did then, to tell the truth, I would still prefer to read the originals. Our journals have interest only for men of letters. We are compelled to glean everything, whether news or ideas, from foreign books; thus we also think in foreign languages (at least all those who do think and who follow the thoughts of mankind). Our most celebrated men of letters admitted this to me. The endless complaints of our writers about the way we neglect Russian books resemble the complaints of Russian merchants, indignant that we go and buy our hats from Sikhler[10] and are not satisfied with the creations of milliners from Kostroma. Now I return to my subject.

Even in epochs of historical significance reminiscences of society life are usually vague and worthless. However, the appearance in Moscow of a certain traveller left a deep impression on me. This traveller was Madame de Staël.[11] She arrived one summer, when the majority of Muscovites had left for the country. Russian hospitality bestirred itself; people just could not do enough to entertain that famous foreigner. Of course, dinners were held in her honour. Ladies and gentlemen gathered to stare at her and were, for the most part, displeased with her. What they saw was a fat, fifty-year-old woman, dressed too youthfully for her years. They did not like her tone, her speeches seemed far too long and her sleeves far too short. Polina's father, who had already known Madame de Staël in Paris, gave a dinner for her, to which she invited all our Muscovite wits. It was here that I saw the author of *Corinne*. She was sitting in the place of honour, elbows on the table, furling and unfurling a roll of paper with her pretty fingers. She seemed in low spirits; on several occasions she started to speak but could not get into the conversation. Our wits ate and drank their fill, and appeared more satisfied with the Prince's fish soup than with Madame de Staël's conversation. The ladies behaved stiffly. They and the others only rarely broke the silence, convinced of the insignificance of their thoughts and inhibited in the presence of the European celebrity. Throughout the dinner

Polina was on tenterhooks. The guests' attention was divided between the sturgeon and Madame de Staël. At any moment they expected a *bon mot* from her; finally a double entendre escaped her lips – and a rather daring one at that. Everyone took it up and roared with laughter and there were whispers of amazement; the Prince was beside himself with joy. I glanced at Polina. Her face was burning, her eyes filled with tears. The guests rose from the table, completely reconciled to Madame de Staël: she had produced a pun which they dashed off to spread all over town.

'What's wrong, ma chère?' I asked Polina. 'Is it possible that a slightly *risqué* little joke could have upset you as much as that?'

'Oh, my dear,' Polina replied. 'I am in despair! How worthless our high society must appear to that remarkable woman! She is used to being surrounded by people who understand her, for whom a brilliant remark, a strong impulse of the heart, an inspired word is never lost; she is accustomed to fascinating conversation, on the highest cultural level. But here . . . My God! Not a single idea, not a single remarkable word in the course of three hours! Dull faces, dull pomposity – and that's all! How bored she was! How weary she seemed! She understood what they needed, what those apes of enlightenment could comprehend, and she tossed them a pun. And they just rushed to snap it up! I was burning with shame and ready to weep . . . But let . . .' Polina continued heatedly, 'let her take away an opinion of our society riff-raff that they deserve. At least she has seen the kind and simple common people and understands them. You heard what she said to that insufferable old buffoon who, in order to gratify a foreign lady, took it into his head to mock our Russian beards: "A nation which stood up for its beards a hundred years ago will, in our times, stand up for its heads as well." How charming she is! How I hate her persecutor!'

I was not alone in noticing Polina's confusion. Another pair of piercing eyes came to rest on her at that same moment: the black eyes of Madame de Staël herself. I do not know what she thought, only that after dinner she went up to my friend and started talking to her. After a few days Madame de Staël wrote her the following note:

Ma chère enfant, je suis toute malade. Il serait bien aimable à vous de venir me ranimer. Tâchez de l'obtenir de m-me votre mère et veuillez lui presenter les respects de votre amie *de S.*[12]

This note is still in my possession. Polina never made clear to me the nature of her relationship with Madame de Staël, despite my curiosity. She idolized that celebrated woman, as good-natured as she was brilliant.

To what extremes a passion for malicious talk can lead! Recently I recounted this story to very respectable company.

'Perhaps,' they pointed out to me, 'Madame de Staël was none other than one of Napoleon's spies and Princess ** was providing her with the information she needed.'

'For goodness' sake,' I said, 'Madame de Staël, persecuted for ten years by Napoleon; noble, kind Madame de Staël, who barely managed to escape, to find refuge under the protection of the Russian Emperor; Madame de Staël, friend of Chateaubriand[13] and Byron – working as a spy for Napoleon! . . .'

'It's highly likely,' retorted the sharp-nosed Countess B. 'Napoleon was such a rogue, and Madame de Staël is a cunning creature!'

Everyone was talking of the imminent war and, as far as I can remember, quite frivolously. Imitation of the French attitude of the time of Louis XV was then in vogue. Love of one's native country seemed pedantry. Contemporary wits praised Napoleon with fanatical servility and joked about our failures. Unfortunately, defenders of the fatherland were rather simple-minded; they were ridiculed (rather amusingly) and had no influence at all. Their patriotism was limited to cruel criticism of the use of the French language in social gatherings, of the introduction of foreign words and to threatening outbursts against Kuznetsky Bridge,[14] and so on. Young people spoke about everything Russian with contempt or indifference and, by way of a joke, predicted for Russia the same fate as that of the Confederation of the Rhine.[15] In brief, society was pretty vile.

Suddenly we were startled by news of the invasion and the Tsar's appeal staggered us. Moscow was in a state of panic. Count Rastopchin's pamphlets[16] for the common people appeared on the scene. The populace braced itself. Society buffoons grew quiet; the ladies became alarmed. Persecutors of the French language and the Kuznetsky Bridge gained what was decidedly the upper hand in society gatherings, and drawing-rooms were filled with patriots; there were those who emptied their boxes of French snuff and started to take Russian; some people burnt French pamphlets by the dozen; some renounced Château Lafite and took to sour cabbage soup. Everyone vowed to give up speaking French; everyone raved about Pozharsky and Minin[17] and started to preach about the people's war while preparing to depart for their Saratov[18] estates with hired horses.

Polina would not conceal her contempt, just as previously she could not conceal her indignation. Such a swift change of attitude and such cowardice made her lose all patience. On the boulevards, at the Presnensky Ponds,[19] she deliberately spoke French; at the dinner-table, in the presence of the servants, she deliberately challenged patriotic bragging, deliberately spoke of the vast numbers of Napoleon's troops, of his military genius. Those present turned pale, fearing they would be reported to the police, and hastened to reproach her for supporting an enemy of the fatherland. Polina smiled disdainfully. 'God grant,' she would say, 'that all Russians shall love their native land as I do.' She amazed me. I always knew Polina as a self-effacing and taciturn person, and I could not understand from whom she had acquired such boldness.

'For heaven's sake,' I once said, 'why do you meddle in matters that do not concern us! Let the men fight and shout about politics; women don't go to war and Bonaparte is no concern of theirs.' Her eyes began to gleam.

'You should be ashamed,' she said. 'Surely women have a fatherland? Don't they have fathers, brothers, husbands? Can Russian blood be alien to us? Or do you suppose that we were born simply to be whirled around in the ballroom and to be made to embroider little dogs on canvas at home? No, I know the kind of influence a woman can have on the opinion of society, or even on the heart of one man. I do not accept the humiliation to which we are condemned. Just take a look at Madame de Staël: Napoleon fought her as he fights enemy forces . . . And my uncle still dares to mock her timidity at the approach of the French army! "Be calm, young lady: Napoleon is fighting Russia, not you . . ." Yes! If Uncle happened to fall into enemy hands they would at least let him stroll in the Palais Royal; but if that were to happen to Madame de Staël she would die in a state prison. What about Charlotte Corday? And our own Marfa Posadnitsa? And Princess Dashkov?[20] Am I in any way inferior to them? To be sure, not in boldness of spirit and resoluteness.' I listened in amazement to Polina. Never had I suspected such fire, such ambition in her. Alas! Where have her rare qualities of spirit, her manly loftiness of mind led to? My favourite writer spoke the truth when he said, '*Il n'est de bonheur que dans les voies communes*.'*[21]

The Tsar's arrival intensified the general excitement. The ecstasy of patriotism finally took hold even of the highest society. Drawing-rooms were turned into debating rooms. Everywhere there was talk of patriotic sacrifice. The immortal speech of young Count Mamonov,[22] who had sacrificed his entire estate, was constantly being retold. After that, several mamas remarked that the Count was no longer such a desirable match, but all of us were in raptures over him. Polina raved about him.

'And what are you going to sacrifice?' she once asked my brother.

'I'm not the owner of the estate yet,' that rake replied. 'All in all I have debts of thirty thousand roubles: I shall sacrifice them on the altar of my fatherland.'

Polina became angry. 'For some people,' she said, 'both honour and fatherland are mere trifles. Their brothers die on the field of battle and they fool around in drawing-rooms. I don't know if there is a woman low enough to permit such a clown to claim that he is in love with her.' My brother flared up.

'You are too severe, Princess,' he retorted. 'You demand that everyone should see a Madame de Staël in you and should recite tirades from *Corinne*. Please understand that while a man can joke about a woman, he cannot joke about his country and its enemies.'

With these words he turned away. I thought that they had fallen out for good, but I was mistaken: Polina found my brother's insolence

---

* Apparently Chateaubriand's words. Editor's note. (Pushkin's note.)

pleasing; she forgave him his inappropriate joke as no more than a noble outburst of indignation, and when she discovered a week later that he had joined the Mamonov regiment, she implored me to reconcile the two of them. My brother was in raptures. He proposed there and then. She accepted, but postponed the wedding until the war was over. Next day my brother set off for the army.

Napoleon advanced on Moscow; our forces retreated; Moscow became exceedingly alarmed. One after the other her citizens left. The prince and princess persuaded my mother to travel with them to their country estate in *** province.

We arrived at **, a large village about fifteen miles from the provincial capital. Around us were numerous neighbours, most of whom had come from Moscow. Every day we would get together; and our life in the country resembled that in the city. Letters from the army arrived almost every day, and old ladies searched on maps for the places where our soldiers encamped and were angry when they could not find them. Polina occupied herself solely with politics, read nothing except newspapers and Rastopchin's proclamations, and did not open one book. Surrounded by people of limited mental capacity, constantly hearing stupid judgements and news without any factual foundation, she fell into a deep depression; a feeling of languor possessed her soul. She despaired of her country's salvation and it seemed to her that Russia was swiftly approaching her fall; every communiqué intensified her hopelessness. Count Rastopchin's police announcements made her lose all patience. Their facetious style struck her as the height of indecency, and the measures he had taken as intolerable barbarity. She could not understand the spirit, so great in its horror, of that epoch, a spirit whose bold execution saved Russia and freed Europe. She spent whole hours with her elbows on a map of Russia, calculating the miles, following the swift movements of the armies. Strange thoughts entered her head. Once she informed me her intention to leave the country, to appear in the French camp, to find her way to Napoleon and then to kill him with her own hands. It was not difficult for me to convince her of the insanity of such an undertaking, but thoughts of Charlotte Corday never left her mind for very long.

Her father, as we already know, was a fairly relaxed person; all he thought about was living a life in the country that was as close as possible to Moscow life. He gave dinner parties, organized a *théâtre de société*, where French *proverbes*[23] were enacted, and he tried in every way to vary our pleasures. Several officer prisoners arrived in town. The prince was delighted to see new faces and sought permission from the governor to have them billeted with us . . .

There were four of them – three rather insignificant men, fanatically devoted to Napoleon, insufferable boasters but who, it must be said, redeemed their boasting with honourable wounds. But the fourth was a really remarkable man.

At that time he was twenty-six years old. He came from a good family. His face was pleasant, his manners excellent. We immediately singled him out from the others. He accepted kindness with a noble modesty. He spoke little, but his conversation was sound. Polina liked him because he was the first person she had known who could give her a lucid interpretation of military operations and troop movements. He set her mind at rest, assuring her that the retreat of the Russian troops was not a senseless flight and that it disturbed the French as much as it embittered the Russians. 'Surely,' Polina asked him, 'you are convinced of the invincibility of our emperor?' Senicourt (I shall call him by the name given him by Mr Zagoskin) – Senicourt, after a brief pause, replied that for someone in his position it would be difficult to be frank. Polina insisted on a reply. Senicourt admitted that the onward drive of the French army into the heart of Russia could become dangerous for them, that the march of 1812 was apparently over, but that did not mean anything decisive.

'Over!' retorted Polina. 'But Napoleon is advancing the whole time and we keep on retreating!'

'So much the worse for us,' Senicourt replied and changed the subject.

Polina, who was tired of both the cowardly predictions and stupid boasting of our neighbours, eagerly listened to these unbiased, factual judgements. I found it impossible to make any sense out of the letters I received from my brother. They were filled with jokes, good and bad ones, questions about Polina, banal assurances of love and so on. Polina grew annoyed as she read them and shrugged her shoulders.

'Admit,' she said, 'that your Aleksey is the shallowest of men. Even in present circumstances he manages to write meaningless letters from the battlefield. What will his conversation be like in the course of a tranquil family life?' She was mistaken. The futility of my brother's letters did not originate from his own worthlessness, but from a prejudice which was most insulting to us: he assumed that with women one should use language adapted to their feeble powers of comprehension and that important topics did not concern us. Such an opinion would be disrespectful anywhere, but in this country it is stupid as well. There is no doubt that Russian women are better educated, read more, and think more than the men, who are busy with God knows what.

News spread of the Battle of Borodino. Everyone was talking about it; everyone had his own, absolutely authentic information, his casualty list of killed and wounded. My brother did not write. We were extremely worried. Finally one of the carriers of news of all kinds arrived to inform us that he had been taken prisoner and at the same time whispered to Polina that he was dead. Polina was deeply upset. She was not in love with my brother and was often annoyed with him, but at that moment she saw him as a martyr, a hero and secretly wept over him. Several times I found her in tears. This did not surprise me; I was aware of how painful was her concern over the fate of our suffering country. I never suspected what was the reason for her grief.

One morning I was strolling in the garden. Senicourt walked by my side; we were talking about Polina. I noticed that he was deeply conscious of her unusual qualities and that her beauty had made a powerful impression on him. Laughing, I pointed out to him that his position was most romantic. Taken prisoner by the enemy, a wounded knight falls in love with the noble chatelaine, touches her heart and finally wins her hand.

'No,' Senicourt told me, 'the princess sees me as an enemy of Russia and will never agree to leave her native land.'

At that moment Polina appeared at the end of the avenue, and we went to meet her. I was struck by her pallor.

'Moscow has fallen,' she told me, without acknowledging Senicourt's greeting; my heart sank, the tears came in floods. Senicourt was silent, his eyes downcast.

'Those noble, enlightened Frenchmen,' she continued, in a voice trembling with indignation, 'have aptly marked their triumph. They have set fire to Moscow – Moscow has been burning for two days already.'

'What are you saying?' cried Senicourt. 'That cannot be possible!'

'Just wait until nightfall,' she coldly replied. 'Perhaps you will see the glow.'

'My God! He has been destroyed,' said Senicourt. 'Can't you see that the fire of Moscow means the ruin of the whole French army, that Napoleon will have nowhere to go, nothing to hold out with, that he will be forced to retreat as fast as he can across ravaged, deserted countryside – and at the approach of winter, with a discontented, disorganized army! And yet you could think that the French dug this hell for themselves! No, no, it was the Russians, the Russians who set fire to Moscow. Such terrible, barbarous magnanimity! All is now decided: your native land is out of danger; but what will become of us, what will happen to our Emperor . . .'

He left us. Polina and I could not collect ourselves.

'Could Senicourt be right,' she said, 'and the burning of Moscow be our handiwork? If that is so . . . Oh, how proud I am to bear the name of a Russian woman! The world will be astounded at our great sacrifice! Now even our fall does not frighten me, our honour has been saved! Never again will Europe dare to fight against a nation which chops off its own hands and burns its capital.'

Her eyes gleamed, her voice rang loud. I embraced her. Our tears of noble ecstasy mingled with ardent prayers for the fatherland.

'Don't you know?' Polina told me with an inspired look. 'Your brother . . . he is happy, he is not in captivity. Rejoice: he died for the salvation of Russia.'

I cried out and fell unconscious into her arms . . .

1831[24]

KIRDZHALI

KIRDZHALI

Kirdzhali was by birth a Bulgarian. In Turkish 'Kirdzhali' means knight, dare-devil. I do not know his real name.

With his brigandage Kirdzhali terrorized the whole of Moldavia. To give you some idea of him I shall recount one of his exploits. One night he and the Albanian Mikhaylaki jointly attacked a Bulgarian village. They set fire to it at both ends and then went from hut to hut. Kirdzhali did the killing, while Mikhaylaki carried off the booty. Both shouted, 'Kirdzhali! Kirdzhali!' The entire village fled.

When Alexander Ypsilanti proclaimed the revolt and started recruiting his army, Kirdzhali brought a few of his old comrades to him. For them the real object of the Hetairists[1] was not at all clear, but war afforded an opportunity of enriching themselves at the expense of the Turks, or perhaps the Moldavians – that was clear enough to them.

Alexander Ypsilanti was personally a brave man, but he did not possess the qualities necessary for that role which he had undertaken with such fervour and lack of caution. He did not know how to handle the people whom he was obliged to lead. They had neither respect for him nor confidence in him. After that unfortunate battle[2] in which the flower of Greek youth perished, Iordaki Olimbioti advised him to withdraw from the scene and stepped into his place himself. Ypsilanti galloped off to the borders of Austria, whence he sent his curses upon those whom he called disobedient, cowards and scoundrels. The majority of these cowards and scoundrels perished within the walls of the monastery of Seko, or on the banks of the

River Prut, desperately defending themselves against an enemy ten times stronger.

Kirdzhali found himself in the detachment of Georgi Kantakuzin,[3] about whom the same could be said as has been said about Ypsilanti. On the eve of the Battle of Skulyani, Kantakuzin asked the Russian authorities for permission to cross into our territory. His detachment was now without a leader, but Kirdzhali, Safyanos, Kantagoni and others had no need of any leader.

The Battle of Skulyani does not appear to have been described by anybody in all its affecting reality. Imagine seven hundred Arnouts,[4] Albanians, Greeks, Bulgarians and all manner of riff-raff with no idea of the art of war retreating at the sight of fifteen thousand Turkish cavalry. This detachment kept close to the banks of the Prut and placed in front of themselves two small cannon found at Jassy[5] in the Governor's courtyard and from which they used to fire salutes at name-day banquets. The Turks would have been glad to use their grape-shot, but dare not without the permission of the Russian authorities: the shot would undoubtedly have landed on our side of the river. The commander of our lines (now deceased) had served forty years in the army without hearing the whistle of a bullet, but God ordained that he should hear it now. Several whizzed past his ears. The old man flew into a terrible rage and for what was happening abused the major of the Okhotsk infantry regiment which was attached to our lines of defence. Not knowing what to do, the major dashed towards the river, on whose far bank commanders of the Turkish crack troops were performing caracoles on their horses, and wagged a threatening finger at them. As soon as they saw this the commanders wheeled round and galloped away, followed by the entire Turkish detachment. The major who had wagged his finger was called Khorchevsky. I do not know what became of him.

Next day, however, the Turks attacked the Hetaerists. Not daring to use either grape-shot or cannon balls, they decided, contrary to their usual practice, to fight with cold steel. The battle was fierce and yataghans[6] were brought into play. The Turks fought with lances, something they had not done before; these lances were Russian. The Nekrasovists[7] fought in the ranks of the Turks. The

Hetaerists, with our Tsar's permission, were able to cross the Prut and take refuge behind our lines. They started to make their way across the river. Kantagoni and Safyanos were the last to leave the Turkish bank. Kirdzhali, wounded the evening before, was already within our lines. Safyanos was killed. Kantagoni, a very plump man, was wounded in the belly by a lance. With one hand he raised his sabre, while with the other he grabbed his enemy's lance and pushed it in deeper: in this way he was able to reach his murderer with his sabre and both fell together.

It was all over. The Turks emerged victorious. Moldavia was cleared of insurgents. About six hundred Arnouts scattered over Bessarabia. Unable to support themselves, they were nevertheless grateful to Russia for her protection. The life they led was idle, but not dissipated. They were always to be seen in the coffee houses of half-Turkish Bessarabia with long chibouks[8] in their mouths, sipping coffee grounds from tiny cups. Their patterned jackets and red, pointed slippers had begun to wear out, but they still wore their crested skull-caps on the side of the head, while yataghans and pistols still stuck out from their broad sashes. No one made any complaints about them. It was hard to believe that these peaceable wretches had been the notorious bandits of Moldavia, comrades of the dread Kirdzhali, and that he himself was amongst them.

The pasha who had been in command at Jassy found out about this and, in accordance with the terms of the peace treaty, requested the extradition of the bandit by the Russian authorities.

The police launched a search. They discovered that Kirdzhali was in fact in Kishinev.[9] They caught him one evening in the house of a fugitive monk while he was eating his supper in the dark with seven comrades.

Kirdzhali was placed under armed guard. He made no attempt to conceal the truth and confessed that he was Kirdzhali. 'But,' he added, 'since crossing the Prut I have not touched the tiniest bit of anyone's property, nor have I given offence to the lowliest gipsy. To the Turks, Moldavians and Wallachians I am of course a brigand, but to the Russians I am a guest. When Safyanos had fired all of his grape-shot and came to collect for his last ammunition, buttons, nails, watch-chains and yataghan knobs from the wounded, I gave him twenty beshlyks[10] and so was left without any money. God knows that I, Kirdzhali, have been living on charity! So why do the Russians now deliver me to my enemies?' After this Kirdzhali fell silent and calmly waited for his fate to be decided.

He did not have to wait long. The authorities, who were not obliged to look on brigands from a romantic point of view and who were convinced of the justice of the pasha's demands, ordered Kirdzhali to be sent to Jassy.

A man of intellect and feeling,[11] at that time a young, obscure civil servant who now occupies an important position, vividly described his departure to me.

At the prison gates stood a *karutsa* . . . Perhaps you do not know what a karutsa is. It is a low, wicker carriage to which, until not long ago, six or eight wretched nags were usually harnessed. A moustached Moldavian in a sheepskin cap, sitting astride one of them, would constantly shout and crack his whip, and his nags would run along at quite a respectable trot. If one of them should happen to tire he would unharness it with terrible curses and abandon it on the road without any concern for its fate. On the return journey he was sure to find it in exactly the same place, quietly grazing on the green steppe. It was quite common for travellers who had departed from one posting-stage with eight horses to arrive at the next with only a pair. This was the case fifteen years ago. Nowadays in Russianized Bessarabia they have adopted the Russian-style harness and the Russian cart.

Such a karutsa was standing at the prison gate in 1821, on one of the last days of September. Jewesses, slovenly dressed and shuffling along in their slippers, Arnouts in ragged, picturesque costumes, shapely Moldavian women with black-eyed children in their arms, surrounded the karutsa. The men remained silent, the women were in a fever of expectation.

The gates opened and several police officials came out into the street; they were followed by two soldiers leading the fettered Kirdzhali.

He seemed about thirty years of age. The features of his swarthy face were regular and severe. He was tall, broad-shouldered and gave the impression of remarkable physical strength. A brightly coloured Turban, worn slantwise, covered the side of his head; a wide sash girded his slim waist; a dolman[12] of thick blue cloth, a loose-fitting knee-length shirt and fine soft shoes completed his costume. His expression was calm and proud.

One of the officials, a red-faced old man in a faded uniform, from which dangled three buttons, pinched with his tin spectacles the purple knob that served him for a nose, unfolded a piece of paper and started reading in Moldavian, with a nasal twang. Now and then he haughtily glanced at the fettered Kirdzhali, to whom the document apparently referred. Kirdzhali listened to him attentively.

The official finished reading, folded the piece of paper and shouted threateningly at the people, ordering them to make way and the karutsa to be brought up. Then Kirdzhali turned to him and spoke a few words of Moldavian; his voice trembled, his expression changed; he burst into tears and fell at the feet of the police official, his fetters rattling. The official recoiled in fright. The soldiers were about to set Kirdzhali back on his feet, but he stood up on his own, gathered up his fetters, stepped into the karutsa and cried, 'Let's go!' A gendarme seated himself beside him, the Moldavian cracked his whip and the karutsa rolled away.

'What did Kirdzhali say to you?' the young civil servant asked the police official.

'He asked me,' replied the police official, smiling, 'to look after his wife and child who live not far from Kiliya in a Bulgarian village. He's afraid they might suffer because of him. These people are so stupid!'

The young civil servant's story affected me deeply. I felt sorry for poor Kirdzhali. For a long time I heard nothing about his fate. Several years later I happened to meet that young civil servant again. We started talking about the past.

'What about your friend Kirdzhali?' I asked. 'Do you know what became of him?'

'Of course I do,' he replied and told me the following story.

After Kirdzhali was taken to Jassy he was brought before the pasha, who condemned him to be impaled. The execution was postponed until some holiday. Meanwhile he was kept in prison.

The prisoner was guarded by seven Turks (simple people and just as much brigands at heart as Kirdzhali); they respected him and, with that avidity typical of all Orientals, listened to his strange stories.

A close link was forged between guards and prisoner. One day Kirdzhali told them,

'Brothers! My hour is near. No one can escape his fate. I shall soon be parting from you. I should like to leave you something to remember me by.'

The Turks pricked up their ears.

'Three years ago,' continued Kirdzhali, 'when I was plundering with the late Mikhaylaki, we buried in the steppe, not far from Jassy, a kettle filled with gold coins. Now, it's clear that neither myself nor he will ever take possession of that kettle. So be it: take it for yourselves and share it like good friends.'

At this the Turks almost went out of their minds. How could they find that secret spot they wondered. They thought long and hard, and at length decided that Kirdzhali himself should lead them to it.

Night fell. The Turks removed the fetters from the prisoner's feet, bound his hands with a rope and left the town for the steppe with him.

Kirdzhali led them, going from mound to mound in the same direction. They walked for a long time. Finally Kirdzhali stopped near a large stone, measured twenty paces towards the south, stamped and said, 'Here.'

The Turks organized themselves. Four of them drew their yataghans and began digging, while three remained on guard. Kirdzhali sat on the stone and watched them work.

'Well? How much longer?' he asked. 'Haven't you reached it yet?'

'Not yet,' the Turks replied, and they worked so hard that the sweat rolled off them in great drops.

Kirdzhali began to show signs of impatience.

'What a crowd!' he said. 'Don't even know how to dig properly.

I would have finished the whole job in a couple of minutes. Untie my hands and give me a yataghan.'

The Turks pondered for a while and started conferring.

'All right!' they decided. 'Let's untie his hands and give him a yataghan. What harm is there in that? He is one — and there are seven of us.'

And the Turks untied his hands and gave him a yataghan.

At last Kirdzhali was free and armed. What must he have felt then! . . . He started digging swiftly, and the guards helped him . . . Suddenly he plunged his yataghan into one of them and, leaving the blade in his chest, snatched two pistols from behind his sash.

The remaining six, seeing Kirdzhali armed with two pistols, fled. These days Kirdzhali is carrying on his plundering near Jassy. Not long ago he wrote to the Governor, demanding five thousand levs[13] from him and threatening, should the money not be paid, to set fire to Jassy and reach the Governor himself. The five thousand levs were brought to him.

That is Kirdzhali for you!

1834

EGYPTIAN NIGHTS

CHAPTER ONE

> — Quel est cet homme?
> — Ha c'est un bien grand talent, il fait de sa voix tout ce qu'il
> veut.
> — Il devrait bien, madame, s'en faire une culotte.[1]

Charsky was a native of St Petersburg. He was not yet thirty years of age; he was not married; he was not burdened with government service. His late uncle, who had been a vice-governor in the good old days, had left him quite a substantial estate. His life could have been most agreeable, but he had the misfortune to write and publish verses. In journals he was called a poet, but in servants' quarters a story-teller.

Despite the great privileges enjoyed by poets (it must be confessed that apart from the right to use the accusative instead of the genitive case and other kinds of so-called poetic licence, we are not aware of Russian poets enjoying any particular privileges), despite the manifold privileges they enjoy, these people are subjected to a great many disadvantages and much unpleasantness. The bitterest misfortune of all, the most intolerable for a poet, is the appellation with which he is branded and which he can never shake off. The public views him as their own property; in their opinion he was born for their *benefit and pleasure*. Should he return from the country, the first person he meets will ask: Haven't you brought us anything new? Should he come to reflect upon his chaotic affairs or the illness of someone dear to him, at once a vulgar smile will accompany the trite exclamation: No doubt he's writing something! Should he fall in love, his fair lady will buy an album in the English shop and then expect an elegy from him. Should he approach someone he hardly knows in order to discuss an important business matter, that person will summon his son and compel him to read the verses of so-and-so; and then the boy will regale the poet with a reading of his own verses, in mutilated form. And these are the flowers of his muse! What then must the disasters be? Charsky acknowledged that the compliments, the questions, the albums and little boys irritated him to such an extent that he was constantly forced to restrain himself from committing some act of rudeness.

Charsky made every possible attempt to rid himself of that insufferable appellation. He shunned the company of his literary brethren and preferred men of the world to them, even the most empty-headed. His conversation was extremely trite and never touched upon literature. In his dress he always followed the very latest fashions with the shyness and superstition of a young Muscovite arriving in St Petersburg for the first time in his life. Nothing in his study, which was furnished like a lady's bedroom, suggested a writer; there were no piles of books on or under the tables; the sofa was not stained with ink; there was no sign of that disorder which reveals the presence of the Muse and the absence of broom and brush. Charsky was in despair if any of his society friends caught him with pen in hand. It is difficult to comprehend to what trifles a man otherwise endowed with talent and soul can stoop. At one time he would pretend to be a passionate horse-lover, at another a desperate gambler, then the most refined gourmet, even though he was quite unable to distinguish between horses of mountain or Arabian breed, could never remember what were trumps and secretly preferred a baked potato to all the many inventions of French cuisine. He led the most distracted existence; he was to be seen at every ball, he overate at every diplomatic dinner, and at every soirée he was as inevitable as Rezanov[2] ice-cream.

However, he was a poet and his passion was invincible: when the 'silly fit' (thus he termed his inspiration) came upon him, Charsky would lock himself in his study and write from morning until late at night. To his genuine friends he admitted that only then did he know real happiness. The rest of the time he passed strolling about, standing on ceremony, dissembling and constantly hearing the famous question: 'Haven't you written anything new?'

One morning Charsky experienced that happy spiritual state when dreams take shape in one's mind and one finds vivid, unexpected words to embody one's visions; when verses easily flow from the pen and sonorous rhymes rush to meet harmonious thoughts. Charsky was plunged heart and soul in sweet oblivion . . . neither the world, nor the world's opinion, nor his own personal fancies existed for him. He was writing poetry.

Suddenly his study door creaked and an unfamiliar head appeared. Charsky started and frowned.

'Who's there?' he asked irritably, inwardly cursing his servants who were never in the hall when they were needed.

A stranger entered.

He was tall, thin and seemed about thirty. The features of his swarthy face were most striking: a pale, high forehead shadowed by black locks of hair, sparkling eyes, an aquiline nose and thick beard surrounding his sunken, brownish yellow cheeks showed that he was a foreigner. He was wearing a black frock-coat that was already turning white at the seams; summer trousers (although the season was late autumn); under his threadbare black cravat, upon a yellowish shirt-front, sparkled an artificial diamond; his shaggy hat, it seemed, had seen both good and bad weather. If you were to meet this man in a forest you would take him for a robber; in society, for a political conspirator; in someone's hall, for a charlatan trading in elixirs and arsenic.

'What do you want?' Charsky asked him in French.

'Signor,' replied the stranger, bowing low. 'Lei voglia perdonarmi se . . .'[3]

Charsky did not offer him a chair and he himself rose to his feet; the conversation continued in Italian.

'I am a Neapolitan artist,' said the stranger. 'Circumstances have compelled me to leave my native country. I have come to Russia, trusting in my talent.'

Charsky thought that the Neapolitan was intending to give some violoncello concerts and was going from house to house to sell tickets. He was about to give him twenty-five roubles to get rid of him as quickly as possible when the stranger added, 'I hope, Signor, that you will render friendly assistance to your confrère and introduce me to those houses where you have entrée.'

It would have been impossible to deal Charsky's vanity a more painful blow. He glanced arrogantly at the man who had called him *confrère*.

'Permit me to ask who you are and for whom you take me?' he asked, controlling his indignation with difficulty.

The Neapolitan observed his annoyance.

'Signor,' he replied, stammering, 'ho creduto . . . ho sentito . . . la vostra Eccelenza mi perdonera . . .'⁴

'What do you want?' Charsky coldly repeated.

'I have heard much about your amazing talent. I am convinced that the gentlemen here consider it an honour to give every possible protection to such an excellent poet,' replied the Italian, 'and this is why I have dared present myself to you . . .'

'You are mistaken, Signor,' Charsky interrupted. 'The calling of poet does not exist here. Our poets do not need the protection of gentlemen. Our poets are gentlemen themselves, and if our Maecenases⁵ (devil take them!) do not realize that, then so much the worse for them. With us there are no abbés in rags whom a musician would take off the streets to compose a libretto for him. With us, poets do not tramp from house to house begging for assistance. Moreover, they were probably joking when they told you I was a great poet. True, at one time I did write some wretched epigrams, but thank God I have nothing in common with our versifying friends, nor do I wish to.'

The poor Italian was confused. He looked around. The paintings, marble statues, bronzes, expensive bric-à-brac displayed on Gothic what-nots amazed him. He understood that between the arrogant dandy standing before him in a tufted brocade skull-cap, gold-coloured Chinese dressing-gown and Turkish sash, and himself, a poor, wandering artist with threadbare cravat and shabby frock-coat, there was nothing in common. He muttered some incoherent apologies, bowed and prepared to leave. His pathetic appearance touched

Charsky who, in spite of some faults in his character, had a kind and noble heart. He was ashamed that his vanity made him so irritable.

'Where are you going?' he asked the Italian. 'Wait . . . I should have renounced any claim to an undeserved title and confessed that I am not a poet. Let us talk about your affairs now. I am ready to be of service to you in any way I can. Are you a musician?'

'No, Eccelenza!' replied the Italian. 'I'm a poor improvvisatore.'[6]

'An improvvisatore!' cried Charsky, conscious of the cruel manner in which he had treated him. 'Why did you not tell me before that you are an improvvisatore?' And Charsky pressed his hand with a feeling of genuine regret.

The Italian was encouraged by his friendly look. He started speaking naïvely of his plans. His appearance was not deceptive: he was in need of money; he hoped that somehow in Russia he would put his domestic affairs in order. Charsky listened to him attentively.

'I hope,' he told the poor artist, 'that you will be successful: society here has never yet heard an improvvisatore. Curiosity will be aroused. True, the Italian language is not in use here and you will not be understood. But that does not matter. The main thing is that you are in fashion.'

'But if none of you understands the Italian language,' said the improvvisatore pensively, 'who will come and listen to me?'

'They will come – have no fear: some of them out of curiosity, others to while away an evening, others to show that they understand Italian. I repeat, all you need is to be in fashion; and you certainly will be – you have my word on it.'

Charsky cordially bade farewell to the improvvisatore, having taken his address, and that same evening went off to canvass on his behalf.

CHAPTER TWO

I am the tsar, I am a slave, I am a worm, I am God.

Derzhavin[1]

Next day, in the dark and dirty corridor of an inn, Charsky sought out room number 35. He stopped at the door and knocked. The Italian whom he had met the previous day opened it.

'Victory!' Charsky told him. 'It's all arranged. Princess *** is offering you her salon. At a reception yesterday I managed to enlist half of St Petersburg; have the tickets and announcements printed. I can guarantee you if not a triumph, at least a profit . . .'

'And that's the most important thing!' cried the Italian, expressing his joy with those lively gestures characteristic of his southern origin. 'I knew that you would help me. Corpo di Bacco![2] You are a poet, like myself, and there's no denying that poets are excellent fellows! How can I express my gratitude? Wait . . . would you like to hear an improvisation?'

'An improvisation! . . . can you manage without an audience, without music, without the thunder of applause?'

'That's all nonsense! Where could I find a better audience? You are a poet. You will understand me better than they do, and your gentle encouragement will be dearer to me than a whole storm of applause . . . Sit down somewhere and give me a theme.'

Charsky sat on a trunk (of the two chairs that stood in that wretched little hole, one was broken, the other piled with papers and linen). The improvvisatore took a guitar from the table and stood before Charsky, running his bony fingers over the strings and awaiting his command.

'Here's a theme for you,' Charsky told him: *'the poet himself selects subjects for his songs; the crowd has no right to direct his inspiration.'*

The Italian's eyes sparkled. He plucked a few chords, proudly raised his head, and the passionate lines, the expression of spontaneous emotion, harmoniously fell from his lips ... Here they are, freely translated by one of our friends from the words memorized by Charsky:

> Behold the poet, his eyes are staring,
> But nothing does he espy;
> And now the garment he is wearing
> Is tugged by a passer-by.
> 'Tell me why you aimlessly wander,
> Having scaled the poetic heights;
> All you do now is ponder
> Your return to earth in downward flight.
> Dimly the orderly world you see,
> You are wearied by fever so sterile.
> Sorely troubled and tempted you appear to be,
> By trivial subjects all the while.'
> To soar on high – that should be the poet's desire;
> That is the true genius' duty;
> To choose some lofty theme, filled with fire,
> And astound us with its beauty.
> Why does the wind whirl in the ravine,
> Bearing away the leaves and dust,
> When the ship on ocean so serene
> Eagerly awaits the fleeting gust?
> Why does the eagle, so grim, so free,
> Fly from mountain and turret to the stump of a tree?
> Him you must ask if you wish to know.
> And why, on the young Arab all aglow
> The young Desdemona bestows all her love.
> Why the moon loves the mist of night.
> Because a maiden's heart knows no law from above –
> Nor do eagle and wind in all their might.

Like Aquilon, the north wind, freely blowing,
The poet takes what he wills, full knowing,
That like the eagle, high in the air,
Of all mortals he is independent;
Choosing, like Desdemona so fair,
An idol for his heart's contentment.

The Italian fell silent . . . Charsky, amazed and deeply touched, said nothing.

'Well?' asked the improvvisatore.

Charsky grasped his hand and pressed it firmly.

'Well?' asked the improvvisatore. 'What do you think?'

'Amazing,' the poet replied. 'Wonderful! Another's thoughts have barely reached your ears, and they have already become your very own, as if you had ceaselessly nursed, cherished and developed them. So, for you there exists no toil, nor cooling-off, nor that restlessness which precedes inspiration? . . . Amazing, amazing!'

The improvvisatore replied, 'Every kind of talent is inexplicable. How does the sculptor see a hidden Jupiter in a block of Carrara marble and, by chipping off its envelope with chisel and hammer, bring it into the world? Why does thought issue from the poet's head already equipped with rhyming quatrains and harmoniously scanning feet? No one, except the improvvisatore himself, can understand that swiftness of response, that close link between his own inspiration and a strange, external will – vainly would I endeavour to explain it. However . . . we must think of my first evening. What do you suggest? What should I charge the public for a ticket which wouldn't be too high and at the same time leave me out of pocket? They say La signora Catalani[3] charged twenty-five roubles a ticket. That's a good price . . .'

Charsky found it disagreeable suddenly to descend from the heights of poesy to the ledger clerk's desk, but he understood the necessities of life very well and started discussing the financial arrangements with the Italian. Here the Italian displayed such savage greed, such ingenuous love of gain, that he disgusted Charsky, who hurried to take leave of him before the feeling of delight inspired in him by the brilliant improvvisatore was completely lost. The preoccupied Italian did not notice this change of mood and led Charsky along the corridor and down the stairs with low bows and with assurances of his eternal gratitude.

CHAPTER THREE

Tickets at 20 roubles; the performance starts at 7 o'clock.
Playbill

Princess *** salon had been placed at the improvvisatore's disposal. A platform had been erected and chairs were arranged in twelve rows. On the appointed day, at seven o'clock, the salon was illuminated. An old, long-nosed woman in a grey hat with broken feathers on it and with rings on all her fingers sat at a small table at the door, selling and collecting tickets. Gendarmes stood near the entrance to the house. The audience began to assemble. Charsky was one of the first to arrive. He had played a major part in organizing the performance, and he wanted to find out from the improvvisatore if everything was to his satisfaction.

He found the Italian in a side-room looking impatiently at his watch. The Italian was wearing theatrical costume: he was in black from head to foot; the lace collar of his shirt was turned back; his bare neck, in its strange whiteness, contrasted sharply with his thick black beard; his hair had been combed forward, overshadowing his forehead and eyebrows. All this was highly displeasing to Charsky, who did not like seeing a poet dressed as a wandering clown. After a brief conversation he returned to the salon which was rapidly filling up.

Soon all the rows of chairs were occupied by glittering ladies; the men crowded on both sides of the platform, along the walls and behind the chairs at the back. The musicians with their stands occupied both sides of the platform. Upon a table in the middle of the platform stood a porcelain vase. The audience was a large one. Everyone impatiently waited for the performance to begin. At last, at half past seven, the musicians stirred themselves, prepared their bows and played the overture from *Tancred*.[1] Everyone took their places and fell silent. The last strains of the overture faded away ... And the improvvisatore, greeted with deafening applause from every corner of the room, approached the very edge of the platform, bowing low.

Charsky anxiously waited to see what impression the first minute would produce, but he noticed that the theatrical costume, which had struck him as so unbecoming, did not have the same effect on the audience. Charsky himself did not find anything ridiculous about it when he saw the Italian on the platform with his pale face brightly illuminated by numerous lamps and candles. The applause died down; the sound of voices ceased. The Italian, expressing himself in poor French, asked the gentlemen in the room to suggest some themes and write them down on separate slips of paper. At this unexpected invitation everyone silently glanced at each other and no one responded. After a pause the Italian repeated his request in a timid and humble voice. Charsky was standing directly under the platform; he was seized by anxiety; he could foresee that without him the performance could not proceed and that he would be compelled to write down a theme himself. In fact, several female heads turned towards him and they started calling out his name, first in hushed tones and then louder and louder. On hearing Charsky's name the improvvisatore sought him out with his eyes and saw that he was standing at his feet. He handed him a pencil and a piece of paper, with a friendly smile. To play a part in this comedy struck Charsky as very unpleasant, but there was nothing he could do; he took the pencil and paper from the Italian's hands and wrote some words on it. Taking the vase from the table, the Italian stepped down from the platform and presented it to Charsky, who dropped his theme into it. His example had the desired effect: two journalists, in their capacity as men of letters, considered it their duty to write down each his own theme; the Secretary of the Neapolitan Embassy and a young man who had recently returned from his travels and who was simply raving about Florence, placed their folded slips of paper in the urn; finally, a rather plain-looking young lady, with tears in her eyes, wrote a few lines in Italian at her mother's command and, blushing to her ears, handed her slip to the improvvisatore, while the other ladies looked on in silence, with barely perceptible smiles. After returning to the platform the improvvisatore placed the urn on the table and started taking out the slips of paper one by one, reading each out aloud:

> La famiglia dei Cenci.
> L'ultimo giorno di Pompeia.
> Cleopatra e i suoi amanti.
> La primavera veduta da una prigione.
> Il trionfo di Tasso.[2]

'What does my honourable audience command?' asked the Italian humbly. 'Will it give me one of the proposed themes itself or allow it to be decided by lot?'

'By lot,' cried a voice from the crowd.

'By lot, by lot,' the audience repeated.

The improvvisatore again stepped down from the platform, holding the urn in his hands. 'Who will be good enough to select a theme?' he asked, casting an imploring look along the front rows of chairs.

Not one of the brilliant ladies who were seated there budged. The improvvisatore, unaccustomed to this Northern indifference, was clearly suffering . . . suddenly he noticed to one side a small, white-gloved, uplifted hand. He eagerly turned and went up to the majestic young beauty seated at the end of the second row. Without the least embarrassment she stood up and with the utmost simplicity lowered her aristocratic hand into the urn and drew out a roll of paper.

'Will you please unroll it and read it out,' the improvvisatore asked her. The beautiful young lady unrolled the piece of paper and read out loud, 'Cleopatra e i suoi amanti.'

These words were spoken in a soft voice, but such deep silence reigned over the salon that everyone heard them. The improvvisatore bowed low to the beautiful young lady with a look of deep gratitude and returned to his platform.

'Gentlemen,' he said, turning to the audience. 'The lot has shown me Cleopatra and her Lovers as the subject for improvisation. I humbly request the person who chose this theme to explain his meaning: which lovers does he have in mind, perché la grande regina n'aveva molto . . .'[3]

At these words many gentlemen laughed loudly. The improvvisatore was rather taken aback.

'I should like to know,' he continued, 'to what historical event the person who chose this theme is alluding . . . I should be very grateful if he would be good enough to explain.'

No one was in any hurry to reply. Several ladies stared at the plain young lady who had written down the theme on her mother's instructions. The poor girl noticed this hostile attention and became so embarrassed that tears hung from her eyes. Charsky could not bear this and, turning to the improvvisatore, told him in Italian:

'It was I who suggested that theme. I had in mind the passage in Aurelius Victor where he writes that Cleopatra designated death as the price of her love and that there were adorers to be found who were neither frightened nor deterred by such a condition . . . However, it seems to me that the subject is rather difficult . . . would you care to choose another . . . ?'

But the improvvisatore already felt the approach of the god . . . He gave the musicians a sign to play . . . His face became dreadfully pale, he trembled as if he were in a fever. His eyes gleamed with a magical fire; with one hand he pushed back his dark hair, wiped his lofty sweat-beaded brow with his handkerchief . . . and suddenly he stepped forward and crossed his hands on his chest . . . the music stopped . . . The improvisation began:

> The palace gleamed, the choir was singing,
> Mingling with sound of flute and lyre;
> To the rich feast the Queen was bringing
> New life, with eyes that were filled with fire.
> All hearts to the throne were turning,
> When suddenly that wondrous head looked down;
> And the Queen, o'ercome with sadness and yearning,
> Leant o'er her golden cup with regal frown.
>
> But the guests into sleep had drifted,
> No more was there singing here;

The Queen, her head again uplifted,
Spake these words, loud and clear.
'Does my love mean perfect bliss?
It is something that can be bought . . .
My love is there for none to miss
And all else is empty sport.
Who craves for love that can be bought?
This love I sell so gladly;
The price is a life: this is a thought
That now must tempt you madly.'

She spake — and all were filled with dread,
Each heart burning with passionate fire;
With cold disdain she turned her head,
Scorning those troubled murmurs of desire.
And she cast a contemptuous glance
At those admirers filled with awe;
When suddenly one seized his chance,
And was immediately followed by two more.
Bold their step, their eyes bright
As she goes to greet them all.
The deal is struck: they have bought three nights,
As they respond to death's grim call.

And now from that fateful urn
By blessed priests the lots are taken,
And each of them awaits his turn,
It is life they have forsaken.
First was Flavius, warrior bold,
Famed for martial deeds untold;
His wife's proud and lofty disdain
No longer could he bear.

He thus accepts the call to pleasure rare,
Like warriors of old glory to gain:
They conquer, only those who dare.
And then Kriton, young sage,

The Muses' noble bard;
Born in Epicurus' age,
Followed in his footsteps hard.
To the Muses he owed all his art,
And like a young flower in spring,
He delighted eyes and heart.
Soft down to his cheeks was clinging,
And delight to his eyes was springing.
Sadly wandered the proud Queen's gaze,
Upon him, innocent of passion's power.
But he looked at her with eyes ablaze
And waited to pluck love's flower.

'To thee I vow, mother of all delight,
To be thy faithful slave.
Never to let thee from my sight;
To give pleasure is what I crave.
Listen, Oh you goddesses above,
And kings in Hades' bourn,
I shall give my eager love
Before the coming of the dawn.
Then with adoring and fervent caress
I shall satisfy my masters' desire;
My lips to theirs I shall tenderly press,
And arouse them with my fire.
But when the early glow of dawn
Fills the sky with rosy light,
Their heads will fall – as I have sworn,
And thus will end their night.'

A JOURNEY TO ARZRUM AT THE TIME OF THE 1829 CAMPAIGN[1]

Recently I came across a book published in Paris last year (1834) with the title *Voyages en Orient entrepris par ordre du Gouvernement Français*.[2] The author, giving a personal account of the campaign of 1829, concludes his observations with the following words:

Un poète distingué par son imagination a trouvé dans tant de hauts faits dont il a été témoin non le sujet d'une poème, mais celui d'une satyre.[3]

Among the poets who were present during the Turkish campaign I knew only of A. S. Khomyakov and A. N. Muravyov.[4] Both were with Count Dibich's army.[5] The first wrote at that time several beautiful lyrical poems, while the second was planning his *Journey to the Holy Land*, which made such a powerful impression. But I have not read any satires on the Arzrum campaign.

Not for one moment would I have thought that the writer was actually alluding to me had I not found in his book my own name amongst those of generals of the Independent Caucasus Corps.[6]

Parmi les chefs qui la commandaient (l'armée du Prince Paskewitch) on distinguait le Général Mouravief ... le Prince Géorgien Tsitsevaze ... le Prince Arménien Beboutof ... le Prince Potemkine, le Général Raiewsky, et enfin – M-r Pouchkine ... qui avait quitté la capitale pour chanter les exploits de ses compatriotes.[7]

I must confess that I was far more irritated by these lines written by that French traveller, despite the flattering epithets, than by the abuse of Russian journals. *To go in search of inspiration* has always struck me as a ludicrous and absurd fantasy: one cannot seek out inspiration – it must find the poet. To go off to war in order to celebrate future exploits in poetry would have been, on the one hand, too egotistical of me and, on the other, most improper. I do not meddle in military judgements. They are none of my business. Perhaps the daring crossing of Sagan-Lu,[8] a manoeuvre by which Count Paskevich[9] cut off the seraskier[10] from Osman-Pasha, the defeat of two enemy corps in one day, the rapid advance on Arzrum – all this, crowned with complete success, might be exceptionally worthy of ridicule in the eyes of military gentlemen (such as, for example, Mr Commercial Consul Fontanier,[11] author of the *Journey to the Orient*); but I would be ashamed to write satires on the renowned commander who warmly received me under the canopy of his tent and who found time, in the midst of serious worries, to flatter me with his attention. The man who has no need of the protection of the powerful, prizes their cordiality and hospitality, for there is nothing else he can ask of them. An accusation of ingratitude must not be left without riposte, as if it were worthless criticism or literary abuse. That is why I have decided to have this preface printed and to publish my travel notes as *everything*[12] I wrote about the campaign of 1829.

A. Pushkin

CHAPTER ONE

The steppes. A Kalmuck tent. A Caucasian spa. The Georgian
Military Highway. Vladikavkaz. An Ossetian funeral. The
Terek. The Darial Gorge. Crossing snow-capped mountains.
First sight of Georgia. Watercourses. Khozrev-Mirza. The
Governor of Dushet.

From Moscow I went to Kaluga, Belev and Oryol, thus making a
detour of one hundred and eighteen miles; however, I did see
Yermolov.[1] He lives in Oryol, close to which his estate is situated.
I arrived at his house at eight o'clock in the morning, but he was
not at home. My driver told me that Yermolov never visited anyone
besides his father, a simple, pious old man, that the only people he
never received were officials from the town, but that everyone else
was welcome at any time. I called back an hour later. Yermolov
received me with his customary affability. At first glance I did not
find in him the least resemblance to those portraits of him that are
usually painted in profile. A round face, fiery grey eyes, bristling
grey hair. The head of a tiger on a Herculean torso. His smile is
unpleasant, since it is not natural. But when he is deep in thought
and frowns, he becomes handsome and bears a striking resemblance
to the poetic portrait painted by Dawe.[2]

He was wearing a green Circassian jacket. Swords and daggers,
souvenirs of his command in the Caucasus, hung on the walls of his
study. Evidently he finds inactivity difficult to endure. Several times
he started speaking about Paskevich — and always sarcastically: he
would compare him to Joshua, before whom the walls fell at the

sound of a trumpet, and called him the Count of Jericho instead of the Count of Yerevan.[3]

'Just let him attack an unintelligent, unskilful pasha – for example, the pasha who was in command at Shumla,'[4] said Yermolov, 'and Paskevich would be finished.'

I told Yermolov of Count Tolstoy's[5] remarks, that Paskevich had performed so well in the Persian campaign that a clever man would have only needed to perform a little worse to distinguish himself from him. Yermolov laughed but he did not agree. 'Men and expense could have been spared,' he said. I think that he is writing, or wants to write, his memoirs. He is dissatisfied with Karamzin's *History*;[6] he would have preferred a fiery pen to have described the transition of the Russian people from insignificance to power and glory. He spoke of Prince Kurbsky's memoirs[7] *con amore*. The Germans caught it. 'In about fifty years,' he said, 'people will think that in the current campaign there was an auxiliary Prussian or Austrian army, commanded by such-and-such German generals.' I stayed a couple of hours with him. He was annoyed at not remembering my full name. He apologized by paying me compliments. Several times our conversation touched upon literature. He said that reading Griboyedov's poetry[8] made his cheek-bones ache. He did not speak one word about government or politics.

My route lay via Kursk and Kharkov; but I turned onto the direct road for Tiflis, thus sacrificing a good dinner in a Kursk tavern (no trifling matter on journeys in Russia) and not at all curious about seeing Kharkov University, which could not compare with any eating-house in Kursk.

Up to Yeletz the roads are terrible. Several times my carriage was bogged down in mud fit to be compared with Odessa mud. Often I could travel no more than thirty miles in twenty-four hours. At last I saw the Voronezh steppes and bowled along freely over the green plain. At Novocherkassk I found Count Pushkin[9] who was also on his way to Tiflis, and we agreed to travel together.

The transition from Europe to Asia is felt more keenly with every hour that passes: forests disappear, hills level out, grass becomes thicker and grows much more luxuriantly; birds appear that are unknown in our forests; as if on guard, eagles sit on the hummocks marking the highway and proudly look down on travellers; over rich pastures

> Herds of indomitable mares
> Proudly wander.[10]

Kalmucks[11] settle themselves around the post-stage huts. By their tents graze their ugly, shaggy horses, familiar to you from Orlovsky's fine sketches.[12]

One day I visited a Kalmuck tent (a wickerwork frame covered with white felt). The entire family was about to have lunch. A cauldron was boiling in the middle and the smoke escaped through an opening at the top of the tent. A young Kalmuck girl, who was not at all bad-looking, smoked tobacco as she sewed. I sat down beside her. 'What's your name?' '***.' 'How old are you?' 'Ten and eight.' 'What are you making?' 'Trouser.' 'For whom?' 'Me.' She handed me her pipe and started eating. Tea was boiling in the cauldron, together with mutton fat and salt. She offered me her ladle. As I did not wish to refuse I took a mouthful, trying to hold my breath. I do not think that any other national cuisine could possibly produce anything more vile. I asked for something to take the taste away. I was given a small piece of dried mare's flesh: I was glad even of that. Frightened by Kalmuck coquetry I escaped from the tent as quickly as I could and rode away from that Circe of the steppes.[13]

In Stavropol I saw clouds on the horizon that precisely nine years before[14] had so vividly captured my imagination. They were still the same, still in exactly the same place: they were the snow-capped peaks of the Caucasus mountains.

From Georgiyevsk I went to visit Goryachiye Vody.[15] Here I found a great change: in my time the baths were in hastily constructed shacks. The springs, mainly in their pristine state, gushed, foamed and flowed down from the mountains in various directions, leaving white and reddish traces. We would scoop the seething water with bark ladles or with the bottom of a broken bottle. Now magnificent baths and houses have been built. A boulevard, lined with lindens, runs along the slope of Mount Mashuk. Everywhere are neat little paths, green benches, symmetrical flower-beds, tiny bridges, pavilions. The springs have been refurbished and faced with stone; police notices are nailed to the walls of the baths. Everywhere there is order, cleanliness, prettification . . .

I must confess that Caucasian spas offer more amenities these days, but I missed their former wild state; I missed the steep stony paths, shrubs and unfenced precipices above which I used to clamber. Sadly I left the spa and started back to Georgiyevsk. Soon night came. The clear sky was studded with millions of stars. I rode along the bank of the Podkumok. It was here that A. Rayevsky[16] once used to sit with me, listening to the melody of the waters. Majestic Beshtu stood out darker and darker in the distance, surrounded by other mountains – its vassals – until finally it disappeared in the gloom.

Next day we pressed on until we reached Yekaterinograd, once ruled by a governor-general.

The Georgian military highway starts at Yekaterinograd; the post-road comes to an end. Here one can hire horses for Vladikavkaz. An escort of Cossack riders and infantry and cannon is provided. The mail leaves twice weekly and travellers join up with it: this is called an *opportunity*.[17] We did not have to wait long. The mail arrived the following day, and at nine o'clock on the third morning we were ready to set off. The whole convoy, consisting of five hundred people or thereabouts, gathered at an assembly point. A drum roll sounded. We moved off. The cannon went in front, surrounded by infantry. Behind it stretched barouches, brichkas and covered wagons filled with soldiers' wives who were moving from one fortress to another; behind them followed a train of creaking two-wheeled bullock-carts. On both sides ran herds of horses and oxen. Around them galloped Nogay[18] guides in felt cloaks and with lassos. At first I found all this most agreeable, but it soon bored me. The cannon moved at walking pace, the wick smoked and the soldiers lit their pipes from it. The slow progress of our journey (in the first day we covered only ten miles), the unbearable heat, the lack of provisions, the restless overnight stays and finally the incessant

creaking of the Nogay bullock-carts, made me lose all patience. The
Tartars pride themselves on the creaking, claiming that they travel
like honest people with nothing to hide. On this occasion I would
have found it more pleasant to travel in less honourable company.

The route is rather monotonous: a plain with hills on either side.
On the horizon are the peaks of the Caucasus, looming higher and
higher every day. The fortresses, which are adequate for this region,
are surrounded by ditches which, in the old days, any one of us
could have leapt across from a standing position; there are rusty
cannon that have not been fired since the time of Count Gudovich[19]
and crumbling ramparts along which a garrison of chickens and geese
wanders. In the fortresses are a few shacks where, with difficulty,
one can obtain a dozen eggs and some sour milk.

The first place of note is the Minaret Fortress. As we approached
it our convoy passed through a delightful valley between burial
mounds overgrown with lime and plane trees. These were the graves
of several thousand plague victims. Here blossomed many-coloured
flowers, born of the infested ashes. On the right glittered the snowy
Caucasus; ahead of us loomed a huge, wooded mountain; beyond it
was the fortress. All around it we could see signs of a ruined village,
formerly called Tatartub and once the most important in Great
Kabarda.[20] A slender, solitary minaret bears witness to the existence
of the now vanished settlement. It rises gracefully between piles of
stones, on the banks of a dried-up stream. The inner staircase has not
collapsed yet. I climbed up to the little platform from which the mullah's
voice no longer rings out. There I found several unfamiliar names
scratched on the bricks by travellers hungry for fame.

Our route became picturesque. The mountains towered above us.
On their peaks wandered barely visible flocks that resembled insects.
We could even make out the shepherd, perhaps a Russian once taken
prisoner and now grown old in captivity. We came across more
burial mounds, more ruins. Two or three headstones stood at the
edge of the road. There, according to Circassian custom, are buried
their horsemen. A Tartar inscription, a sword, a brand mark, carved
in the stone, have been left by predatory grandsons in memory of
their predatory ancestors.

The Circassians hate us. We have forced them out of their wide open pastures; their villages have been destroyed, entire tribes annihilated. They are constantly withdrawing deeper into the mountains, whence they direct their raids. The friendship of pacified Circassians is not to be relied upon: they are always ready to help their unruly fellow tribesmen. The spirit of their wild chivalry has noticeably declined. Rarely do they attack Cossacks of equal numbers, never infantry, and they flee at the sight of a cannon. On the other hand, they never miss an opportunity of attacking a weak detachment or the defenceless. This part of the country is full of talk of their evil deeds. There is practically no way of pacifying them until they are disarmed as the Crimean Tartars were, an exceptionally difficult undertaking by reason of the hereditary feuds and vendettas prevailing among them. The dagger and sword are essentially (bodily) limbs and infants start to use them before they can even babble. With them killing is a simple bodily movement. They keep prisoners in the hope of gaining a ransom for them, but they treat them with dreadful inhumanity, forcing them to work beyond their strength, feeding them on raw dough, beating them when the fancy takes them; to guard them they employ boys who have the right to hack them to pieces with their children's swords if they utter one wrong word. Recently a pacified Circassian who had fired at a soldier was captured. He tried to defend himself by claiming that his rifle had been undischarged for too long. What can one do with such people? One must hope, however, that the annexation[21] of the eastern part of the Black Sea, by cutting off the Circassians' trade with the Turks, will force them closer to us. The effect of luxury might favour their subjugation: the samovar would be an important innovation in this respect.

But there is a method that is more powerful, more moral, more consistent with our enlightened century: the preaching of the gospels. The Circassians adopted the Mohammedan faith only very recently. They were carried away by the energetic fanaticism of the apostles of the Koran, among whom a certain Mansur[22] distinguished himself – an extraordinary man who had long been stirring up the Caucasus against Russian dominion and who was finally captured by us and died in the Solovetsky Monastery. The Caucasus awaits Christian missionaries. But it is easier for us, in our laziness, to pour out dead letters in place of the living word and to send mute books to people who cannot read or write.

We reached Vladikavkaz, formerly Kapkaz, the gateway to the mountains. It is surrounded by Ossetian villages. I visited one of them and happened upon a funeral. People were crowding around a hut. In the yard stood a cart, harnessed with two oxen. Relatives and friends of the deceased rode in from all directions, and with loud lamentations they entered the hut, beating their foreheads with their fists. The women stood submissively. The corpse was carried out on a felt cloak . . .

> . . . like a warrior taking his rest
> With his martial cloak around him;[23]

and they laid him in the cart. One of the guests took the deceased's rifle, blew the powder from the firing pan and placed it beside the body. The oxen moved off; the guests followed. The body was to be buried in the mountains, about twenty miles from the village. Unfortunately no one could explain this ceremony to me.

The Ossetians are the poorest tribe amongst the nations inhabiting the Caucasus; their women are beautiful and, it is said, very well disposed towards travellers. At the fortress gates I met the wife and daughter of an imprisoned Ossetian. They were taking his dinner to him. Both appeared calm and bold. However, when I approached, both of them looked down and covered their faces with their tattered yashmaks. In the fortress I saw Circassian hostages, sprightly and handsome boys. They are constantly getting up to mischief and running out of the fortress. They are kept in a pitiful state, going around in rags, half-naked and disgustingly filthy. On some of them I saw wooden shackles. Probably, once they are released, these hostages have no regrets about their stay in Vladikavkaz.

The cannon left us. We set off with the infantry and the Cossacks. The Caucasus received us into its sanctuary. We heard a dull roar and saw the Terek, flowing in different directions. We rode along its left bank. Its turbulent waves set in motion the wheels of the squat Ossetian mills resembling dog kennels. The further we went into the mountains the narrower the gorge became. The confined Terek tosses its turbid waters over the crags barring its way. The gorge winds its way along the river's course. The rocky feet of the mountains have been worn smooth by its waves. I made my way on foot, constantly stopping, astounded by the gloomy charms of nature. The weather was overcast; thick banks of cloud hung over the black peaks. As they looked at the Terek, Count Pushkin and Shernvall[24] recalled the Imatra[25] and accorded superiority to the 'river thundering in the North'.[26] But I found nothing with which I could compare the spectacle that lay ahead.

Before we reached Lars, I dropped behind the convoy, lost in contemplation of the huge cliffs between which the Terek gushes with indescribable fury. Suddenly a soldier came running towards me, shouting from the distance, 'Don't stop, Your Honour! They'll kill you!' As I was unaccustomed to such warnings, it struck me as extremely strange. The fact is, Ossetian bandits, secure within those narrow confines, fire at travellers across the Terek. The evening before we crossed they had attacked General Bekovich,[27] who galloped through their fire. On a cliff can be seen the ruins of some castle; clinging all around them like swallows' nests are the huts of pacified Ossetians.

We stayed the night at Lars. Here we found a French traveller who frightened us with his account of the road ahead. He advised us to leave our carriages at Kobi and proceed on horseback. With him we drank for the first time Kakhetian wine from a stinking goatskin, which reminded me of the carousing in the *Iliad*:

And in goatskins is wine, our delight![28]

Here I found a soiled copy of the *Prisoner of the Caucasus*[29] and, I must confess, read it with great pleasure. It was all so feeble, youthful, incomplete; but much of it was faithfully observed and expressed.

Next morning we pressed on. Turkish prisoners were working on the road. In no way could they accustom themselves to Russian black bread. This reminded me of the words of my friend Sheremetev[30] on his return from Paris: 'It's rotten living in Paris, my friend: there's just nothing to eat. You can't get black bread for love or money!'

About four miles from Lars is the Darial post. The pass bears the same name. Cliffs stand on both sides like parallel walls. Here it is so narrow, so very narrow, writes one traveller, that one not only sees but actually feels the narrowness, it seems. A patch of blue sky appears like a ribbon above one's head. Streams, falling from the heights of the mountains in thin spurts of spray, reminded me of *The Abduction of Ganymede*, that strange painting by Rembrandt.[31] Moreover, the pass is illuminated entirely in his taste. In some places the Terek is eroding the very feet of the cliffs, and rocks are piled high on the road, like a dam. Not far from the post a small bridge has been boldly thrown across the river. Standing on it is like being on a mill. The whole bridge shakes, while the Terek roars, producing a sound like wheels driving a millstone. Opposite Darial can be seen the ruins of a fortress on a steep cliff face. According to tradition a certain Queen Dariya took refuge there, thus giving her name to the pass: this is a fairy-tale. In ancient Persian *darial*[32] means gates. According to the testimony of Pliny the Caucasian Gates, erroneously called the Caspian Gates, were situated here. The pass was closed with real gates, made of wood and ribbed with iron. Beneath them, writes Pliny, flows the River Diriodoris.[33] Here was erected another fortress to resist the raids of wild tribes; and so on. Consult the *Journey* of Count J. Potocki,[34] whose scholarly investigations are as diverting as his Spanish novels.

From Darial we set off for Kazbek. We saw the Trinity Gates (an arch formed in the rock face by a gunpowder explosion) – beneath them the road once ran, but now the Terek flows there, often changing its course.

Not far from the settlement of Kazbek we crossed the Frenzied Gorge, a ravine which turns into a raging torrent when there is heavy rain. At this time of year it was completely dry, and resounding only in name.

The village of Kazbek is at the foot of Mount Kazbek and belongs to Prince Kazbek. The Prince, a man of about forty-five, is taller than a fugleman[35] of the Preobrazhensky Regiment. We found him in a *dukhan* (the name for taverns in Georgia, which are far poorer and no cleaner than Russian ones). In the doorway lay a pot-bellied wineskin (an oxhide), its four legs spread wide. The giant drew some *chikhir*[36] from it and asked me a few questions, to which I replied with the respect due to one of his rank and height. We parted the best of friends.

Impressions soon become dulled. Scarcely one day had passed and no longer did the roar of the Terek and its unattractive waterfalls, those cliffs and precipices, attract my attention. My impatience to reach Tiflis took hold of me to the exclusion of all else. I rode past Kazbek as indifferently as I had once sailed past Chatyrdag.[37] The truth was the rainy, misty weather prevented me from seeing its snowy mass which, as the poet puts it, 'props up the horizon'.[38]

A Persian prince was expected. A short distance from Kazbek we met several carriages, which hampered our progress along the narrow road. While the carriages were passing each other, the convoy officer announced that he was escorting a Persian court poet and, in accordance with my wishes, introduced me to Fazil-Khan.[39] With the help of an interpreter I embarked on a high-flown Oriental-style welcome; but how mortified I felt when Fazil-Khan replied to my inappropriate elaboration with the simple, intelligent politeness of a decent fellow! He hoped to see me in St Petersburg, he regretted that our acquaintance would be so short-lived and so on. To my shame I was compelled to abandon my mock-serious tone and descend to normal European phraseology. This was a lesson for Russian facetiousness. In future I shall not judge a man by his *papakha** and his painted nails.

The post of Kobi lies at the very foot of the Krestov Mountain, which we now had to cross. Here we stopped for the night and began to wonder how we were to accomplish that fearful exploit: should we abandon our carriages and ride on Cossack horses, or should we send for Ossetian oxen? To be on the safe side I wrote an official request, on behalf of all our convoy, to Mr Chilyayev, who was in command in this region, and we went to bed, expecting carts to arrive.

* Thus Persian fur caps are called. (A. S. Pushkin)

Next day, around noon, we heard a loud noise and shouting, and witnessed an unusual spectacle: eighteen pairs of skinny, undersized oxen, urged on by a crowd of half-naked Ossetians, were hauling, with difficulty, the light Viennese carriage belonging to my friend O**. This spectacle at once dispelled all my doubts. I decided to send my heavy St Petersburg carriage back to Vladikavkaz and ride to Tiflis on horseback. Count Pushkin had no wish to follow my example. He preferred to harness a whole herd of oxen to his brichka, which was laden with all kinds of provisions, and to ride in triumph over the snowy ridge. We parted, and I set off with Colonel Ogaryov, who was inspecting the roads in the area.

Our road went over a landslide that had come down at the end of June 1827. Such incidents usually occur every seven years. The enormous mass of rock and earth that had crashed down had buried the pass for as much as half a mile and dammed the Terek. The sentries who were stationed lower down had heard a terrible rumbling and saw that the river was swiftly growing shallower, and within quarter of an hour it was completely drained and silent. It took the Terek two hours to burrow through the landslide. Then it indeed looked terrifying!

We climbed ever higher up the steep slope. Our horses sank into the loose snow, beneath which one could hear little streams. I looked in amazement at the road and could not understand how travelling along it on wheels was at all possible.

Just then I heard a hollow rumbling. 'It's an avalanche,' Mr Ogaryov told me. I looked around and to one side I saw a pile of snow which was crumbling and slowly sliding down the steep slope. Small avalanches are not uncommon here. Last year a Russian carrier was driving along Krestov Mountain. An avalanche started; the dreadful mass piled into his wagon, swallowing up wagon, horse and man, rolled across the road and continued rolling down into the abyss with its booty. We reached the very summit of the mountain. Here stands a granite cross, an old monument, restored by Yermolov.

At this point travellers usually leave their carriages and proceed on foot. Recently a certain foreign consul was passing through: he was so faint-hearted that he ordered himself to be blindfolded; they then led him by the arm, and when the blindfold was removed he went down on his knees, thanked God, and so on, which absolutely amazed his guides.

The instant transition from awe-inspiring Caucasus to pretty Georgia is enchanting. The air of the South suddenly begins to waft over the traveller. From the heights of Mount Gut the Kayshur valley opens out with its inhabited rock faces, its orchards, its bright Aragva, winding like a silver ribbon – and all this visible on a reduced scale, at the bottom of a two-mile long abyss, along which runs a dangerous road.

We descended into the valley. A new moon appeared in the bright sky. The evening air was calm and warm. I spent the night on the banks of the Aragva, in Mr Chilyayev's house. Next day I parted from my amiable host and went on further.

Here Georgia begins. Bright valleys, watered by the cheerful Aragva, replaced those gloomy defiles and the menacing Terek. Instead of bare cliffs I saw green hills all around and fruit trees. Watercourses revealed the presence of civilization. One of them struck me as the very perfection of an optical illusion: the water, so it appeared, was flowing uphill.

At Paysanur I stopped to change horses. Here I met a Russian officer who was accompanying the Persian prince.[40] Soon I heard the tinkle of small bells and a whole line of *katars* (mules), tied one to the other and laden Asian style, stretched along the road. I proceeded on foot, without waiting for the horses; and about a quarter of a mile from Ananur, at a turn in the road, I met Khozrev-Mirza. His carriages had stopped. He looked out of his barouche and nodded to me. A few hours after our meeting the prince was attacked by tribesmen from the mountains. When he heard the whistle of bullets Khozrev leapt from his barouche, mounted his horse and galloped off. The Russians who had been accompanying him were amazed at his boldness. The fact was, the young Asian, unaccustomed to a carriage, viewed it more as a trap than a refuge.

I reached Ananur without any feeling of fatigue. My horses had not arrived. I was told that the town of Dushet was no more than six miles away and once again I set off on foot. But I did not know that the road was uphill. These six miles were equal to a good thirteen.

Evening set in. I moved on, climbing higher and higher. It was impossible to lose one's way; but in places the clayey mud, formed by springs, reached up to my knees. I was completely exhausted. The darkness thickened. I heard the howling and barking of dogs and I was glad, imagining that the town could not be far away. But I was mistaken: the barking was of Georgian shepherds' dogs, while the howling came from jackals, which are quite common in these parts. I cursed my impatience, but there was nothing I could do. Finally I saw lights and towards midnight found myself close to some houses with trees overhanging them. The first person I came across offered to lead me to the mayor, for which service he asked one *abaz*.[41]

My appearance at the house of the mayor – an old Georgian officer – produced a great deal of commotion. Firstly, I requested a room where I could undress; secondly, a glass of wine; thirdly, an *abaz* for my guide. The mayor just did not know how he should receive me and looked at me in bewilderment. When I saw that he was in no hurry to carry out my request, I started undressing in front of him, asking him to excuse *de la liberté grande*. Luckily I found in my pocket an order for fresh horses that proved I was a law-abiding traveller and no Rinaldo-Rinaldini.[42] That blessed charter immediately had the desired effect: a room was provided, a glass of wine was brought and an *abaz* handed to my guide, together with a paternal reprimand for his cupidity that was an insult to Georgian hospitality. I threw myself on the divan, hoping to sleep soundly after my heroic exploit. No hope of that! Fleas, which are far more dangerous than jackals, attacked me and did not give me a moment's peace the whole night. In the morning my man came and announced that Count Pushkin had safely traversed the snowy mountains with his oxen and had arrived in Dushet. I had to hurry! Count Pushkin and Shernvall called on me and suggested we all set off together again. I left Dushet with the pleasant thought that I would be spending that night in Tiflis.

The road was just as pleasant and picturesque, although we rarely saw any signs of habitation. A few miles from Gartsiskal we crossed the River Kura by a wooden bridge, a monument to Roman campaigns, and at a round trot, sometimes even at a gallop, we rode on to Tiflis where we arrived inconspicuously at about eleven o'clock at night.

CHAPTER TWO

I stayed at an inn and next day went off to the famous Tiflis baths.
The city struck me as very populous. The Asian styles of architecture
and the market reminded me of Kishinev. Along the narrow, crooked
streets ran donkeys, laden with a basket on each side; carts harnessed
to oxen blocked the road. Armenians, Georgians, Circassians crowded
the irregular square. Among them rode young Russian civil servants
on Karabakh stallions. At the entrance to the baths sat the owner,
an old Persian. He opened the door and I entered a spacious room
– and what did I see? More than fifty women, young and old, half
and completely naked, sitting or standing, were undressing and
dressing on benches arranged along the walls. I hesitated. 'Come on,
come on,' the owner told me, 'it's Tuesday, women's day. Don't
worry, it doesn't matter.' 'Of course it doesn't matter,' I replied.
'On the contrary.' The appearance of men made no impression
whatsoever. They continued laughing and chatting among themselves. Not one of them was in any hurry to cover herself with her
chadra;[1] not one stopped undressing. It seemed that I had entered

invisibly. Many of them were indeed beautiful and justified the imagination of T. Moore:

> a lovely Georgian maid,
> With all the bloom, the freshen'd glow
> Of her own country maiden's looks,
> When warm they rise from Teflis' brooks.
> 'Lalla Rookh'[2]

On the other hand I know of nothing more repellent than old Georgian women: they are witches.

The Persian led me into the baths: a hot ferrous sulphide spring was pouring into a deep basin carved out of the rock face. Never in my life had I encountered, whether in Russia or Turkey, anything more luxurious than the Tiflis baths. I shall describe them in detail.

The owner left me in the care of a Tartar bathhouse attendant. I have to tell you that he had no nose; this did not prevent him from being master of his trade. Hassan (this was the noseless Tartar's name) began by making me lie outstretched on the warm stone floor. After this he started beating my limbs, stretched out my joints and thumped me violently with his fist. I did not feel the least pain, only an amazing sense of relaxation. (Asian bath attendants usually go into raptures, jumping on one's shoulders, sliding their feet over one's ribs and performing a squatting dance on one's back, *e sempre bene*.)[3] After this he rubbed me for a long time with a woollen mitten and, having splashed me violently with warm water, started washing me with a soapy inflated linen bladder. The sensation is indescribable: the hot soap washes over one like air!

Note The woollen mitten and linen bladder should certainly be introduced into Russian baths: connoisseurs would be grateful for such an innovation.

After the bladder Hassan released me into the bath; with that the ceremony ended.

In Tiflis I was hoping to find Rayevsky, but when I discovered that his regiment was already on the march I decided to ask Count Paskevich's[4] permission to join up with the army.

I spent about two weeks in Tiflis and met local society. Sankovsky,[5] publisher of the *Tiflis Gazette*, told me many curious things about these parts, about Prince Tsitsianov,[6] A. P. Yermolov and so on. Sankovsky loves Georgia and foresees a brilliant future for it.

Georgia resorted to Russia's protection in 1783, which did not prevent the renowned Aga-Mohammed[7] from capturing and destroying Tiflis and taking away 20,000 of its inhabitants as prisoners (1795). Georgia came under Alexander's sceptre in 1802. The Georgians are a bellicose nation. Under Russian banners they have shown their courage. Their intellectual abilities await further development. In general they are of a cheerful and sociable disposition. On holidays the men drink and make merry in the streets. Black-eyed boys sing, skip and perform somersaults; the women dance the *lezginka*.[8]

The sound of Georgian songs is pleasant. One of them was translated for me word for word; apparently it was written in modern times; it contains some Oriental nonsense, which does have its own poetic merit. Here it is:

My soul, recently born in paradise! My soul, created for my happiness!
  From thee, immortal soul, I await life.
From thee, blossoming spring, two-week-old moon, from thee my
  guardian angel, I await life.
Thy face is radiant and thou cheerest with thy smile. I do not wish to
  possess the world; I desire thy glance. From thee I await life.
Mountain rose, refreshed with dew! Chosen favourite of Nature!
  Silent, hidden treasure! From thee I await life.[9]

Georgians do not drink as we do and are amazingly strong. Their wines do not travel well and soon spoil, but are excellent where they are made. Kakhetian and Karabakh are as good as some burgundies. They keep their wines in *maranas*, enormous jugs buried in the ground. They are opened to the accompaniment of solemn ritual. Not long ago a Russian dragoon who secretly dug up one of the jugs fell into it and was drowned in Kakhetian wine, like the hapless Clarence in a butt of malaga.

Tiflis is on the banks of the Kura, in a valley surrounded by rocky mountains. They protect it on all sides from the wind and as they grow hot in the sun do not simply heat the motionless air but bring it to boiling-point. This is the reason for the intolerable heat that prevails in Tiflis, despite the fact that the city is located only just below forty-one degrees of latitude. Its very name (Tbilis-kalar) means Hot City.

Most of the city is built Asian style: the houses are low, the roofs flat. In the northern part, European-style houses are going up and near them regularly shaped squares are beginning to appear. The market is divided into several arcades; the shops are full of Turkish and Persian goods which are comparatively cheap if one considers the generally high prices. Tiflis weapons are highly prized throughout the Orient. Count Samoylov[10] and V., renowned as heroes here, usually tested their new swords by cutting a sheep in half or decapitating a bull at one stroke.

In Tiflis Armenians make up the major part of the population: in 1825 there were as many as 2,500 families here. During the current wars their number has increased even further. There are reckoned to be up to 1,500 Georgian families. Russians do not look upon themselves as local residents. Military men, following the call of duty, live in Georgia because they have been ordered to. Young titular counsellors come here to obtain the much sought-after rank of assessor. Both types consider Georgia a place of exile.

The Tiflis climate is said to be unhealthy. Malarial fever here is dreadful; it is treated with mercury, which is quite harmless on account of the searing heat. Doctors administer it to their patients without any pangs of conscience. General Sipyagin,[11] they say, died because his personal physician, who had travelled from St Petersburg with him, took fright at the dose recommended by the local doctors and did not give it to the sick man. Common fevers are like those in the Crimea and Moldavia and are treated similarly.

The inhabitants drink water, which is muddy but pleasant, from the River Kura. In all the wells and springs the water has a strong taste of sulphur. Wine, however, is so commonly drunk here that any shortage of water would pass unnoticed.

I was surprised to see how little money was worth in Tiflis. Having gone down two streets in a cab and sent it away after half an hour,

I had to pay two silver roubles. At first I thought that the driver wanted to take advantage of a newcomer's ignorance; but I was told that I had been charged exactly the right price. Everything else is proportionately expensive.

We drove to the German colony, where we dined. We drank the beer they make there, which has a most unpleasant taste, and paid an exorbitant price for a very bad dinner. I was fed just as expensively and poorly at my inn. General Strekalov,[12] a celebrated gastronome, invited me to dinner one day; unfortunately his guests were served according to their rank, and seated at the table were English officers with generals' epaulettes. The servants missed me out so diligently while serving that I left the table hungry. The devil take that Tiflis gastronome!

Impatiently I waited for my fate to be decided. At last I received a note from Rayevsky. He wrote that I should hurry to Kars, since in a few days the army would have to move on. I left the very next day.

I went on horseback, changing horses at Cossack posts. Around me the earth was scorched by the heat. From the distance Georgian villages resembled beautiful gardens, but as I drew nearer I could see a few poor huts standing in the shade of dusty poplars. The sun had set, but the air was still stifling:

> Sultry nights!
> Foreign stars! . . .

The moon was shining; all was quiet; the clatter of my horse's hoofs rang out in the nocturnal silence. I rode for a long time without finding any sign of habitation. At length I saw an isolated hut. I started knocking at the door. The owner came out. I asked for some water, first in Russian, then in Tartar. He did not understand me. What amazing indifference! Only twenty miles from Tiflis, on the main road to Persia and Turkey, and he did not know a word of either Russian or Tartar.

After spending the night at a Cossack post I pressed on further at dawn. The road ran through mountains and forests. I came across some travelling Tartars; among them were a few women. They were on horseback and were wrapped in yashmaks; only their eyes and heels were visible.

I began the ascent of Bezobdal, the mountain that separates Georgia from ancient Armenia. The wide road, shaded by trees, winds its way past the mountain. At the summit of Bezobdal I rode through a narrow defile called, I think, the Wolf's Gate and found myself on the natural border of Georgia. New mountains, a new horizon came into view; below me stretched lush green cornfields. I glanced once more at scorched Georgia and began my descent of the mountain slope to the fresh plains of Armenia. To my indescribable pleasure I noticed that the torrid heat had suddenly abated: the climate was already different.

My man with the pack-horses was lagging behind. I rode on alone in the flowering wilderness, which was surrounded by distant mountains. In a fit of absent-mindedness I rode past the post where I should have changed horses. More than six hours passed, and I began to feel amazement at the great distance between the staging-posts. To one side I saw some piles of rocks resembling huts and I set off towards them. I had in fact ridden into an Armenian village. A few women in colourful rags were sitting on the flat roof of an underground hut. Somehow I managed to make myself understood. One of them went down into the hut and brought me cheese and milk. After a few moments' rest I pressed on and saw opposite me, on the high river bank, the fortress of Gergery. Three torrents, roaring and foaming, came crashing down from the high bank. I crossed the river. Two oxen, yoked to a cart, were climbing the steep road. Several Georgians were accompanying the cart.

'Where are you from?' I asked them.

'From Teheran.'

'What are you taking?'

'Griboyed.'

It was the body of the slain Griboyedov[13] which they were conveying to Tiflis.

Never had I imagined that I would meet our Griboyedov again! I had parted from him the previous year in St Petersburg, before he left for Persia. He was sad and had strange forebodings. I wanted to set his mind at rest; he told me, 'Vous ne connaissez pas ces gens-là: vous verrez qu'il faudra jouer des couteaux.'[14] He assumed that the cause of any bloodshed would be the death of the Shah and the consequent strife between his seventeen sons. But the aged Shah is still alive, and Griboyedov's prophetic words came true. He perished under Persian daggers, the victim of ignorance and treachery. His mutilated corpse, the play-thing of the Teheran rabble for three days, was recognizable only from one hand that had once been pierced by a pistol bullet.

I became acquainted with Griboyedov in 1817. His melancholy character, his embittered mind, his good nature, his very weaknesses and vices, those inevitable companions of mankind – everything about him was unusually attractive. Born with an ambition equal to his talents, he was long caught up in the meshes of petty needs and obscurity. The abilities of a statesman were not put to any use; the talent of a poet was not recognized; even his steely and brilliant courage was for some time under suspicion. A few friends knew his worth and met with an incredulous smile, a stupid and insufferable smile, whenever they happened to speak of him as an extraordinary person. People trust only in fame and do not understand that in their midst might be some Napoleon who has never commanded so much as one *chasseur* company, or another Descartes who has never even published a single line in the *Moscow Telegraph*. However, our respect for fame possibly originates from vanity: after all, it is our own voice too that contributes to that fame.

Griboyedov's life was darkened by several clouds, the consequence of violent passions and powerful circumstances. He felt the necessity of settling accounts once and for all with his youth and turning his life in a completely different direction. He bade St Petersburg and idle dissipation farewell and travelled to Georgia, where he spent eight years in solitary, unceasing activity. His return to Moscow in 1824[15] was a turning-point in his fortunes and the beginning of unbroken success. His comedy, *The Misfortune of Being Clever*, while still in manuscript, had an indescribable effect and immediately put him on a level with our leading poets. Not long afterwards his perfect knowledge of that region where war was commencing opened up a new career for him: he was appointed envoy. After arriving in Georgia he married the woman he loved[16] ... I know of nothing more enviable than the last years of his stormy life. Death itself, which claimed him in the middle of a courageous, unequal combat, held nothing terrible, nothing agonizing for Griboyedov. It was instantaneous and beautiful.

What a pity that Griboyedov did not leave any memoirs! To have written his biography should have been the concern of his friends; but with us, remarkable people disappear without trace. We are lazy and incurious ...

At Gergery I met Buturlin[17] who, like myself, was on his way to the army. Buturlin travelled with every possible luxury. I dined with him as if we were in St Petersburg. We decided to travel together; but once again the demon of impatience took possession of me. My man asked for permission to rest. I set off alone, without a guide even. The road was the same the whole way and completely safe.

After crossing the mountain and descending into a valley shaded by trees, I saw a mineral spring flowing across the road. Here I encountered an Armenian priest travelling from Erivan to Akhaltsyk. 'What's new in Erivan?' I asked him. 'In Yerevan they've the plague,' he replied. 'And what's the news from Akhaltsyk?' 'In Akhaltsyk they've the plague,' I replied. After exchanging this pleasant news we parted.

Now I was riding amidst fertile cornfields and flowering meadows. The crops were swaying, awaiting the sickle. I admired the beautiful soil, whose fertility has become proverbial in the East. Towards evening I arrived at Pernike. Here was a Cossack post. The sergeant predicted a storm and advised me to stay the night, but I wanted to reach Gumry that same day, come what may.

Facing me was a journey across some low mountains, the natural border of the *pashalyk*[18] of Kars. The sky was filled with clouds. I was hoping that the wind, which was strengthening every minute, would disperse them. But it began to drizzle, and then the rain became heavier and more persistent. From Pernike to Gumry is about eighteen miles. I tightened the straps around my felt cloak, put the hood over my cap and entrusted myself to providence.

More than two hours passed. The rain did not stop. Water streamed off my cloak which was now heavy from the rain and off my sodden hood. Eventually a cold trickle began to make its way under my necktie, and soon I was soaked to the skin. It was a dark night; the Cossack rode on ahead, showing me the way. We started climbing into the mountains; meanwhile the rain had stopped and the clouds dispersed. It was still another six miles to Gumry. The freely blowing wind was so strong that in about a quarter of an hour it had completely dried me. I did not think I would avoid a fever. Finally I reached Gumry at around midnight. The Cossack took me straight to the post. We stopped by a tent and I hurried into it. Here I found twelve Cossacks sleeping side by side. I was given a place; I collapsed on to my cloak, completely numb with fatigue. That day I had ridden fifty miles. I slept like a log.

The Cossacks awoke me at dawn. My first thought was: did I have a fever? But I felt very well, thank God, and in the best of spirits; there wasn't a trace either of illness or fatigue. I went out of the tent into the fresh morning air. The sun was rising. Against the clear sky stood a white, snow-capped mountain. 'What mountain is that?' I asked, stretching myself, and I received the reply, 'That's Ararat.' How powerful an effect a few vowels can have! I glanced at the biblical mountain, and I saw the ark moored to its summit in the hope of life's renewal – and the raven and the dove flying forth from it, symbols of punishment and reconciliation.

My horse was ready. I set off with a guide. It was a beautiful morning. The sun was shining. We rode across a broad meadow, over lush green grass sprinkled with dew and drops of yesterday's rain. Before us gleamed a small river that we had to cross. 'And there is Arpachay,' the Cossack told me. Arpachay! Our frontier! This was as good as Ararat. I galloped towards the river with an indescribable feeling. Never had I set eyes on foreign soil. A frontier held some kind of mystery for me, and since childhood travelling had been my fondest dream. Long afterwards I led a nomadic existence, wandering first in the South, then the North, but not until now had I broken out of the bounds of vast Russia. I gaily rode into the cherished river and my worthy steed carried me out on to the

Turkish bank. But this bank had already been conquered: I was still in Russia.

It was another fifty miles to Kars. I was hoping to see our camp by evening and I did not stop anywhere. Halfway, in an Armenian village built in the hills on the banks of a small river, I ate instead of dinner that damned Armenian bread called *churek*, which is baked in the form of a flat cake – half with ashes – and for which those Turkish prisoners in the Darial Pass were pining so much. I would have given anything for a slice of the Russian black bread, that they found so revolting. I was accompanied by a young Turk, a dreadful chatterbox ... The whole way he kept jabbering in Turkish, unconcerned whether I understood or not. I concentrated as hard as I could and tried to make out what he meant. He seemed to be abusing the Russians and, accustomed to seeing them all in uniform, took me for a foreigner because of my clothes. Then we happened to meet a Russian officer. He was travelling from our camp and informed me that the army had already moved out of Kars. I can find no words to describe my despair: the thought that I would have to return to Tiflis after having exhausted myself to no purpose in desolate Armenia left me utterly dejected. The officer went on his way; the Turk recommenced his monologue, but I no longer had any time for him. I changed from an amble to a round trot and arrived that evening at a Turkish village twelve miles from Kars.

Having jumped down from my horse I wanted to enter the first hut, but the owner appeared in the doorway and pushed me away with a shower of abuse. I responded to his welcome with my whip. The Turk started bellowing; a crowd gathered. My guide, it seemed, had interceded on my behalf. I was shown a caravan-serai;[19] I entered a large hut resembling a cattle shed; there was nowhere to spread my cloak. I demanded a horse. The Turkish headman came over to me. To all his incomprehensible words I gave the same reply: *verbana at* (give me a horse). The Turks would not agree. Finally I had the sense to show them money (which I should have done in the first place). A horse was brought immediately and I was given a guide.

I rode along a wide valley, surrounded by hills. Soon I saw Kars, standing out white on one of them. My Turk kept pointing it out to me, repeating 'Kars, Kars!' and put his horse into a gallop. I followed him, tormented by anxiety: it was in Kars that my fate would be decided. There I would discover the whereabouts of our camp and if there was still any chance of catching up with the army. Meanwhile the sky clouded over and it started raining again; but I was not worried about the rain.

We rode into Kars. As we approached the city gates I heard a Russian drum: they were sounding the retreat. A sentry took my pass and went to the commandant. I stood in the rain for about half an hour. Finally they let me enter. I instructed my guide to take me straight to the bathhouse. We rode along steep, crooked streets; our horses kept slipping on the wretched Turkish paving. We stopped at a building of somewhat squalid appearance. It was the bathhouse. The Turk dismounted and started knocking at the door. No one answered. The rain bucketed down on me. Eventually a young Armenian emerged from a nearby house and after a discussion with my Turk called me over to him, expressing himself in quite pure Russian. He led me up a narrow staircase to the second floor of his house. In a room furnished with low divans and ancient carpets sat an old woman – his mother. She came over and kissed my hand. Her son told her to make a fire and prepare some supper for me. I took my things off and sat in front of the fire. My host's younger brother, a lad of about seventeen, came in. Both brothers were frequently in Tiflis and lived there for a few months at a time. They told me that our army had marched out the previous day and that our camp was sixteen miles from Kars. At this I was completely reassured. In no time the old woman prepared some mutton and onions for me, which struck me as the height of culinary art. We all lay down to sleep in the same room; I stretched out in front of the dying fire and fell asleep in the pleasant expectation of seeing Count Paskevich's camp the next day.

In the morning I went to look round the city. The younger of my hosts volunteered to be my cicerone. As I inspected the fortifications and citadel, built on an inaccessible cliff, I was at a loss to understand how we had succeeded in capturing Kars. My Armenian explained to me, to the best of his ability, the military actions which

he himself had witnessed. Observing his liking for war, I suggested
he travel with me to the army. He agreed at once. I sent him to fetch
some horses. He reappeared with an officer who asked for my written
order. Judging from his Asiatic features I did not think it necessary
to rummage around in my papers and took from my pocket the first
piece of paper I found there. After solemnly inspecting it the officer
immediately ordered some horses for 'his honour' in accordance with
the written order and handed me back my piece of paper: it was a
verse epistle[20] I had scribbled at one of the Cossack post-stages. Half
an hour later I rode out of Kars, and Artemy (this was my Armenian's
name) was already galloping beside me on a Turkish stallion, with
a flexible Kurdish javelin in one hand and a dagger in his belt, raving
about Turks and battles.

I rode over soil sown everywhere with grain; around me I could
see villages, but they were deserted: the inhabitants had fled. The
road was excellent and in marshy areas was paved . . . stone bridges
had been built across the small streams. The land rose perceptibly –
the first foothills of the Sagan-Lu (ancient Taurus) ridge were
beginning to appear. About two hours passed; I rode up a long
incline and suddenly saw our camp pitched on the banks of the
Kars-chay; within a few minutes I was in Rayevsky's tent.

CHAPTER THREE

March over Sagan-Lu. Cross-fire. Camp life. The Yazidi. Battle
with the Seraskier of Arzrum. A hut blown up.

I arrived in good time. That same day (June 13th) the army received
orders to advance. While I was dining with Rayevsky I listened to
some young generals discussing the movements they had been
directed to make. General Burtsov's[1] forces were to be detached to
the left, on the great Arzrum road directly opposite the Turkish
camp, while the remainder of the army was to outflank the enemy
from the right.

Before five o'clock the troops advanced. I rode with the Nizhny
Novgorod dragoon regiment, chatting with Rayevsky, whom I had
not seen for several years. Night fell; we stopped in a valley where
the whole army made a halt. Here I had the honour of being
introduced to Count Paskevich.

I found the count in his tent in front of a bivouac fire, surrounded
by his staff. He was in a cheerful mood and greeted me warmly.
Since I was ignorant of the art of war, I did not suspect that the
outcome of the campaign was being decided that very minute. Here
I saw our Volkhovsky,[2] covered in dust from head to foot, with a
thick growth of beard, and worn out with worry. However, he did
find time to chat with me as if I were an old comrade. Here I also
saw Mikhayl Pushchin,[3] who had been wounded the previous year.
He is loved and respected as a wonderful comrade and a brave
soldier. Many of my old friends gathered round me. How they had
changed! How quickly time passes!

Heu! fugaces, Posthume, Posthume,
Labuntur anni . . .[4]

I returned to Rayevsky and spent the night in his tent. In the middle of the night I was awakened by terrible shouting: one would have thought that the enemy had made a surprise attack. Rayevsky sent someone to find out the reason for the commotion: a few Tartar horses had broken loose from their tethers, were running around the camp and the Muslims (that is the name for the Tartars serving in our army) were trying to catch them.

At dawn the army advanced. We approached thickly forested mountains. We rode into a gorge. The dragoons were telling each other, 'Watch out, my friend, sit tight. They could get you any minute with grape-shot.' And in fact the terrain favoured ambushes; but the Turks, diverted by General Burtsov's manoeuvres in another direction, did not put their advantage to good use. We safely passed through the dangerous gorge and halted on the heights of Sagan-Lu, about six miles from the enemy camp.

Nature all around was gloomy. The air was cold, the mountains covered with sad pine trees. Snow lay in the gullies.

. . . nec Armeniis in oris,
Amice Valgi, stat glacies iners
Menses per omnes . . .[5]

We had barely managed to rest and have dinner when we heard rifle shots. Rayevsky sent men to find out what was happening. They reported that the Turks had started exchanging rifle fire with our advance pickets. I rode off with Semichev to look at a scene that was quite new to me. We met a wounded Cossack: pale and bloody, he swayed as he sat in his saddle. Two Cossacks were supporting him. 'Are there many Turks?' Semichev asked. 'Teeming like swine, Your Honour,' one of them replied.

After passing through the gorge we suddenly saw on the slope of the mountain opposite us about two hundred Cossack cavalry loosely deployed, while above them were about five hundred Turks. The Cossacks were slowly retreating; the Turks attacked them with increasing audacity, taking aim at twenty paces and then galloping back to their positions after firing. Their tall turbans, fine tunics and the glittering trappings of their horses contrasted sharply with the Cossacks' dark blue uniforms and simple harness. About fifteen of our men were already wounded. Lieutenant-Colonel Basov[6] sent for help. At that moment he himself was wounded in the leg. The Cossacks were about to panic, but Basov remounted his horse and stayed in command. The reinforcements arrived in time. As soon as the Turks saw them they vanished, leaving behind on the mountain the naked corpse of a Cossack, decapitated and hacked to pieces. The Turks send severed heads to Constantinople, while they dip the hands in blood and make imprints from them on their banners. The firing died down. Eagles, those companions of armies, soared above the mountain, seeking out booty from on high.

Just then a crowd of generals and officers appeared. Count Paskevich had arrived, and he set off up the mountain behind which the Turks had disappeared. They were reinforced by four thousand cavalry, hidden in a depression and in gullies. From the heights of the mountain the Turkish camp, separated from us by gullies and high ground, came into view. It was late when we returned. As I rode through our camp I saw some of our wounded, five of whom died that same night or the following day. In the evening I called on young Osten-Saken,[7] wounded that same day in another engagement.

I found camp life most agreeable. A cannon would wake us at sunrise. Sleeping in a tent is amazingly healthy. At dinner we would wash down Asian shashlik[8] with English beer and champagne chilled in the snows of Taurus. Ours was a varied company. In General Paskevich's tent the commanders of the Moslem regiments would gather; conversation was conducted through an interpreter. In our army there were also men of different nationalities from our Trans-Caucasian provinces and inhabitants of recently conquered regions. I looked with particular curiosity at the Yazidis,[9] reputed in the East to be devil-worshippers. About three hundred families live at the foot of Mount Ararat. They have recognized the sovereignty of the Russian emperor. Their leader, a tall, ugly man in a red cloak and black cap, would sometimes come to pay his compliments to General

Rayevsky, commander of all the cavalry. I tried to find out from the Yazid the truth about their creed. To my questions he replied that stories of the Yazids worshipping Satan were pure fabrication; that they believed in the one God; that, according to their law, it is indeed considered improper and ignoble to curse the Devil, since he is now an unfortunate, but in the course of time he might be forgiven, for the mercy of Allah knows no bounds. This explanation reassured me. I was very pleased for the Yazidis, in that they do not worship Satan, and their aberrations struck me now as much more excusable.

My man turned up in the camp three days after myself. He arrived with a baggage train which, although in full view of the enemy, had safely joined up with our army.

Note   Throughout the whole campaign not one cart from our large baggage train was seized by the enemy. The orderliness with which this train followed the army was truly amazing.

On the morning of June 17th we once again heard cross-fire and two hours later we saw the Karabakh regiment returning with eight Turkish banners: Colonel Fridericks[10] had engaged the enemy which had consolidated its position behind some stone obstructions, forced it out and driven it away. Osman-Pasha, who was commanding the cavalry, barely managed to escape.

On June 18th the camp moved to another position. On the 19th, the cannon had hardly awakened us when the whole camp was in motion. The regiments lined up; officers stood by their platoons. I was left alone, not knowing which way to go, and I let my horse gallop where God willed it to. I met General Burtsov, who told me to join the left flank. 'What is the left flank?' I wondered and rode on. I saw General Muravyov,[11] who had been deploying the cannon. Soon the Turkish cavalry appeared, wheeling along the valley and exchanging fire with our Cossacks. Meanwhile a dense mass of their infantry was moving along the low-lying ground. General Muravyov gave orders to fire. The grape-shot struck the mass right in the middle. The Turks poured to one side and hid behind some high ground. I caught sight of Count Paskevich, surrounded by his staff officers. The Turks rounded our troops, who were separated from them by a ravine. The count sent Pushchin to inspect the ravine.

Pushchin galloped off. The Turks took him for a raider and fired a salvo at him. Everyone burst out laughing. The count ordered the cannon to be brought forward and fired. The enemy scattered over the mountain and the low-lying areas. On the left flank, to which Burtsov had summoned me, fierce fighting was taking place. In front of us (opposite the centre) the Turkish cavalry was galloping. To deal with it the count sent General Rayevsky, who led his Nizhny Novgorod Regiment into the attack. The Turks vanished. Our Tartars surrounded their wounded and quickly stripped off their clothes, leaving them naked in the middle of the field. General Rayevsky stopped at the edge of the ravine. Two squadrons, having broken off from the regiment, pursued them much too far; they were rescued by Colonel Simonich.[12]

The fighting died down; right before our eyes the Turks started digging and dragging up rocks, fortifying their position in their usual manner. They were left in peace. We dismounted and dined on whatever there was to eat. Just then some prisoners were brought to the count; one of them was severely wounded. They were questioned. At about five o'clock the troops were once again ordered to attack the enemy. The Turks stirred behind their barricades, met us with cannon fire, after which they soon began to retreat. Our cavalry rode in front; we began to make our descent into the ravine; the earth kept crumbling and falling away under our horses' hoofs. My horse could have fallen at any moment, and then the Combined Uhlan Regiment would have ridden over me. But God brought me through safely. Hardly had we come out on to the broad road that runs through the mountains when our entire cavalry began to gallop at full speed. The Turks fled; the Cossacks lashed the cannon that had been abandoned on the road with their whips and tore past. Now the Turks were rushing into the gullies on both sides of the road; no longer did they fire; at least, not one bullet whistled past my ears. Leading the pursuit were our Tartar regiments, whose horses are distinguished for speed and strength. My own horse, chafing at the bit, did not lag behind; I could hardly hold her back. She stopped by the body of a young Turk lying across the road. He was about eighteen, I think, and his pale, girlish face was not disfigured. His turban lay in the dust; the shaven nape of his neck had been pierced by a bullet. I rode on at walking pace; soon Rayevsky caught up with me. On a scrap of paper he wrote a message in pencil for Count Paskevich, about the complete rout of the enemy, and rode on. I followed him at a distance. Night began to fall. My weary horse fell behind and stumbled at every step. Count Paskevich ordered the men not to discontinue the pursuit and directed it himself. I was overtaken by our cavalry detachments; I caught sight of Colonel Polyakov, commander of the Cossack artillery, which had played an important role that day, and we arrived together at the abandoned settlement where Count Paskevich had stopped after calling a halt to the pursuit because of nightfall.

We found the count before a fire, on the roof of an underground hut. Prisoners were being brought to him. He was cross-examining them. Almost all their leaders were there. The Cossacks held their horses by the reins. The fire illuminated the scene, which was worthy of Salvatore Rosa; the sound of a small river could be heard in the darkness. At that moment the count was informed that stores of gunpowder had been found in the village and that an explosion was to be feared. The count left the hut with all his suite. We set off for our camp, which was about twenty miles from the place where we had spent the night. The road was filled with cavalry detachments. No sooner did we arrive than the sky was suddenly lit up as if by a meteor and we heard the dull thud of an explosion. The hut that we had left just quarter of an hour before had been blown sky-high: it was there that the gunpowder had been stored. The scattered rocks crushed a few Cossacks.

That is all that I was able to observe at the time. In the evening I discovered that in this battle the seraskier of Arzrum, who had gone to join Gaki-Pasha with thirty thousand troops, had been defeated. The seraskier fled to Arzrum; his army, scattered beyond Sagan-Lu, had been put to flight, his artillery captured and Gaki-Pasha alone remained on our hands. Count Paskevich did not give him time to rally his forces.

Battle with Gaki-Pasha. Death of the Tartar commander. A hermaphrodite. A captive Pasha. Araks. The Shepherd's Bridge. Hassan-Kale. A hot spring. March to Arzrum. Negotiations. Capture of Arzrum. Turkish prisoners. A dervish.

Next day, after four o'clock, the camp awoke and the order was given to move out. After leaving my tent I met Count Paskevich, who had risen earlier than anyone else. When he saw me he asked, 'Êtes-vous fatigué de la journée d'hier?' 'Mais un peu, m. le Comte.' 'J'en suis fâché pour vous, car nous allons faire encore une marche pour joindre le Pacha, et puis il faudra poursuivre l'ennemi encore une trentaine de verstes.'[1]

We moved off and towards eight o'clock reached some high ground, from which Gaki-Pasha's camp was clearly visible. The Turks fired innocuously from all their batteries. Meanwhile, a great deal of movement was noticeable in their camp. Fatigue and the morning heat forced many of us to dismount and lie down on the fresh grass. I wound the reins around my hand and fell into a sweet slumber, awaiting the order to move on. A quarter of an hour later I was woken up. Everything was on the move. On one side columns advanced on the Turkish camp; on the other the cavalry was preparing to pursue the enemy. I wanted to follow the Nizhny Novgorod regiment, but my horse was limping. I fell behind. A regiment of uhlans swept past me. Then Volkhovsky galloped past with three cannon. I found myself all alone in the wooded mountains. A dragoon came towards me and announced that the woods were full of the enemy. I turned back and met General Muravyov with an infantry regiment. He had detached one squad into the woods to clear them. As I drew near the low-lying ground I witnessed an extraordinary scene. Under a tree lay one of our Tartar commanders, mortally wounded. Beside him was his favourite, sobbing. A mullah was kneeling and reciting prayers. The dying commander was extraordinarily calm and stared motionlessly at his young friend. In the low-lying area about five hundred prisoners had been assembled. Several captive Turks motioned to me, probably taking me for a doctor and asking for help which I was unable to give. Out of the woods came a Turk, pressing a bloody rag to his wound. Some soldiers went up to him with the intention of finishing him off with their bayonets, perhaps out of humanity. But this disturbed me beyond all measure; I interceded for the poor Turk and with great difficulty managed to lead him, exhausted and dripping with blood, to a small group of his comrades. With them was Colonel Anrep.[2] He was amicably smoking from their pipes, despite rumours that plague had broken out in the Turkish camp. The prisoners sat there, calmly chatting among themselves. Almost all of them were young men. After a rest we pushed on. The whole road was littered with bodies. After about nine miles I found the Nizhny Novgorod regiment which had halted on the bank of a small river flowing between crags. The pursuit continued for several hours longer. Towards evening we reached a valley surrounded by dense forest, and at last I was able to sleep to my heart's content, having galloped in these two days more than fifty miles.

Next day the troops who had been pursing the enemy received orders to return to camp. There we discovered that among the prisoners was a hermaphrodite. At my request Rayevsky ordered him to be brought to us. I saw a tall, fairly stout man with the face of an old, snub-nosed Finnish woman. We examined him in the presence of a doctor. Erat vir, mammosus ut femina, habebat t. non evolutos, p. que parvum et puerilem. Quaerebamus, sit ne exsectus? – Deus, respondit, castravit me.[3] This illness, known to Hippocrates according to the testimony of travellers, is often found among Nomadic Tartars and Turks. *Khoss* is the Turkish name for these so-called hermaphrodites.

Our troops remained in the Turkish camp captured the day before. Count Paskevich's tent was situated close to the large green tent of Gaki-Pasha, who had been taken prisoner by our Cossacks. I went up to him and found him surrounded by our officers. He was sitting cross-legged, smoking a pipe. He seemed to be about forty. His handsome face was a picture of dignity and profound tranquillity. When he had surrendered he had asked for a cup of coffee and to be spared any questioning.

We were encamped in a valley. The snow-capped and wooded mountains of Sagan-Lu were already behind us. We moved on, no longer encountering the enemy anywhere. The settlements were deserted. The surrounding countryside is dreary. We saw the Araks, swiftly flowing between its stony banks. About ten miles from Hassan-Kale there is a bridge, beautifully and boldly built on seven unequal arches. Legend ascribes its construction to a shepherd who had become rich and who had died a hermit on the top of a hill, where his grave, shaded by two pines, is pointed out to this day. The neighbouring villagers flock there to pay their respects. The bridge is called Chaban-Kepri (Shepherd's Bridge). The road to Tabriz runs across it.

A few paces from the bridge I visited the dark ruins of a caravan-serai. I found no one there, apart from a sick donkey, probably abandoned by fleeing villagers.

On the morning of June 24th we set off for Hassan-Kale, an ancient fortress occupied the previous day by Prince Bekovich. It was about ten miles from the place where we had spent the night. Those long marches had exhausted me. I was hoping for a rest, but things turned out differently.

Before the cavalry moved out, some Armenians who lived in the mountains came to our camp to ask for protection from the Turks, who had driven their cattle away three days before. Colonel Anrep, who had difficulty understanding what they wanted, concluded that a detachment of Turks was in the mountains and galloped off in that direction with a squadron from the Uhlan regiment, having left word for Rayevsky that in the mountains were three thousand Turks. Rayevsky followed him in order to provide reinforcements should danger threaten. I considered myself attached to the Nizhny Novgorod Regiment and, sorely vexed, galloped off to liberate the Armenians. After we had advanced about thirteen miles, we entered a village, where we saw several uhlan stragglers hurriedly pursuing a few chickens with bared sabres. One of the villagers there managed to convey to Rayevsky that the whole fuss was about three thousand oxen which had been driven away by the Turks three days before and which could very easily be caught within a couple of days. Rayevsky ordered the uhlans to discontinue their pursuit of the chickens and sent Colonel Anrep instructions to return. We rode back and after emerging from the mountains encamped outside Hassan-Kale. In consequence we had made a detour of about twenty-six miles just to save the lives of a few Armenian chickens, which did not strike me as at all funny.

Hassan-Kale is considered the key to Arzrum. The town is built at the foot of a cliff crowned with a fortress. There are as many as one hundred Armenian families living there. Our camp stood on the broad plain that unfolds before the fortress. Here I visited a circular stone building that houses a hot ferrous sulphide spring.

The round basin is about six feet in diameter. I swam across it twice and suddenly, feeling dizziness and nausea, barely had the strength to clamber out on to the stone edge. These waters are famed in the East but, lacking decent doctors, the inhabitants use them without thinking and probably without much success.

Beneath the walls of Hassan-Kale flows the little River Murts; its banks are covered with ferrous springs which gush from under the stones and flow into the river. They are not so pleasant to the taste as Caucasian *narʐan*[4] and remind one of copper.

On June 25th, the birthday of our Sovereign Emperor, the regiments held services of thanksgiving in our camp, beneath the fortress walls. During dinner at Count Paskevich's, when we drank the Sovereign's health, the count announced that we would be marching on Arzrum. By five o'clock that afternoon the troops had already moved out.

On June 26th we halted in the mountains three miles from Arzrum. These mountains are called Ak-Dag (white mountains); they are of chalk. The caustic white dust made our eyes smart; their melancholy appearance induced sadness. The proximity of Arzrum and the certainty that the march would soon be over consoled us.

That evening Count Paskevich rode out to inspect the position. The Turkish raiders who had been circling in front of our pickets all day started firing at him. The count threatened them several times with his whip, without interrupting his discussion with General Muravyov. We did not return their fire.

Meanwhile there was great confusion in Arzrum. The seraskier, who had fled to the city after his defeat, had spread the rumour that the Russians had been utterly routed. Following in his footsteps, some released prisoners had conveyed news of Count Paskevich's appeal. The fugitives established that the seraskier had been lying. Before long they learnt of the rapid approach of the Russians. The people began to talk of surrender. The seraskier and his troops considered defending themselves. A mutiny broke out. A few Franks[5] were killed by the infuriated rabble.

A deputation from the people and the seraskier appeared in our camp on the morning of the 26th; the day was spent in negotiations; at five o'clock in the afternoon the envoys set off for Arzrum, and with them went General Prince Bekovich, who was well versed in Asian languages and customs.

Next morning our troops advanced. To the east of Arzrum, on the heights of Top-Dag, a Turkish battery was in position. Our regiments moved towards it, answering the Turkish fire with drum rolls and music. The Turks fled and Top-Dag was taken. I arrived there with the poet Yuzefovich.[6] At the abandoned battery we found Count Paskevich with his entire suite. From the height of the mountain, in a hollow, Arzrum with its citadel, its minarets, its green roofs glued together, opened up before us. The count was on horseback. Before him, seated on the ground, were some Turkish envoys who had come with the keys to the city. But the agitation in Arzrum was plain to see. Suddenly fire flashed on the city ramparts, there was a cloud of smoke and cannon-balls came flying towards Top-Dag. Several of them whizzed over Count Paskevich's head. 'Voyez les Turcs,' he told me, 'on ne peut jamais se fier à eux.'[7] Just then Prince Bekovich, who had been at the negotiations in Arzrum since the previous day, galloped up to Top-Dag. He announced that the Turkish commander and the people had agreed to surrender long ago, but that a few unruly Arnauts[8] under the command of Topcha-Pasha had seized the city batteries and were rebelling. The generals rode up to the count, asking permission to silence the Turkish batteries. The dignitaries of Arzum, exposed to the fire of their own cannon, repeated the selfsame request. For some time the count hesitated; finally he gave the order to fire, with the words, 'That's enough of their clowning!' Cannon were immediately brought up, firing commenced and the enemy fire gradually died down. Our regiments advanced to Arzrum and on June 27th, the anniversary of the battle of Poltava,[9] at six o'clock in the evening, the Russian banner was unfurled over the citadel of Arzrum.

Rayevsky rode off to the city, and I went with him. We rode into the city, which presented an amazing spectacle. Turks gloomily surveyed us from their flat roofs. Armenians noisily thronged the narrow streets. Their little boys ran in front of our horses, crossing themselves and repeating, 'Christians! Christians! . . .' We rode up to the fortress which our army was entering. To my utter astonishment here I met my Artemy, who was already riding around the city, despite strict orders that no one from our camp should absent himself without special permission.

The city streets are narrow and crooked. The houses are fairly tall. Large numbers of people were walking about – the shops had been closed. After spending a couple of hours in the city I returned to the camp; the Turkish commander and four pashas who had been taken prisoner were already there. One of the pashas, a skinny old man and a terrible busybody, was talking very excitedly to our generals. On seeing me in my tailcoat he asked who I was. Pushchin accorded me the title of poet. The pasha crossed his arms on his chest and bowed to me, telling me through his interpreter, 'Blessed is the hour when we meet a poet. The poet is brother to the dervish. He has neither fatherland, nor earthly blessings; and whereas we, poor wretches, worry ourselves about glory, power, treasures, he is the equal of the lords of the earth, and they bow down to him.'

This Oriental greeting on the part of the pasha delighted us all. I went to have a look at the Turkish commander. As I entered his tent, I met his favourite page, a black-eyed boy of about fourteen, dressed in rich Albanian clothes. The Turkish commander, a grey-haired old man of most ordinary appearance, was sitting in a state of profound dejection. Around him was a crowd of our officers. As I left his tent, I saw a young man, half-naked, in a sheepskin cap, with a club in one hand and a wineskin (*outre*) on his shoulders. He was shouting at the top of his voice. I was told that he was my brother, the dervish, who had come to welcome the victors. They had difficulty driving him away.

CHAPTER FIVE

Arzrum. Asian luxury. The climate. The cemetery. Satirical
verse. The seraskier's palace. The Turkish pasha's harem. The
plague. Death of Burtsov. Departure from Arzrum. Return
journey. A Russian journal.

Arzrum (incorrectly called Arzerum, Erzrum, Erzron) was founded
about AD 415 in the time of Theodosius the Second[1] and named
Theodosiopolis. Nothing of historical note is connected with its
name. All I knew about it was that here, according to the testimony
of Hadji-Baba,[2] calves' ears, rather than human ones, were presented
to the Persian consul as reparation for some insult.

Arzrum is considered the principal city of Asiatic Turkey. It is
estimated to have as many as 100,000 inhabitants, but this figure
appears to be exaggerated. Its houses are of stone, the roofs covered
with turf, which gives the city an extremely strange appearance if
one looks on it from high up.

The main overland trade route between Europe and the East runs
through Arzrum. But few goods are sold there; they are not put out
for sale here, as Tournefort[3] observed when he wrote that in Arzrum
a sick person could die from the impossibility of obtaining a spoonful
of rhubarb, while whole sackfuls of it were in stores in the city.

I know of no expression more meaningless than the words: Asiatic
luxury. This saying probably came into existence at the time of the
Crusades, when poor knights, having left the bare walls and oak
chairs of their castles, saw for the very first time red divans, colourful
carpets, daggers with coloured gemstones on their hilts. Nowadays
one can say, Asiatic poverty, Asiatic swinishness and so on; but

luxury, of course, is one of Europe's possessions. In Arzrum you cannot buy for any money what you can easily find in a grocer's in any small town in Pskov province.

The Arzrum climate is severe. The city is built in a depression, lying about seven thousand feet above sea level. The surrounding mountains are covered with snow for most of the year. The land is treeless, but fertile. It is irrigated by a great number of springs and is criss-crossed in every direction by watercourses. Arzrum is famous for its water. The Euphrates flows two miles from the city. But everywhere there are fountains. At each one a tin ladle hangs on a chain, and the worthy Muslims drink it and cannot praise it too highly. Timber is obtained from Sagan-Lu.

In the Arzrum arsenal we found a large number of ancient firearms, helmets, chain-mail armour, sabres that had probably been rusting since the time of Godfrey.[4] The mosques are low and dark. The cemetery is outside the city. Usually the headstones consist of columns adorned with stone turbans. The graves of two or three pashas are distinguished by greater ornamentation, but there is nothing elegant about them: no taste, no imagination ... One traveller writes that of all the cities in Asia only in Arzrum did he find a tower clock – and that was broken. Innovations devised by the sultan have not yet reached Arzrum. The troops still wear their picturesque Eastern costume. Between Arzrum and Constantinople there exists the same rivalry as that between Kazan and Moscow. Here is the beginning of a satirical poem written by the janissary Amin-Oglu.[5]

> The giaours now do Stambul's praises sing,
> But tomorrow they will crush it
> With iron heel, like a sleeping serpent,
> And departing will leave it thus.
> Stambul fell asleep before disaster struck.
>
> Stambul has renounced the Prophet,
> There the cunning West has darkened
> The wisdom of the ancient East.
> Stambul, for the sweet delights of vice,
> Has forsaken prayer and sabre.

Stambul has forgotten the sweat of battle
And quaffs wine during hours of prayer.

There the pure zeal of faith has faded,
There wives walk the cemeteries;
They send old women to the crossroads,
And they bring husbands to the harems.
And the bribed eunuch slumbers on.

But lofty Arzrum is not like that,
Our Arzrum where many roads do meet.
We do not sleep in shameful luxury,
We do not dip our unruly goblet into wine
To scoop out debauchery, fire and commotion.

We fast: with their sober stream
The holy waters do give us drink;
Our warrior horsemen fly into battle
A fearless and mettlesome host.
There is no access to our harems,
The eunuchs are strict and incorruptible,
And the wives do humbly dwell there.

I stayed in the seraskier's palace, in the rooms where the harem
was situated. For a whole day I wandered along countless passages,
from room to room, from roof to roof, from staircase to staircase.
The palace appeared to have been pillaged; the seraskier, deciding
to flee, took away whatever he could. Divans were stripped of their
covering and carpets taken up. While I was wandering around the
city the Turks would beckon to me and poke their tongues out.
(They took every Frank for a doctor.) This became tiresome and I
was ready to answer in kind. I spent the evenings with the clever
and amiable Sukhorukov:[6] the similarity of our pursuits brought us
together. He told me of his literary projects, of his historical research
which he had once embarked upon with such zeal and success. The
modest nature of his aspirations and needs is truly touching. It would
be a pity if they are not fulfilled.

The seraskier's palace presented a constantly lively scene: there, where the gloomy pasha used to smoke in silence amongst his wives and shameless boys, his conqueror was receiving reports of the victories of his generals, distributing pashaliks[7] and discussing the latest novels. The Pasha of Mush went to Count Paskevich to ask if he could have his nephew's place. As he walked through the palace the solemn Turk stopped in one of the rooms, uttered a few words with great animation and then became very pensive: in that very room his father had been beheaded on the seraskier's orders. Here are truly Oriental impressions for you! The glorious Bey-Bulat,[8] terror of the Caucasus, has arrived in Arzrum with two village-elders from Circassian settlements that had rebelled during the recent wars. They dined with Count Paskevich. Bey-Bulat is a man of about thirty-five, stunted and broad-shouldered. Either he does not speak Russian, or he pretends not to. His arrival in Arzrum really delighted me: he had already been my guarantee for my safe passage through the mountains and Kabarda.

Osman-Pasha, taken prisoner near Arzrum and sent to Tiflis together with the seraskier, pleaded with Count Paskevich for the safety of the harem he had left behind in Arzrum. For the first few days it seemed to have been forgotten, but once, over dinner, when we were discussing how quiet was the Muslim city, now occupied by ten thousand troops and where not one of its inhabitants made a single complaint of attempted rape against any of our soldiers, the count remembered Osman-Pasha's harem and ordered Mr Abramovich to call at the pasha's house and ask his wives if they were content and if they had been insulted in any way. I asked permission to accompany Mr A. We set off. Mr A. took as interpreter a Russian officer whose story is most interesting. At the age of eighteen he was captured by the Persians. He was castrated and for over twenty years he served as eunuch in the harem of one of the Shah's sons. He told of his misfortune, of his stay in Persia with touching candour. From a physiological point of view his testimony was invaluable.

We arrived at Osman-Pasha's house; we were led into an open room, furnished very decently, tastefully even – in the stained glass windows were passages from the Koran. One of them struck me as most ingenious for a Muslim harem: 'It behoves you to tie and to untie'. We were brought coffee in small cups inlaid with silver. An old man with a venerable white beard, Osman-Pasha's father, had come on behalf of the wives to thank Count Paskevich – but Mr A. said flatly that he had been sent to interview Osman-Pasha's wives and wanted to see them, to have their personal assurance that, in their husband's absence, everything was to their satisfaction. Hardly had the Persian prisoner managed to translate all this when the old man, to show his indignation, clicked his tongue and declared that in no way could he accede to our demands and that if the pasha were to discover on his return that other men had seen his wives he would order that the old man, together with all the harem servants, had his head chopped off. The servants, among whom there was not one eunuch, confirmed the old man's words, but Mr A. was immovable. 'You fear your Pasha,' he told them, 'and I my seraskier, and I dare not disobey his orders.' There was nothing one could do about it. We were led through a garden, where two feeble little fountains were flowing. We approached a small stone building. The old man stood between us and the door, cautiously opened it without taking his hands off the catch, and we saw a woman covered in a white yashmak from her head to her yellow slippers. Our interpreter repeated the question to her: we heard the mumbling of a seventy-year-old woman; Mr A. interrupted her. 'She's the Pasha's mother, but I've been sent to speak to his wives. Bring me one of them.' Everyone was astonished at the giaour's quick-wittedness. The old woman went away and a minute later returned with a woman covered just as she was; from beneath her veil came a pleasant young voice. She thanked the count for his concern for the poor widows and praised the behaviour of the Russians. Mr A. was skilful enough to engage her in further conversation. Meanwhile, as I looked around me, I suddenly saw, right over the door, a small round window, and in this small round window were five or six round heads with inquisitive black eyes. I wanted to tell Mr A. of my discovery, but the little heads started nodding and winking, and several tiny fingers started threatening me, giving me to understand that I must keep quiet. I did as I was told and did not share my discovery. All of them had pleasant faces, but there wasn't a single beauty among them; the woman at the door who was conversing with Mr A. was probably mistress of the harem, the treasury of hearts, the Rose of Love – at least, that's what I imagined.

Finally Mr A. concluded his questioning. The door closed. The faces at the window disappeared. We looked around the garden and the house, and returned extremely satisfied with our diplomacy.

And so I saw a harem: few Europeans have succeeded in doing that. There's the basis of an Oriental novel for you!

The war appeared to be over. I started making preparations for the return journey. On July 14th I went to the public baths and I did not feel happy with life. I cursed the filthiness of the towels, the wretched service and so on. How can one compare Arzrum baths to those in Tiflis!

When I returned to the palace I learned from Konovitsyn, who was on guard duty, that the plague had broken out in Arzrum. At once I visualized all the horrors of quarantine and that same day decided to leave the army. The thought that the plague is nearby can be very unpleasant for one who is not used to it. Wishing to shake off these feelings I went for a stroll in the bazaar. I stopped in front of an armourer's and had begun to inspect a dagger, when suddenly someone struck me on the shoulder. I looked round: before me stood a dreadful beggar. He was as pale as death; tears streamed from his red, festering eyes. The thought of the plague once again flashed through my mind. I pushed the beggar away with a feeling of indescribable revulsion and returned home extremely unhappy with my stroll.

Curiosity, however, prevailed; next day I went off with a doctor to the camp where plague victims were kept. I did not dismount and took the precaution of standing with my back to the wind. A sick man was led to us from a tent; he was very pale and staggered as if he were drunk. Another victim lay unconscious. After inspecting the plague victim and assuring the poor wretch of a speedy recovery, I turned my attention to the two Turks who led him under the arms, undressed him, and touched him as though the plague were nothing worse than a cold. I must confess that I felt ashamed of my European timidity in the presence of such indifference and hastily returned to the city.

On July 19th, when I went to bid Count Paskevich farewell, I found him deeply distressed. He had received the sad news that General Burtsov had been killed at Bayburt.[9] It was a pity about the valiant Burtsov, but the incident could prove equally disastrous for our entire small army which had penetrated deeply into foreign territory and was surrounded by hostile people ready to rise up the moment they heard rumours of the first defeat. And so war resumed! The count suggested I witness further military undertakings. But I was in a hurry to return to Russia . . . The count presented me with a Turkish sabre as a souvenir. I keep it now as a memento of my journeying in the footsteps of that brilliant hero across the conquered wastes of Armenia. That very same day I left Arzrum.

I travelled back to Tiflis along a road that was already familiar to me. Places that not long before had been enlivened by the presence of fifteen thousand troops were now silent and melancholy. I crossed Sagan-Lu and could barely recognize the place where our camp had stood. In Gumry I had to endure a three-day quarantine. Once again I saw Bezobdal and left the high plains of cold Armenia for sultry Georgia. I arrived in Tiflis on August 1st. Here I stayed for several days in amiable and cheerful company. I spent a few evenings in the gardens, to the sound of music and Georgian songs. Then I pushed on further. My crossing of the mountains was memorable for the fact that near Kobi I was overtaken by a storm during the night. In the morning, as I rode past Kazbek, I witnessed a wonderful sight. Ragged white clouds were drifting across the summit of the mountain and a solitary monastery,[10] lit up by the sun's rays, seemed to be floating in the air, borne along by the clouds. The Frenzied Gorge also appeared to me in all its grandeur: the gully, filled with rain water, surpassed in its ferocity the Terek itself which was thundering menacingly close by. The banks had been torn to pieces; huge rocks had been shifted and blocked the flow of water. A large number of Ossetians were working on the road. I crossed safely. At last I emerged from the narrow defile into the open expanses of the broad plains of Great Kabarda. At Vladikavkaz I found Dorokhov[11] and Pushchin. Both had travelled to the spa to receive treatment for wounds inflicted in the current campaigns. On a table in Pushchin's room I found some Russian journals. The first article I came across was a review of one of my works. In it myself and my poetry were reviled in every conceivable way. I started reading it aloud. Pushchin stopped me, demanding that I read it with greater mimetic skill. I should point out that the review[12] was embellished with the usual conceits of our critics: it was a conversation between a sacristan, a woman baker of communion bread and a proof-reader, the Zdravo-mysl of this little comedy. Pushchin's request struck me as so amusing that the annoyance aroused in me by reading the article disappeared completely and all of us roared with whole-hearted laughter.

Such was the first welcome I received in my dear fatherland.

NOTES

THE TALES OF THE LATE IVAN PETROVICH BELKIN

FROM THE EDITOR

1. *The Minor*: Comedy (1782) by Denis Fonvizin (1745–92).
2. *corvée*: Compulsory service due to a landowner.
3. *quit-rent*: Money payments in lieu of service.

THE SHOT

1. *Baratynsky*: From the poem *The Ball* (1828) by E. A. Baratynsky (1800–44).
2. '*An Evening on Bivouac*': A military sketch (1822) by A. Bestuzhev-Marlinsksy (1797–1837).
3. *Burtsov . . . his poetry*: A. P. Burtsov (died 1813), hussar officer, friend of the poet Denis Davydov (1784–1839) and famous for his dissolute life. Davydov addressed to him the verse epistles 'To Burtsov. Invitation to Lunch' (1804) and 'To Burtsov' (1804).
4. *honeymoon*: Pushkin uses the English word.
5. *Battle of Skulyani . . . Alexander Ypsilanti*: The battle (1821) is described in the story 'Kirdzhali'. Ypsilanti (1792–1828) was leader of the *Philike Hetairia*, the Greek movement for independence.

THE BLIZZARD

1. *Zhukovsky*: From the ballad *Svetlana* (1813) by V. A. Zhukovsky (1783–1852).
2. *Boston*: A card-game, related to whist.

3. *Tula*: A town south of Moscow famous for its metalwork.

4. *Borodino*: The Battle of Borodino, which took place on 7 September 1812, saw the defeat of the Russians by Napoleon. Soon afterwards the French marched into Moscow.

5. *Artemisia*: Queen of Halicarnassus who erected a monument (one of the seven wonders of the world) in memory of her husband Mausolus.

6. *Vive Henri-Quatre*: From the historical comedy *La Partie de chasse de Henri IV* (1774) by Charles Collé (1709–83). The soldiers of Napoleon sing the lines in *War and Peace*.

7. *Joconde*: A comic opera (1814) by Niccolò Isouard (1775–1818), an Italian–French composer.

8. *And tossed their bonnets into the air*: From the comedy, *Misfortune of Being Clever* (1823–4), by A. S. Griboyedov (1795–1829).

9. *Se amor . . . dunque*: S'amor non è che dunque?: 'If it be not love, then what?' From Petrarch's sonnet, 'S'amor non è, che dunque è quel ch'io sento?' ('If it be not love, then what is it I feel?')

10. *St Preux*: Hero of Jean-Jacques Rousseau's novel *Julie, ou la Nouvelle Héloïse* (1761).

THE UNDERTAKER

1. *Derzhavin*: From the ode *The Waterfall* (1794), by G. R. Derzhavin (1743–1816).

2. *to Nikitskaya Street*: i.e. right across Moscow.

3. *Razgulyai*: A quarter of Moscow close to Basmannaya Street, where the undertaker used to live.

4. *Pogorelsky's postman*: Hero of *The Poppyseed-Cake Woman of Lafertovo* (1825), a fantastic tale by Antony Pogorelsky (A. A. Perovsky, 1787–1836).

5. *axe . . . cloth*: From the poem *Dura (the Fool) Pakhomovna* (1824) by A. E. Izmaylov (1779–1831).

6. *unserer Kundleute*: Our customers.

7. *seemed . . . morocco*: A line, slightly altered, from the comedy *The Boaster* (1786) by Y. B. Knyazhnin (1742–91).

THE POSTMASTER

1. *Prince Vyazemsky*: From the poem *The Post-station* (1825) by Prince Vyazemsky (1792–1878), a close friend of Pushkin.

2. *scriveners of old*: Refers to clerks in the old Muscovite administration, notorious for their skulduggery.

3. *Murom*: Refers to brigands from the forests of Murom in Vladimir province.

4. *rank*: Postmasters held a rank equivalent to that of collegiate registrar in the civil service. Grade fourteen was the lowest in the Table of Ranks instituted by Peter the Great.

5. *allowance for two horses only*: This allowance covered all expenses for anyone travelling on official business. The higher the official's rank the greater the number of horses he could pay for. As a result he could ride in a larger, more comfortable carriage.

6. *passed over . . . dinner-table*: Pushkin describes an instance of this in 'A Journey to Arzrum', Chapter Two.

7. *Demut's hotel*: Very fashionable hotel, where Pushkin often stayed. It was established by a Frenchman.

8. *Avdotya*: The Christian name of which Dunya is a diminutive.

9. *Dmitriev's beautiful ballad*: Caricature (1791) by I. I. Dmitriyev (1760–1837).

THE SQUIRE'S DAUGHTER

1. *Bogdanovich*: From the poem *Dushenka* (1783) by I. F. Bogdanovich (1743–1803).

2. *Senate Gazette*: A kind of official government gazette, published weekly.

3. *But Russian . . . observed*: From the poem *Satire*, by Prince A. A. Shakhovskoy (1777–1846); the line has been slightly altered.

4. *Board of Guardians*: A state institution which undertook financial transactions, such as mortgages. It was also concerned with the protection of widows, orphans and illegitimate children.

5. *moustache grow . . . need one*: In the event of his joining a hussar regiment, where moustaches were compulsory.

6. *Jean-Paul's opinion*: Jean-Paul Friedrich Richter (1763–1825), German romantic novelist. Pushkin had been reading the *Pensées de Jean-Paul* *extraites de tous ses ouvrages* (Paris, 1829), which was given to him in Moscow in August 1830. The passage to which Pushkin is referring is: 'Respectez l'individualité dans l'homme; elle est la racine de tout ce qu'il a de bien' ('Respect individuality in man; it is the root of everything that is good').

7. *capital cities*: Moscow and St Petersburg.

8. *nota nostra manet*: We stand by our observation.

9. *Pamela*: *Pamela, or Virtue Rewarded* (1740–41), a novel by Samuel Richardson (1689–1761), has as its theme the resistance of a virtuous servant to her master's attempts to seduce her. Extremely popular in Russia in the eighteenth century, it was translated into Russian from a French version.

10. *sarafan*: Peasant woman's long, sleeveless dress.

11. '*Tout beau, Sbogar, ici . . .*': 'Steady, Sbogar, come here . . .' The dog is named after the eponymous hero of *Jean Sbogar* (1818), by the French novelist Charles Nodier (1780–1844). The novel describes the adventures of an Illyrian 'Robin Hood'-style bandit, and was one of Tatyana's favourites in *Eugene Onegin* (III.12).

12. *à l'imbécile*: Wide sleeves, gathered at the wrist, with small leaden weights at elbow level to make them hang down.

13. *Madame de Pompadour*: Jeanne Antoinette Poisson, Marquise de Pompadour (1721–64), mistress of Louis XV.

14. *Lancaster system*: Method of teaching, devised by G. J. Lancaster (1778–1838), which was very popular in Russia at the beginning of the nineteenth century. In it, older pupils were responsible for educating the younger ones.

15. *Natalya the Boyar's Daughter*: Historical story (1792) by N. M. Karamzin (1766–1826). A boyar was a member of the old Russian aristocracy, before the time of Peter the Great (1672–1725).

16. *Taras Skotinin*: character in Denis Fonvizin's comedy *The Minor*.

17. *Mais . . . êtes-vous fou?*: '(But) let go of me, sir; are you mad?'

THE HISTORY OF THE VILLAGE OF GORYUKHINO

1. *Manual of Letter Writing*: First published in 1769, the *Manual* was compiled by N. G. Kurganov (1726–96) and went through several editions. It contained anecdotes, sample letters, grammar and a wide range of information on astronomy and other subjects. Pushkin parodies this popularizing work in the 'History'.

2. *General Plemyannikov*: Inept general (d. 1775) who served under Empress Elizabeth, daughter of Peter the Great.

3. *Niebuhr*: B. G. Niebuhr (1776–1831), German historian, author of *Roman History* (1811–32), considered the first example of modern scientific historical writing.

4. *the Twelve Nations*: Napoleon's Grande Armée was composed of battalions from twelve nations.

5. *brichka*: Light open carriage.

6. *Hatred and Repentance*: Melodrama (1789) by the German playwright August Friedrich Ferdinand von Kotzebue (1761–1819), whose works were extremely popular in Russia.

7. *B.*: Faddei Venediktovich Bulgarin (1789–1859), writer and journalist of Polish origin, fought against France with Alexander I's army, and then changed sides. A police informer, he attacked in his journal *Northern Bee* almost all writers of note, including Pushkin, who effectively demolished his reputation in a series of devastating satires. An unquestioning supporter of the autocracy, Bulgarin was termed the 'reptile journalist'. (Police inspectors of the time wore pea-green coats.)

8. *Rurik*: Prince Rurik (d. 879), semi-legendary Viking founder of the ruling house of Rurikids in Novgorod, in 862. The princes and grand princes of Kiev and of Vladimir, and the grand princes of Muscovy, belonged to this house until 1598.

9. *The Dangerous Neighbour*: Comic poem (1811) by V. L. Pushkin (1770–1830), a salon poet and uncle of Pushkin.

10. *Critique of a Moscow Boulevard, Presnensky Ponds*: Anonymous satirical poems circulating in manuscript.

11. *Abbé Millot's*: C. F. X. Millot (1726–85), prominent French historian, whose *Histoire universelle* was translated into Russian in 1785.

12. *Tatishchev*: V. N. Tatishchev (1686–1750), whose *History of Russia from the Earliest Times* (1768–74) laid the foundation of modern Russian historiography. Boltin and Golikov were also leading historians.

13. *a certain historian*: Edward Gibbon (1737–94), author of *The History of the Decline and Fall of the Roman Empire*, 6 vols. (1776–88), had voiced similar sentiments on its completion.

14. *Great Russian*: Great Russia is the central part of Russia. Great Russian is the language of the principal ethnic group.

15. *the two-headed eagle*: The symbol of Tsarist Russia, with one head looking to the East and the other to the West.

16. *Mr Sumarokov*: A. P. Sumarokov (1718–77), an important contributor to the development of the Russian literary language and versification; he wrote in an extremely wide variety of genres – idylls, odes, ballads, eclogues, satires, etc.

ROSLAVLEV

1. *Roslavlev*: *Roslavlev or the Russians in 1812*, historical novel by M. N. Zagoskin (1789–1852), published in 1831. Pushkin was deeply critical of this work's pseudo-patriotism, agreeing with his friend Vyazemsky's statement that 'in Zagoskin's *Roslavlev* there is no truth in a single thought, in a single feeling, in a single situation'. The novel was strongly influenced by Sir Walter Scott.

2. *a key and a star*: The key was the emblem of a court chamberlain; a star designated an order of the first degree.

3. *Montesquieu*: Charles Louis de Secondat, Baron de la Brède et de Montesquieu (1689–1755), French writer on the nature of the state and the science of law. His *Persian Letters* (1721) satirized contemporary political and social institutions in France.

4. *Crébillon*: Claude-Prosper Jolyot de Crébillon (1707–77), minor French novelist.

5. *Rousseau*: Jean-Jacques Rousseau (1712–78), French philosopher, political and educational writer, and novelist.

6. *Sumarokov*: see p. 184 n. 16.

7. *Yury Miloslavsky*: *Yury Miloslavsky, or the Russians in 1612* (1829), historical novel by Zagoskin, also showing strong influence of Scott.

8. *Lomonosov*: Mikhail Vasilyevich Lomonosov (1711–65), the first great Russian scientist and poet.

9. *Karamzin's History*: N. M. Karamzin (1766–1826), leader of the Sentimental school in Russian literature and author of *The History of the Russian State*, 12 vols. (1818–26).

10. *Sikhler*: Fashionable milliner in Moscow.

11. *Madame de Staël*: Madame de Staël (1766–1817) visited Russia in 1811. Pushkin wrote a brief article about her in 1825. *Corinne* (1807) was her most famous novel, one in which she championed the cause of intellectually gifted women.

12. *Ma chère . . . amie de S.*: 'My dear child, I am quite ill. It would be very kind on your part if you came to cheer me up. Try and get your mother's permission and please convey to her the respects of your friend *de S.*'

13. *Chateaubriand*: François-René, Vicomte de Chateaubriand (1768–1848), French author and statesman.

14. *Kuznetsky Bridge*: Many fashionable shops belonging to foreigners (especially the French) were situated there, a highly fashionable street in Moscow.

15. *Confederation of the Rhine*: Formed by Napoleon in 1806, uniting Bavaria, Württemberg, Baden and other German states as a bastion against Prussia and Austria. It collapsed in 1813, after the defeat of Napoleon.

16. *Count Rastopchin's pamphlets*: Count F. V. Rastopchin (or Rostopchin) (1763–1826) was Governor-General of Moscow during the Napoleonic War. He was concerned with keeping up the morale of the people of Moscow by issuing posters in which he tried to convince them that all was going well. The posters and pamphlets were written in a racy, popular Russian, aimed at the populace.

17. *Pozharsky and Minin*: They ejected the Poles from Moscow in 1612.

18. *Saratov*: City on the Volga, about 400 miles south of Moscow.

19. *Presnensky Ponds*: Fashionable part of Moscow where the aristocracy loved to take a stroll.

20. *Charlotte Corday ... Marfa Posadnitsa ... Princess Dashkov*: Charlotte Corday (1768–93), French revolutionist who stabbed Marat to death in his bath. Marfa Posadnitsa, widow of the leader of the republic of Novgorod, unsuccessfully opposed the union of Novgorod with Moscow. Princess Ekaterina Romanovna Dashkov (1743–1810) took an active part, at the age of nineteen, in the palace revolt of 1762. She was a supporter of Catherine the Great.

21. *'Il n'est ... communes.'*: 'Happiness can be found only along well-trodden paths', from Chateaubriand's *René* (1805).

22. *Count Mamonov*: Count M. A. Dmitriev-Mamonov (1790–1863), a very wealthy Moscow aristocrat who, in 1812, formed a regiment at his own expense.

23. *proverbs*: *Proverbes*, or *proverbes dramatiques*, a short dramatic sketch, written to illustrate a point, originating in the salons of seventeenth-century France.

24. *1831*: This story was never completed.

KIRDZHALI: A TALE

1. *Hetairists*: *Philike Hetairia* (Society of Friends) founded in 1814 for the Liberation of Greece from the Turks. Ypsilanti, a Greek, was an officer in the Russian army, who initiated risings in the Peloponnese and on the mainland north of the Gulf of Corinth. His forces were eventually crushed.

2. *unfortunate battle*: At Skulyani, in Moldavia, on 29 June 1821. The Hetaerists were defeated by the Turks, near the River Prut. Iordaki Olimbi-oti, one of the main leaders of the Greek revolt, took refuge at the Monastery of Seko, in Moldavia, after the defeat. Rather than surrender, the Hetairists committed suicide, blowing up the gunpowder magazine.

3. *Georgi Kantakuʒin*: Prince Georgi Kantakuzin (d. 1857), one of the leaders of the Greek revolt. Pushkin had known him in Kishinev.

4. *Arnouts*: Turkish name for Albanians.

5. *Jassy*: Jassy (or Iasi), cultural centre of Moldavia.

6. *yataghans*: Muslim swords without guards and usually with a double-curved blade.

7. *Nekrasovists*: Cossack Old Believers who fled to Turkey after the rout of their uprising under Kondraty Bulavin. They took their name from Ignat Nekrasa, one of Bulavin's chieftains.

8. *chibouks*: Long Turkish pipes.

9. *Kishinev*: Capital of Moldavia, where Pushkin lived 1821–3, during his first exile.

10. *beshlyks*: Small Turkish silver coins.

11. *man of intellect and feeling*: This was M. I. Leks, serving on the staff of General Inzov, who gave Pushkin information about Kirdzhali in Kishinev and later in St Petersburg.

12. *dolman*: Long Turkish robe, worn open in the front.

13. *levs*: Bulgarian coins (principal monetary unit).

EGYPTIAN NIGHTS

CHAPTER ONE

1. *Quel . . . culotte*: From the French *Almanac of Puns* (1771).

Who is this man?
Ha, he's a great talent, he can do anything he wants with his voice.
In that case, Madame, he should make himself a pair of trousers from it.

2. *Reʒanov*: A fashionable patisserie.

3. *Signor . . . Lei voglia perdonarmi se . . .*: 'Sir . . . please forgive me if . . .'

4. *ho creduto . . . mi perdonera*: 'I believed . . . I thought . . . your Excellency, forgive me . . .'

5. *Maecenases*: Maecenas was a lavish patron of literature and the arts in Ancient Rome, friend of the Emperor Augustus and patron of Horace and Virgil.

6. *improvvisatore*: One prototype for the Italian *improvvisatore* is possibly the Polish poet Adam Mickiewicz who gave a dazzling performance at the

salon of Princess Zinaida Volkonskaya. Pushkin is said to have exclaimed, 'Quel génie, quel feu sacré, que suis-je auprès de lui!' ('What genius, what divine fire, what am I next to him!') However, the best-known *improvvisatore* of the time was one Tommaso Sgricci, who had in fact once improvised on the theme of Cleopatra's death and who, like Pushkin's character, was notorious for his avarice.

CHAPTER TWO

1. *Derzhavin*: from the ode 'God' (1784).
2. *Corpo di Barcco*: 'Good God!'
3. *La signora Catalani*: Angelica Catalani (1780–1849), famous Italian opera singer. In 1820 she performed in St Petersburg.

CHAPTER THREE

1. *Tancred*: Opera (1813) by G. Rossini (1792–1868).
2. *La famiglia . . . di Tasso*:

> The Cenci Family.
> The Last Day of Pompeii.
> Cleopatra and her Lovers.
> Spring Seen from a Prison.
> The Triumph of Tasso.

The themes suggested are connected with topics of the day: *The Cenci Family* is possibly linked either with Shelley's *The Cenci* (1819), or with Adolphe Custine's *Beatrix Cenci* (1830). *The Last Day of Pompeii* was the subject of a painting by K. P. Briullov, exhibited in St Petersburg in 1834. *Spring Seen from a Prison* bears a relationship to Silvio Pellico's *Le Mie Prigioni* (1832), in which Pellico's fellow-prisoner Maroncelli improvises a hymn, bemoaning their fate. A play by N. N. Kukolnik entitled *Torquato Tasso* was performed in St Petersburg in 1833.
3. *perché la grande regina n'aveva molto . . .*: 'Because the great queen had many . . .'

A JOURNEY TO ARZRUM AT THE TIME OF THE 1829 CAMPAIGN

PREFACE

1. *1829 Campaign*: During the war between Russia and Turkey, conducted on two fronts, the Balkans and Eastern Turkey, Russia acquired considerable territories in north-east Turkey, including the ancient fortress-city of Arzrum (Erzurum).

2. *Voyages . . . Français*: By Victor Fontanier.

3. *Un poète . . . d'une satyre*: 'A poet distinguished by his imagination has found, in the many glorious deeds to which he has been witness, not the subject for a poem, but for a satire.'

4. *A. S. Khomyakov and A. N. Muravyov*: Khomyakov (1804–60), minor poet, philosopher and theologian. Muravyov (1806–74), poet and travel writer. Author of *Journey to the Holy Land* (1832), sympathetically reviewed by Pushkin.

5. *Count Dibich's army*: Count I. I. Dibich (1785–1831), Field Marshal, of German birth, took part in the war against Napoleon, defeated the Turks at Sliven and occupied Adrianople in the 1829 Campaign. He commanded the Russian army during the Polish uprising of 1830–1.

6. *Independent Caucasus Corps*: Largely made up of Decembrists.

7. *Parmi les . . . ses compatriotes*: 'Among the military chiefs who commanded it (Prince Paskevich's army), there stood out General Muravyov . . . The Georgian Prince Tsitsevaze . . . the Armenian Prince Bebutov . . . Prince Potemkin, General Rayevsky, and finally Monsieur Pushkin . . . who had left the capital to sing of the exploits of his compatriots.'

8. *Sagan-Lu*: Mountain ridge in eastern Turkey.

9. *Count Paskevich*: Count I. F. Paskevich (1782–1856), commander of Russian army in the war against Turkey.

10. *seraskier*: Turkish commander-in-chief and war minister.

11. *Fontanier*: He was rumoured to be a spy for the French government.

12. *everything*: Pushkin had in fact written several poems about Georgia and the Caucasus, as well as his travel notes *The Georgian Military Highway*, published in the *Literary Gazette* in 1830.

CHAPTER ONE

1. *Yermolov*: A. P. Yermolov (1772–1861), commander-in-chief of the Russian army in the Caucasus before being replaced by Paskevich, whom he strongly criticized. In 1827 he had been pensioned off by Nicholas I, after which he lived in retirement on his estate near Oryol.

2. *Dawe*: George Dawe (1771–1829), English portrait painter, created the Military Gallery in the Winter Palace at St Petersburg, and painted many portraits of Russian generals during the Napoleonic War.

3. *Erivan*: Erivan (Yerevan), capital of Armenia.

4. *Shumla*: Fortress in the Balkans that had not been captured by the Russians.

5. *Count Tolstoy's*: Count F. I. Tolstoy (1782–1846), nicknamed the 'American', notorious duellist and gambler. A great-nephew of Leo Tolstoy.

6. *Karamzin's History*: See 'Roslavlev' note 9.

7. *Prince Kurbsky's memoirs*: Prince A. M. Kurbsky (1528–83), fierce opponent of the autocratic rule of Ivan IV; author of the celebrated *Correspondence* with Ivan IV.

8. *Griboyedov's poetry*: Besides being the author of one of the most famous Russian comedies, *The Misfortune of Being Clever*, Griboyedov also wrote a few lyric poems. See Chapter Two note 13.

9. *Count Pushkin*: V. A. Musin-Pushkin (1789–1854), Decembrist. Son of the famous manuscript collector.

10. *Herds . . . wander*: From the poem 'Peter the Great in Ostrogozhsk' (1823) by K. F. Ryleyev (1795–1826).

11. *Kalmucks*: Kalmucks (Kalmyks), a semi-nomadic Mongol-speaking Buddhist people who lived in East Turkestan until the seventeenth century, after which they moved west, occupying territory near the Lower Volga.

12. *Orlovsky's fine sketches*: A. O. Orlovsky (1777–1832), Polish war artist famous for his drawings of horses.

13. *Circe of the steppes*: Pushkin's poem 'To a Kalmuck Girl' (1829) is based on this encounter.

14. *nine years before*: Pushkin had spent the summer of 1820 in the Caucasus, during his exile.

15. *Goryachiye Vody*: 'Hot Springs', later named Pyatigorsk.

16. *A. Rayevsky*: A. N. Rayevsky (1795–1868), elder of the two Rayevsky brothers. Pushkin was a close friend of the family and was looked after by the father, General N. N. Rayevsky (1771–1829), a hero of the 1812 War, when taken ill during his first exile to the South of Russia in 1820. Pushkin

spent two happy months with the Rayevskys in the Caucasus and Crimea, forming a lasting friendship with the general's two sons, and a deep attachment towards his daughter Maria.

17. *opportunity*: I.e. an opportunity of travelling with military escort.

18. *Nogay*: Turkic-speaking people living in the North Caucasus.

19. *Count Gudovich*: I. V. Gudovich (1741–1820), Field Marshal who commanded Russian troops in three wars against Turkey.

20. *Kabarda*: Republic on northern slopes of Caucasus; it became Russian in 1825.

21. *annexation*: The eastern coast of the Black Sea had been conquered by Catherine the Great in 1783. It was again declared Russian after the Treaty of Adrianople (1829), which concluded the Russo-Turkish War.

22. *Mansur*: Follower of Islam who was captured by the Russians in 1791 and died in the Schlusselburg Fortress.

23. *like a warrior . . . him*: From 'The Burial of Sir John Moore at Corunna' (1817) by Charles Wolfe (1791–1823).

24. *Shernvall*: E. K. Shernvall-Walleen, who was travelling to the Caucasus with his brother-in-law, Count Musin-Pushkin. He was an officer on Paskevich's staff.

25. *Imatra*: Waterfall in Finland.

26. *'river thundering in the North'*: From *The Waterfall*, by Derzhavin.

27. *General Bekovich*: F. A. Bekovich-Cherkassky, a Kabardinian by birth, entered the Russian army and was in command of the Turkish fortress of Kars after its capture in 1828.

28. *And in . . . delight*: From a Russian translation of *The Iliad*, by E. Kostrov.

29. *Prisoner of the Caucasus*: One of Pushkin's early Byronic 'Southern' narrative poems, written 1820–1.

30. *Sheremetev*: Probably P. V. Sheremetyev (1799–1837), who was attached to the Russian embassy in Paris.

31. *strange painting by Rembrandt*: Pushkin appears to be mocking the conventional Romantic attitude to mountain scenery here, when he compares the spurts of water falling from the mountains to a Rembrandt painting that depicts a terrified boy urinating from on high as he is carried off by an eagle.

32. *darial*: More fully, 'Gate of the Alans'. 'Alan' was the medieval name for the Ossets, a mountain tribe in the Caucasus.

33. *Diriodoris*: Of foul odour.

34. *Count J. Potocki*: Refers to *Voyage dans les steps d'Astrakhan et de Caucase* (1829), by Count Jan Potocki (1761–1815), who travelled widely in the

Caucasus (trans. Ian Maclean (Viking, 1995)). His 'Spanish' novels include *The Manuscript found in Saragossa*, written in French.

35. *fugleman*: A soldier placed in the front row of a squad to direct drill.

36. *chikhir*: A Georgian red wine.

37. *Chatyrdag*: A mountain near the southern coast of the Crimea, past which Pushkin had sailed with the Rayevsky family in 1820.

38. *'props up the horizon'*: From the poem 'Half-soldier' (1826) by Denis Davydov.

39. *Fazil-Khan*: Lived in Tiflis (d. 1852). In 1829 Pushkin wrote a poem 'Blessed be your new exploit' to commemorate their meeting.

40. *the Persian prince*: Khozrev-Mirza (1821–78), travelling to St Petersburg to make an apology for the massacre of the Russian mission in Teheran in January 1829, in which the playwright Griboyedov perished (see Chapter Two note 13).

41. *abaz*: Georgian silver coin.

42. *Rinaldo-Rinaldini*: Robber-hero of novel of that title (1798) by German writer C. A. Vulpius (1762–1827).

CHAPTER TWO

1. *chadra*: Veil, yashmak worn by Moslem women.

2. *a lovely . . . brooks*: (1817). The original reads 'maiden's' and 'Teflis' is all in capitals.

3. *e sempre bene*: 'And all is well', or 'that's excellent!'

4. *Count Paskevich's*: Count I. F. Paskevich (1782–1856), General who commanded the Russian troops in the war against Turkey, 1828–9. Count Benkendorf, Chief of the Secret Police, had been informed of Pushkin's intentions to travel from St Petersburg to the Caucasus, and instructed Paskevich to keep the poet under close surveillance. Paskevich communicated with the authorities in Tiflis and every move of Pushkin's was closely watched.

5. *Sankovsky*: P. S. Sankovsky (1793–1832), editor of first Russian newspaper in Transcaucasia, the *Tiflis Record*, which was published in Russian, Persian and Georgian.

6. *Prince Tsitsianov*: General P. D. Tsitsianov (1754–1806), himself of Georgian origin, had been sent in 1802 to pacify Georgia after its annexation. He provoked war with Persia in 1804 by attacking Erivan. He was murdered during negotiations with the Persians at Baku.

7. *Aga-Mohammed*: Shah of Persia, murdered in 1797.

NOTES

8. *lezginka*: A courtship dance.

9. *My soul . . . await life*: From the poem 'Spring Song' by the Georgian poet D. Tumanishvili (d. 1821).

10. *Count Samoylov*: Count N. A. Samoylov (d. 1847), was an officer in the Preobrazhensky Regiment, formerly adjutant to Yermolov and first cousin of the Rayevsky brothers and sisters.

11. *General Sipyagin*: Military governor of Tiflis.

12. *General Strekalov*: Became military governor of Tiflis after the death of Sipyagin. He was ordered by Count Paskevich to keep Pushkin under secret surveillance.

13. *Slain Griboyedov*: A. S. Griboyedov (1785–1829), author of *The Misfortune of Being Clever*, had been appointed Russian minister to Persia. The Peace of Turkmenchai (1828) created great resentment in Teheran, particularly the clause providing for the repatriation of Armenian women in Persian harems. After an Armenian eunuch took refuge in the Russian legation, it was stormed by a fanatical Persian mob on 30 January 1829. All but one in the legation were killed. Griboyedov was recognizable only by his crooked finger, mutilated in a duel some years earlier.

14. *Vous ne . . . des couteaux*: 'You don't know these people: you'll see, in the end it will come to knives.'

15. *1824*: Actually 1823.

16. *woman he loved*: Nina, daughter of prince Alexander Chavchavadze, a celebrated Georgian poet.

17. *Buturlin*: M. B. Buturlin, adjutant to Chernyshev, Minister of War.

18. *pashalyk*: Area governed by a pasha.

19. *caravan-serai*: Public building providing shelter for caravans and travellers.

20. *verse epistle*: This was 'To a Kalmuck Girl'.

CHAPTER THREE

1. *General Burtsov's*: General I. G. Burtsov (1794–1829) had been arrested in 1826 for Decembrist sympathies. After one year's imprisonment he was transferred to the Caucasus.

2. *Volkhovsky*: V. D. Volkhovsky (1798–1841), lycée friend of Pushkin's. Sent to Caucasus after Decembrist rebellion to serve under Paskevich.

3. *Mikhayl Pushchin*: Brother of Pushkin's close lycée friend.

4. *Heu . . . anni*: Horace, *Odes* 3.14: 'Alas! Postumus, Postumus, the fleeting years are slipping by . . .'

5. *nec Armeniis . . . omnes*: Horace, *Odes* 2.9: '. . . Valgus, my friend, the mountains of Armenia are not covered all year round with motionless ice . . .'

6. *Lieutenant-Colonel Basov*: P. T. Basov commanded a Don Cossack regiment bearing his name.

7. *Osten-Saken*: Commander of the Independent Caucasus Corps.

8. *shashlik*: A kebab of muttons and garnishings.

9. *Yazidis*: (Or Yezidis) members of a religious sect of Iraq and Iran. The religion is syncretistic and postulates belief in a Satan who, although formerly evil, is now good, and chief of the angelic hosts.

10. *Colonel Fridericks*: B. A. Frideriks (1797–1874) commanded the Erivan Regiment of light cavalry.

11. *General Muravyov*: General N. N. Muravyov (1794–1866), superior officer at the time.

12. *Colonel Simonich*: I. O. Simonich, commander of Georgian regiment of grenadiers.

CHAPTER FOUR

1. '*Êtes-vous fatigué . . . de verstes.*': 'Are you tired after yesterday's journey?' 'Just a little, Count.' 'I'm angry on your behalf, since we shall be on the march again to join up with the pasha, and then we shall have to pursue the enemy another thirty versts.'
('verst' is about 1.06 kilometres)

2. *Colonel Anrep*: R. R. Anrep (d. 1830), commander of Combined Uhlan Regiment.

3. *Erat . . . me*: 'He was a man with the breasts of a woman, underdeveloped testicles, a small and boyish penis. We asked him if he had been castrated. "God," he replied, "castrated me."'

4. *narzan*: Strong Caucasian mineral water from the spring of the same name.

5. *Franks*: West Europeans.

6. *Yuzefovich*: M. V. Yuzefovich (1802–89), adjutant to General Rayevsky. A minor poet, and an archaeologist, he left interesting memoirs of Pushkin in the Caucasus.

7. '*Voyez . . . à eux.*': 'You see what the Turks are like . . . you can never trust them.'

8. *Arnauts*: Turkish name for an Albanian.

9. *Poltava*: City in the Ukraine where, in 1709, Peter the Great defeated Charles XII of Sweden, and Mazeppa.

CHAPTER FIVE

1. *Theodosius the Second*: (401–50), Byzantine emperor.

2. *Hadji-Baba*: Pushkin is referring to an episode from *The Adventures of Hadji Baba of Ispahan*, by the English diplomat James Morier (1780–1849). A Russian translation was published in 1830.

3. *Tournefort*: Joseph Pitton de Tournefort (1656–1708), French botanist. Pushkin cites his *Relation d'un voyage du Levant* (1717–18).

4. *Godfrey*: Godfrey (Godfred, Gottfried) of Bouillon, *c.* 1060–1100, took part in the First Crusade, and his deeds are mentioned in Tasso's *Gerusalemme Liberata*.

5. *Amin-Oglu*: Fictional name. The poem was written by Pushkin. (A 'giaour' was a non-Moslem, especially a Christian.)

6. *Sukhorukov*: V. D. Sukhorukov (1795–1841), journalist and historian.

7. *pashaliks*: District governed by a pasha.

8. *Bey-Bulat*: Bey-Bulat Taimazov, leader of tribal warfare in the Caucasus. In 1828 he went over to the Russian side and served as guarantee for safe passage along the Georgian military highway.

9. *Bayburt*: Small town in north-east Turkey, sixty miles north-west of Arzrum.

10. *a solitary monastery*: The ancient church of Tsmind Sameb, also described in Pushkin's poem, 'A Monastery in Kazbek' (1829).

11. *Dorokhov*: R. I. Dorokhov (1801–52), celebrated duellist and rake. Possibly the prototype of Dolokhov in Tolstoy's *War and Peace*.

12. *the review*: Pushkin is referring to a hostile review by the critic N. I. Nadezhdin, in the 'Herald of Europe' (1829), of his narrative poem *Poltava*. The review is in the form of a comedy, where the actors are the author (a classicist), a romantic and an old university press proof-reader. Pushkin replaced the first two with the sacristan and baker. 'Zdravomysl' is common sense.

READ MORE IN PENGUIN

In every corner of the world, on every subject under the sun, Penguin represents quality and variety – the very best in publishing today.

For complete information about books available from Penguin – including Puffins, Penguin Classics and Arkana – and how to order them, write to us at the appropriate address below. Please note that for copyright reasons the selection of books varies from country to country.

In the United Kingdom: Please write to *Dept. EP, Penguin Books Ltd, Bath Road, Harmondsworth, West Drayton, Middlesex UB7 0DA*

In the United States: Please write to *Consumer Services, Penguin Putnam Inc., 405 Murray Hill Parkway, East Rutherford, New Jersey 07073-2136.* VISA and MasterCard holders call 1-800-631-8571 to order Penguin titles

In Canada: Please write to *Penguin Books Canada Ltd, 10 Alcorn Avenue, Suite 300, Toronto, Ontario M4V 3B2*

In Australia: Please write to *Penguin Books Australia Ltd, 487 Maroondah Highway, Ringwood, Victoria 3134*

In New Zealand: Please write to *Penguin Books (NZ) Ltd, Private Bag 102902, North Shore Mail Centre, Auckland 10*

In India: Please write to *Penguin Books India Pvt Ltd, 11 Community Centre, Panchsheel Park, New Delhi 110017*

In the Netherlands: Please write to *Penguin Books Netherlands bv, Postbus 3507, NL-1001 AH Amsterdam*

In Germany: Please write to *Penguin Books Deutschland GmbH, Metzlerstrasse 26, 60594 Frankfurt am Main*

In Spain: Please write to *Penguin Books S. A., Bravo Murillo 19, 1°B, 28015 Madrid*

In Italy: Please write to *Penguin Italia s.r.l., Via Vittorio Emanuele 45/a, 20094 Corsico, Milano*

In France: Please write to *Penguin France, 12, Rue Prosper Ferradou, 31700 Blagnac*

In Japan: Please write to *Penguin Books Japan Ltd, Iidabashi KM-Bldg, 2-23-9 Koraku, Bunkyo-Ku, Tokyo 112-0004*

In South Africa: Please write to *Penguin Books South Africa (Pty) Ltd, P.O. Box 751093, Gardenview, 2047 Johannesburg*